Arrow

praise for KNIFE

'Love, fear, compassion and courage
are woven into a magical story'
Amanda Craig, *The Times*

'Both a thriller and a romance...
this is a lively and engrossing debut novel'
Books for Keeps

'A compelling adventure/love story'
Financial Times

'This is the best kind of fantasy:
a book that makes fairies wonderfully real'
Sarah Prineas, author of *The Magic Thief*

Arrow

R J ANDERSON

ORCHARD BOOKS

ORCHARD BOOKS
338 Euston Road, London NW1 3BH
Orchard Books Australia
Level 17/207 Kent Street, Sydney, NSW 2000

First published in the UK in 2011 by Orchard Books

ISBN 978 1 40831 262 9

Text © R J Anderson 2011

The right of R J Anderson to be identified as the author of this work has been
asserted by her in accordance with the Copyright, Designs and Patents Act, 1988.

A CIP catalogue record for this book is available from the British Library.

3 5 7 9 10 8 6 4 2

Printed in Great Britain

Orchard Books is a division of Hachette Children's Books,
an Hachette UK company.

www.hachette.co.uk

To my husband,
A man of peace and integrity

prologue

'Faeries of the Oak,' said Rob, 'we are at war.'

The young rebel leader paced the dais, torchlight glinting in his dark eyes and turning his fox-coloured hair to flame. Above him soared the high ceiling of the Queen's Hall, braced by the roots of the living Oak, while below and before him the great chamber was crowded with faeries.

There must have been two hundred of Rob's followers standing or leaning or even sitting at the back of the room, looking almost human in their modern clothes. After them came the upright but markedly smaller group of the Children of Rhys – Garan and his men from the magical Green Isles of Wales – who could have been extras from a Robin Hood film. But at the front of the crowd stood forty or so females dressed in simple, homespun clothing of a style that had not been popular since Jane Austen. It was to this last group that Rob was speaking, and judging by the tense lines of their bodies and the slight quiver of their wings, the

Oakenfolk were listening. Standing in the shadows along the wall, Timothy Sinclair – the lone human in the room – silently marvelled. After nearly two centuries of isolation, he hadn't thought the Oakenfolk would respond well to being addressed by a stranger, but they'd all come to attention the moment Rob opened his mouth.

'About a hundred and fifty years ago,' Rob continued, 'a faery calling herself the Empress rose to power in the world beyond this Oak. With cunning and dark magic, she enticed our forebears into giving her one drop each of their blood. By tasting that blood, the Empress learned all their true names...and so bound them, and their children, and their children's children, to obey her every command, forever.'

As Rob spoke that last sentence, Timothy watched for the faeries' reaction. The rebels who had followed Rob here from London looked resigned; they had grown up under the Empress's rule, after all. Garan and the other Children of Rhys wore expressions of grave pity. But the Oakenfolk, who had never heard this story before, were wide-eyed and trembling with horror.

'The Empress's ambition,' Rob told them, 'is to control every faery in Great Britain, and ensure that they do only what she believes is best for them. And so, when she learned of the Oak's existence and found that your people had escaped her power, she swore that she would either conquer you...or stamp you out.'

That last part was a little oversimplified, but Timothy could understand why. If Rob explained the whole truth about the Empress's origins and her connection to the Oak, the Oakenfolk would be more frightened than ever. And if they knew that what she wanted most was to stop faeries from being friendly with human beings, some of them might even be tempted to side with her. There were more than a few Oakenfolk who disliked humans, even now.

'But you are not alone,' Rob told the Oakenfolk. 'Like your new allies from the Green Isles, who have sacrificed so much to join with you and help you in your struggles—' he nodded to Garan and his men— 'we rebels believe in this Wyld's right to remain free, and are ready to support you in any way we can.' He straightened his shoulders, resolute. 'We may be strangers to you, but make no mistake about our loyalties. Every one of us is prepared to fight to the death, rather than allow this Oak to fall.'

In the hush that followed, Timothy had to resist the urge to applaud. Beside him Linden, the brown-haired girl who was his closest friend among the Oakenfolk, gazed at Rob with shining eyes and lips parted in admiration; and even Thorn, a stocky female who was the most sarcastic faery Timothy had ever met, looked grudgingly impressed. Had Rob succeeded in winning the Oakenfolk over? Timothy hoped so, but he knew better than to count on anything yet.

'It's easy for you to talk of fighting,' spoke up a harsh

voice, and the faeries in the front row scuttled aside as Mallow – a broad, tough-looking faery who was the Oak's Chief Cook and troublemaker – pushed her way towards the dais. 'But some of us have better things to do than waste time waving swords about. What makes you think we want to get involved in this war of yours?'

'You are already involved,' said Rob, 'whether you wish it or not. Soon the Empress is going to attack the Oak, and when she does you will either have to fight, or become her slave.'

'And whose fault is that?' Mallow demanded. 'None of us Oakenfolk would be in danger at all if those two—' she jabbed a finger at Linden and Timothy— 'hadn't been fool enough to go haring off into the Empress's territory and make a spectacle of themselves.' She folded her arms dismissively. 'So let *them* fight with her. Leave the rest of us out of it.'

Timothy had meant to stay out of the discussion, but that was too outrageous to let pass. 'So you'd rather Linden had stayed in the Oak and let you all die,' he said, 'instead of risking her life to find other faeries and get you back your magic?'

'What business is it of yours, human boy?' retorted Mallow. 'You don't know what it's like to be a faery, with magic or without. Who brought you in here anyway?'

'I did.' Queen Valerian rose from her throne at the back of the dais, regal despite her plain robes and mild appearance. 'I gave Timothy a charm that would make him small enough to visit us. And I asked him to be present at this meeting, so that he might report the outcome to the rest of our human allies.'

Which made it sound as though there were a whole horde of humans ready to defend the Oak, so it was no wonder the newcomers in the audience looked impressed. But the truth was, all they had was Timothy, his cousin Paul, and Paul's wife Peri, also known as Knife – who had once been a faery herself.

'Is that so?' said Mallow. 'Well, if Knife's so interested in what we're up to, why isn't she here? I think we all know where her loyalties really lie.'

'How dare you?' Linden rounded on her, small fists clenched. 'Knife's done more for our people than anyone. For years she's protected us, hunted food for us, brought us knowledge and ideas from the outside world. Without her, we'd have died out a long time ago.' Her voice quavered with emotion. 'She's given up so much to help us – and it makes me *so angry* that nobody seems to care!'

Linden was one of the shortest faeries in the Oak, and at fifteen she was certainly the youngest. But at that moment she looked as fierce as Knife herself, and everyone around her took a hasty step back, even Mallow.

'Knife's loyalties are not in question,' said Queen Valerian. 'She has her own plans for how to protect the Oakenwyld against attack, and has already begun training her fellow humans to fight with her. Is that not so, Timothy?'

Timothy nodded gingerly. He still had a pulled muscle in his neck from sparring with Peri that morning.

'Mallow, you have every right to ask questions. But if you cannot be civil, then you will be asked to leave.' Valerian turned to Rob. 'Please continue. How can we Oakenfolk, few as we are, defend ourselves against such a powerful enemy?'

'My people are skilled in magical combat and the use of weapons,' said Rob. 'We are willing to train anyone who wishes to fight.'

A hand crept up from the midst of the crowd, and everyone turned to look at the tiny red-haired faery who had raised it. 'But what if some of us aren't good at fighting? Or just…can't bear to hurt anyone?'

'Coward,' muttered a male voice behind Timothy, and Timothy had to resist the urge to whip around and punch the rebel flat. Wink – short for Periwinkle – might be fluttery and timid-seeming at times, but no one who knew her would ever accuse her of cowardice.

'It takes more than swords to win a battle,' said Rob. 'We will need faeries to set protective wards about the Oakenwyld, to craft arrows and supply provisions, and to treat the injured. Even the least warlike among you can make a difference, if you are willing.' He inclined his head to Wink, and she beamed back.

'That's nice,' Mallow said dryly. 'But if this Empress controls all the other faeries, then she's got us far outnumbered already. There's no way we can win.'

'If I believed that,' Rob replied, 'I would never have brought my people here. This Oak is an excellent stronghold, with room for twice as many faeries as we have with us today. I believe that once the news of our stand against the Empress begins to spread, it will not be long before this Wyld is full of our allies.'

'Full of fools wishing for a quick death, you mean,' said Mallow. 'Who'd get involved in a war unless they have to? And how are your so-called allies – or even you and your rebels, for that matter – supposed to stand up against the Empress, when she could call your names and tell you to go stick your heads in the privy at any minute?'

'I can think of someone's head *I'd* like to stick in the privy,' muttered Thorn, and Timothy had to pretend he was coughing to hide a laugh. Trust Thorn to be unimpressed by Mallow, even when the rest of the Oakenfolk were intimidated.

'The Empress may call all she likes,' said Rob, 'but we will no longer answer. The Stone of Naming, which Linden and Timothy brought back with them from the Green Isles, gives a new name to any faery who holds it – a name which the Empress does not know.'

He gestured to Garan, who held up the ordinary-looking white pebble for the Oakenfolk to see. 'My followers and

I have already touched the Stone, and can vouch for its power. And I am confident that once the faeries in the surrounding Wylds learn of the Stone's existence, they will be eager to join us, if only we can set them free.'

Mallow looked sceptical, but made no further protest. The faeries in the audience began to whisper to each other, and the buzz in the chamber grew until Queen Valerian motioned them all to silence.

'I have set three faeries in charge of defending the Oak,' she said. 'Rob will lead the rebels, and Garan the Children of Rhys; and as for the Oakenfolk, your commander will be Thorn.'

There was a general murmur at this, most of it approving. The Queen went on: 'At all times my three generals will work together, along with myself and my council and also with the humans in the House, to ensure that the Oakenwyld is protected.'

She spread out her hands to the crowd, taking them all in with a single gesture. 'The Empress could come upon us at any moment. We must be prepared, but above all we must be united, if we are to survive. And so I ask you all to set aside your prejudices and fears, and trust each other. For if we do not have that trust, then even the Stone of Naming will not be enough to keep us from falling into the Empress's power.'

All the faeries were silent. At last Queen Valerian said, 'You may go,' and they scattered like blown feathers, out the double doors and into the corridor beyond.

A few minutes later, Timothy sat at the table in Queen Valerian's study with Linden on one side and Campion on the other, feeling slightly ridiculous. What sort of wisdom did he have to contribute to a faery council of war? Only a few weeks ago he'd been just another teenage boy at boarding school, with no idea that faeries even existed. When he'd come to stay at his cousin Paul's house in the Kentish countryside, he'd known that the huge old oak at the bottom of the garden was hollow, but never guessed that there was a colony of six-inch-tall magical people living inside. And when Linden had popped up out of his rucksack and dragged him into the wildest and most dangerous adventure of his life, he'd had no clever strategy to save her, or the Oakenfolk, or even himself. All they could do was keep running until they found help, and hope the Empress didn't catch them first.

But Knife — more and more Timothy found himself thinking of her by that name, even though he'd grown up calling her Peri — was counting on him to give her a full report of this meeting when he came back to the house. So here he was, shrunk down to a tenth of his usual size, trying not to make a face as Wink poured them all cups of hot chicory. Sitting uncomfortably in his low-backed chair, because unlike the female faeries for whom all the furniture had been built, he didn't have wings. And telling himself to stop thinking about the e-mail he'd got from Miriam that morning, because finding out that a girl he'd liked only thought of him as a brother was really not that important. Not compared to what was happening here.

'...except for Mallow poking the bees' nest,' said Thorn, and Timothy realised he'd missed part of the conversation. He took a sip of chicory to punish himself, and resolved to listen more carefully.

'Mallow's attitude is the least of our concerns,' Queen Valerian said. 'What we need now is to determine our next course of action. Once we have finished arming and preparing the Oak against attack, what then? Garan, your thoughts?'

'As long as the Empress is still mustering her forces,' Garan said, 'the Stone of Naming is our best weapon against her. I believe we should send emissaries to all the Wylds within flying distance, and free as many of the Empress's subjects as we can.'

'I agree, but we will have to move carefully,' said Rob. 'I can tell you where most of the Wylds are in this part of England, but I also know that the Empress has spies and lieutenants in every one of them. Our emissaries will have to be not only persuasive, but also discreet. And they will need to be skilled in self-defence, or the Stone may be taken from us before we can use it.'

'Any of my people would be capable,' replied Garan. 'But

give me a little time, and I will find you the best. There is only one thing I ask: that when we offer the Stone to those enslaved by the Empress, we do so without condition. The gift of Rhys the Deep cannot be bought or bargained for, and it was his teaching that faeries should be generous with one another.'

'Maybe that works in those Green Isles of yours,' Thorn said. 'But here, we bargain. And there's nothing dishonourable about that. Every faery knows that if you want something valuable, you have to be prepared to give something equally valuable in return. Otherwise, what's to keep us from being cheated?'

'Besides,' Rob added, 'you gave up the right to control the Stone of Naming when you gave it away to Linden. We owe you a great debt, but—'

'I gave Linden the Stone,' Garan said, 'because I knew that she had been raised among humans as well as faeries, and so would appreciate the nature of a gift. And I think that Timothy knows that some things are too precious *not* to be given away.'

Timothy did, but he could also see why Rob and Thorn were concerned. He was just about to say so when Valerian spoke:

'This is too deep a matter to be settled by debate. As your Queen, and the only one here who is gifted with the Sight, the final decision about how to use the Stone, and the consequences of that decision, should be mine.' Her searching grey eyes moved from Thorn to Rob, and finally to Garan. 'Will you allow me to bear this burden?'

It was hard to argue when she put it like that. After a brief hesitation, all the commanders nodded.

'But if we do not send out the Stone quickly,' said Rob, 'we may not have the chance to use it at all. It is not in the Empress's nature to be indecisive, or over-cautious. As soon as she is able, she will strike.'

Garan nodded. 'Then we must be sure the Oakenwyld is warded on every side, and watched by night and day. Our resistance may be feeble, but at least the Empress will not catch us unawares.'

'Well, aren't you two cheerful,' said Thorn. 'Nice to know my fellow commanders take such a positive view of our chances. Wither and gall!' She shoved her chair back from the table and stood, glowering. 'Even without her magic – even *human* – Knife is worth ten of you. She'd take on the Empress single-handed if she had to, and not waste a moment complaining about it.' Then she stomped out.

'It appears,' said Valerian, 'that our discussion has come to an end.' But she did not seem distressed by Thorn's reaction. Timothy suspected that the Queen also regretted that Peri could not lead the faeries into battle, but they all knew that would never work. The Oakenfolk were still uneasy with the choice Peri had made by becoming human to marry Paul, and few of them would be willing to follow her orders.

The Queen dismissed the council, and they all headed off to their various duties. But as Rob passed by Linden, he whispered something in her ear that made her blush and smile. And when Timothy glanced at Garan, the blonde faery's brow was furrowed, as though something troubled him.

'What is it?' Timothy asked, when the others had gone.

'It may be folly even to say it,' replied Garan, 'for it is no business of mine. Yet I cannot help wondering why Rob takes such an interest in Linden. Not that she is unworthy of his notice,' he added hastily, 'but they are so different.'

'I asked him that myself, only a couple of days ago. He says that he finds her lack of cynicism refreshing. But if you're worried about his intentions, I wouldn't worry too much.'

'Why is that?' asked Garan.

'Because,' said Timothy, 'Linden is Knife's foster-daughter, and if Rob so much as hurts her feelings, then Knife will skin him and leave him for the crows.'

Garan's mouth curled in a reluctant smile, and too late Timothy remembered that the Children of Rhys had a hard time seeing humour in violence. He was about to apologise when Garan said, 'It is not merely concern for Linden that moves me, I admit. It is that when I look at her and Rob, I am reminded of some things I left behind, when I came here from the Green Isles. Things I did not even realise I would miss, until they were gone.'

Timothy was about to say *I know what you mean*, but he

swallowed the words. Yes, he missed his home in Uganda, where his parents still lived as missionaries – but at least there was a chance that he could go back there some day. Garan and his fellow exiles didn't have that option. By helping the Oakenfolk against their Elders' will, they had cut themselves off from their homeland and people forever.

It was probably better just to change the subject. 'That reminds me,' Timothy said. 'We've all been talking about using the Stone of Naming to free the Empress's slaves, but your people weren't exactly happy when they found out you'd taken it. What are we going to do if they decide they want it back?'

'The Children of Rhys will not come after the Stone,' said Garan. 'To journey so far onto the mainland would expose them to all the violence and corruption they have pledged themselves to avoid. Besides, my people are sworn to peace, and pursuing the Stone would bring them into conflict with us, if not with the Empress as well. Naturally they grieve the loss of such a precious artefact, but to fight us for it . . .' He shook his head.

Timothy knew he ought to be relieved. But with an evil faery Empress plotting his death and the deaths of all his friends, it was hard to be happy about anything. And if they ever lost the Stone of Naming...well, all of them might as well just give up, because there was no way they could win this war without it.

'I hope you're right,' he said.

one

'Rhosmari! Look what we found!'

Rhosmari daughter of Celyn stood on the front steps of the House of Learning, smiling as the faery children pelted over the grass towards her. The sea wind blew loose spirals of hair about her face, and automatically she undid the clasp at the nape of her neck and twisted the clove-coloured strands back into submission again.

She had only just finished when her students came panting up the steps and crowded around her, pressing shells and bits of sea-glass into her hands for her inspection. Fioled trailed after them, dishevelled and looking exhausted. 'Your turn,' she said.

'Come inside,' Rhosmari told the children. 'It's time for a story.'

Soon they were all settled in the Teaching Room, the students wriggling like seal pups on the carpet by her feet while Fioled arranged their newly gathered treasures on the shelves behind them. 'I have exciting news to tell you,' she whispered to Rhosmari, 'but it can wait.'

Rhosmari folded her hands together, assuming her most scholarly posture. 'Today,' she told her students, 'we are going to learn about the Rhysian Games, and how they came to be. None of you are old enough to compete in them yet, but—' A small hand went up, surprising her; it was not like any of the children to interrupt. 'Yes, Bleddyn?'

'Did Garan really steal the Stone of Naming and give it away to strangers?'

For a moment she was speechless at the question. She glanced back at Fioled, but the other girl was absorbed in picking seaweed off a piece of driftwood and did not meet her gaze.

'Yes,' said Rhosmari at last. 'But we aren't here to talk about that right now—'

'My father said he and the others left to join a war,' said another boy. But before Rhosmari could intervene, the girl next to him demanded, 'What's *war*?'

It was the wrong time to be discussing this, thought Rhosmari helplessly. They were too young for such dark subjects. But how could she blame them for being curious about what Garan had done, when half the population of the Green Isles was talking about it?

'It's when faeries disagree so strongly, they take up weapons against each other,' she said.

'Like in the Games?' asked the smallest of the girls, her nose wrinkled in confusion.

'No, Merywen, not for sport.' Rhosmari could hear the strain in her own voice now; it was an effort to keep it level. 'To hurt, and to – to kill.'

'Are Garan and the others going to be killed?'

Very likely, thought Rhosmari, but she could not bring herself to say it. 'I hope not.'

'Will we ever see them again?'

The soft voice belonged to Cudyll, the youngest of Garan's cousins. She wanted to change the subject, but this child at least deserved an answer. 'If Garan repents and brings back the Stone before anyone is hurt,' she told him, 'then the Elders may give him another chance.'

What she did not add was that if Garan or any of his men had shed blood, no penance would be enough: they would be barred from the Green Isles forever. And that after the harsh things he had said to the Elders, he might as well have committed murder in their eyes.

'But what if we don't get back the Stone? Will other faeries be able to see our islands? Will they come here and try to fight us too?' The questions flew at her from every side, so quickly that she could not tell which of the children had spoken. Had they been plaguing Fioled like this all morning? No wonder she looked tired.

'No,' said Rhosmari with all the firmness she could muster, 'the *Gwerdonnau Llion* is still safe. The Stone's power is only to give new names to faeries who have had theirs taken away, and no one is going to do that to us. The Elders keep watch over our people, and maintain the wards that protect us. And you all know about the herb we call Rhys's Blessing, which keeps our islands invisible to strangers. The Stone is very precious and we are sorry to lose it, but no enemy can hurt us here.' She regarded them levelly. 'Now, are you ready to get back to our lesson?'

The children nodded, but they did not look satisfied. And though they stayed quiet after that, Rhosmari could tell that they were not really paying attention to her stories about the Rhysian Games. At last she gave up and sent them outside to play.

As their chattering voices faded, the House of Learning settled back into its usual tranquility. Even Fioled had disappeared for the moment, and Rhosmari was alone in her favourite place: a low-ceilinged rectangle of weathered beams and plastered stone, open windows brimming with sunlight, curtains rippling in the ocean breeze. All around her, on shelves and pedestals, were the marvellous objects that the Children of Rhys had brought back from their visits to the human world: a jellyfish sculpted from iridescent glass, a slim book of poetry bound in tooled leather, a silken scarf dyed all the colours of flame. And on the far wall, just beside the doorway to the Archive, hung a harp, light and elegant as a gull's wing.

Her father had brought back that harp from Milford

Haven when Rhosmari was a small child, and for a few glorious hours he had remembered how to play it. She had sat beside him all the while, entranced by the notes rippling like magic from her father's fingertips – and when the music ended, she had wept. It seemed so cruel to her then that faeries had no creativity of their own, and that the talents they absorbed from their visits to the human world could not last once they returned to the Green Isles. But her father had cupped her chin in his hand and brushed away her tears, and told her that he had put all those songs into a loreseed for her, so she could listen to them again as often as she liked…

The floorboards creaked behind her, and Rhosmari turned. Fioled had come back, in fresh clothes and hair still damp from her bath. 'Are you all right?' the other girl asked. 'That can't have been easy for you.'

'I'm fine,' said Rhosmari. 'But if the children are talking like this, then their parents must be as well. Have our people become so ignorant about what the Stone of Naming is? Do they really think we're in danger without it?'

'I don't know.' Fioled wrung out the end of one pale braid and tossed it back over her shoulder. 'But everyone's been shaken up by what Garan did. Taking the Stone was bad enough, but flying off to the mainland and taking half the single males in the *Gwerdonnau Llion* with him? It's the biggest shock we've had since…'

She stopped before she could say the words, but to

Rhosmari she might as well have shouted them. *Since your father died.*

'So of course people are upset,' Fioled continued, reddening a little, 'and afraid that something even worse is going to happen next. That's only natural. What I don't understand—' she gave Rhosmari a sidelong look— 'is how you can be so calm about it. Especially after what Garan did to you.'

Rhosmari pressed her lips together in annoyance. Why did everyone want to talk about that? He was gone, and there was nothing she could do about it. 'You said you have exciting news?' she asked.

'Oh, yes!' Fioled was instantly transfigured. 'Lady Arianllys told me this morning that I've been chosen!'

There was no need to ask what the other girl meant. Every month the Children of Rhys cast lots for the privilege of going to the Welsh mainland, to buy goods from the humans and witness their amazing powers of creativity. Only five or six Rhysians were sent each time, and they never stayed longer than a day, but even a brief visit to the human world was said to be an unforgettable experience.

'I'm happy for you,' Rhosmari said, and meant it, because if someone had to take her place she would rather it be Fioled than anyone else. But it was hard to hide the bitter knowledge that her name had been drawn first, and then for some reason the Elders had forbidden her to go.

Or at least, her mother had.

26

'Oh, Rhosmari.' Fioled's face softened with pity. 'I'm sorry. But your turn will come soon, I'm sure of it. And I promise I'll tell you all about it when I get back.'

Rhosmari nodded. 'Did Lady Arianllys say anything else, when you talked?' she asked. 'I haven't seen her today, and she didn't leave any instructions.'

'She was called away to a meeting with the Elders,' Fioled told her. 'But she did ask if we would recopy a few of the older loreseeds, because they're beginning to wear out. Here.' She led Rhosmari into the Archive and pulled out a tray of sleek oval pods, worn smooth and dark by the touch of many hands. 'These top ones were cast by your father. Maybe you should do those, so the quality will be better.'

From a scholarly viewpoint, Fioled was right. Loreseeds were magical recordings of important events, but they tended to weaken with repeated viewings and had to be renewed. Rhosmari's father had been a great lorecaster, saving many of their people's most ancient records from destruction – but his speciality had been the history of the Children of Rhys before the Green Isles, and the loreseeds he had spent his life preserving were records of battle and war. Once as a young child Rhosmari had sneaked into his workshop and touched one of those seeds, and the images that exploded in her mind had given her nightmares for weeks.

She had witnessed death already. She did not care to see it again.

'I can't,' she said. 'Not those ones. Give them to someone else. Maybe Broch—' She caught Fioled's eye and stopped, embarrassment flooding her as she remembered that Broch had left with Garan and would not be coming back. 'Well, one of the others anyway. I'll take these.'

She pulled out another tray, this one full of proceedings from the Hall of Judgment, and sat down at the table with it. Watching the Elders settle disputes between neighbouring farmers or announce the winners of the two hundred and forty-eighth Rhysian Games might be dull, but at least she would sleep tonight.

Long after Fioled had left for the day, Rhosmari remained in the Archive with her tray of loreseeds, copying one after another. But when the last of the sunlight on the waters of Cardigan Bay flickered and went out, she realised that she could not avoid her mother any longer. The evening meal would be served at any moment, and it was her duty to be there.

Reluctantly she slid the tray back onto its shelf, closed up the building, and walked out into the night. Waves surged and hissed against the nearby shore, while the lonely cry of a seabird echoed from the other side of the strait. Rhosmari closed her eyes and inhaled, drawing deep of the salt-spiced air. Then she Leaped.

In an eye-blink the meadow vanished and her ancestral home rose up before her, an airy-looking cottage with sandstone walls and generous windows overlooking the sea. She went in, to find Lady Celyn waiting for her in the dining room.

At first glance this room could have been part of the House of Learning, with its age-darkened timbers and creamy walls. But in other ways the two places could not have been more different. The brass and pottery artefacts displayed upon the shelves had been in the family for centuries, but all were surrounded by spells that rendered them untouchable, so that not even a fingerprint or a speck of dust could mar their appearance. The dishes and cutlery were arranged at precise intervals, and even the fireplace glowed more steadily than any natural flame ought to burn. It was a place of order, and even beauty – but not of comfort.

'You look tired,' her mother remarked as she gathered her silken robes and sat down. 'Was it a teaching day?'

'Yes,' said Rhosmari, taking her own seat at the other end of the table. She waited as the servant girl dished out the first course, a creamy fish soup delicately threaded with saffron, then joined her mother in spreading out her hands in gratitude to Rhys and the Great Gardener before picking up her spoon and beginning to eat.

As always, they dined in silence, for it was Lady Celyn's belief that each dish should be savoured without distraction, to show respect for the hands that had prepared it. Which was why Rhosmari's mother had no difficulty keeping servants, despite her exacting standards; they all knew she took notice of good work, and rewarded it accordingly.

If only Rhosmari could find her so easy to please.

What did I do wrong? she wanted to ask. *How did I fail you, that you would punish me this way?* But her courage failed when she looked up and met Lady Celyn's eyes, cool as jet in the smooth chestnut mask of her face. Rhosmari and her mother resembled each other closely, with the same warm skin, full lips and rippling abundance of hair. But at this moment they might as well have been strangers.

'Now,' said her mother when the last crumb of berry tart had been consumed and the golden plates whisked away. 'I have been considering what we are to do now that Garan is gone.'

'Do?' asked Rhosmari.

'I believe it would be hasty to try and arrange another betrothal for you straightaway,' her mother said, 'but perhaps in a few months...'

Rhosmari's hand closed hard around her napkin, crumpling it. 'That is what you want to talk about?' she said. 'Another marriage contract? You think I am old enough to be betrothed, but not old enough to go to the mainland when my name is drawn?'

'It is not a matter of age,' Lady Celyn told her. 'It is simply not the right time for you to go. The next time you are chosen, perhaps.'

Which sounded reasonable on the surface, but they both knew that it might be years, or even decades, before her name was drawn again. 'I don't understand,' said Rhosmari. 'Why is it the right time for Fioled, but not for me?'

'Because Fioled is not my daughter.' Celyn spoke mildly, but her tone was edged with warning. 'There are evils in the human world that you know nothing about.'

'I am sixteen years old,' said Rhosmari, 'and I am being trained as a scholar. I am not ignorant of—'

'Of some things,' Lady Celyn cut in, 'you are indeed ignorant, and I hope you always will be. But this matter is not under debate. I am your Elder as well as your mother, and it is your duty to accept my judgment.'

Rhosmari knew better than to press the matter further. She lowered her gaze.

'Besides,' her mother continued, 'the situation here is unstable, and we Elders have many decisions to make. It may be that we must delay our visits to the human world for a time, in order to concentrate on more urgent matters.'

'Such as?' Rhosmari asked, not really expecting an answer.

'Such as how to recover the Stone of Naming,' replied Lady Celyn.

Rhosmari's surprise overcame her resentment. 'You think we can?'

'I think we must. The loss of the Stone has thrown our people into chaos. There are all kinds of superstitions about its powers, and many consider its disappearance to be a bad sign. It has even been claimed that Rhys is angry with us and that we are under a curse.' Lady Celyn leaned back in her chair, the amber pendant at her throat glowing in the firelight. 'The Elders have been blamed for not guarding the Stone more closely, and for allowing Garan and his followers to escape. There has been talk of a conspiracy to protect Garan, and suspicion has fallen on everyone who was close to him...including you.'

A cold stone dropped into Rhosmari's stomach. 'Me? Why?'

'You were seen speaking privately with Garan, only a short time before he declared his treachery to the Council and disappeared.'

'He was asking me to release him from our vows of betrothal! Everyone knows that!'

'Perhaps, but they also think you must have known why he was asking. To break his pledge to you so soon after Timothy and Linden came to us for help in their war against the Empress? Surely you suspected something was wrong?'

She had, but not in the way her fellow faeries seemed to think. *I cannot love you as a husband should*, Garan had told her, *and it would be wrong to pledge myself to you when my heart lies elsewhere.* What could Rhosmari make of that, except that he had been enchanted by Linden's wide-eyed prettiness, and wanted to be with her instead?

But when Garan admitted to stealing the Stone of Naming and flew off to help the Oakenfolk, Rhosmari realised she had been mistaken. Being attracted to someone you'd just met, even strongly, was not enough to make you betray your own people, disgrace your family, and leave the only homeland you'd ever known. And it certainly wouldn't be enough to talk thirty-seven other faeries into coming with you.

'I did not help Garan ap Gwylan or support him in any way,' said Rhosmari, willing her voice not to shake. 'I will swear that in the Hall of Judgment, if you like.'

Celyn dismissed this with a gesture. 'There is no need. Whatever foolish talk may arise, the other Elders are satisfied that no daughter of mine could have taken any part in Garan's crimes. And we have already taken steps to assure our people that we do not tolerate thieves and traitors, or those who sympathise with them.' She sipped her wine slowly, as though savouring some private triumph. 'All we need now is to find the Stone and bring it back.'

'How can we do that?'

'I cannot say for certain until I have the support of the other Elders,' replied her mother. 'But I know what I mean to recommend. We must send out an armed party to find Garan and his fellow rebels, and make them give us back the Stone…if necessary, by force.'

'Force!' Rhosmari's mouth went dry with shock. She pushed back her chair from the table, trying to put as much distance between herself and Lady Celyn as possible. 'No!

How could we do such a thing, without breaking every law Rhys and our ancestors laid down for us?'

'We have sworn not to shed blood in violence,' said her mother. 'But nothing prevents us from restraining other faeries, or even taking them captive if need be. Why do our people train for the Rhysian Games each year, if not to ensure that we never lose our ability to defend ourselves? Even you have—'

'The Games were meant to be an alternative to fighting, not preparation for it! I know the Stone is precious, but nothing can be worth taking up arms against our own people!'

'If Garan is prepared to be reasonable, then neither he nor any of his allies will have anything to fear.' Lady Celyn's fingers coiled about the stem of her goblet, turning it slowly on the table. 'All they need do is hand over the Stone, and we will depart as peacefully as we came.'

'But what about the Empress?' asked Rhosmari, pleading now. 'Linden and Timothy told us that she controls nearly all the faeries on the mainland. How can you send a band of armed warriors into her territory and expect her not to notice?'

'She may,' said her mother. 'But if we are challenged, we will explain that we have no plan to interfere in her conflict with the rebels, and that this is a private matter. If she is sensible, she will let us pass without further hindrance. And even if she chooses to oppose us, I think three hundred

Children of Rhys should be enough to withstand any attack.'

Three hundred. Rhosmari felt faint. 'But…if there is fighting, some of them will die.' She closed her eyes, seeing in memory the image of her father's broken body. 'Mother, you cannot do this.'

'It is not for you to tell me, *daughter*, what I should do.' Celyn rose from the table, a pillar of topaz and obsidian in the firelight. 'I chose to tell you of my plan because I believed you were mature enough to appreciate its wisdom. Clearly I was mistaken, but that is of no account. My fellow Elders will decide what is best for our people, and I am confident that they will agree with me.'

And without waiting for a reply, she swept out, leaving Rhosmari staring blindly into the flames.

The cottage was dark, darker even than the cloud-veiled sky outside. The servants had left, and Lady Celyn had retired for the night. But Rhosmari paced the floor of her bedroom, unable to sleep.

Would the council of Elders agree to Lady Celyn's proposal? Would they really endanger the lives of so many Children of Rhys, just to get back the Stone? To Rhosmari it was unthinkable, but if they believed that there was no other way to restore peace and win back their people's confidence, they might be willing to take the risk. Lady Celyn was not only eloquent and persuasive, but she was one of the strongest leaders the Green Isles had. If she wanted an army, she would very likely get one.

But an army was not just a collection of individuals: it was made up of fathers and brothers, mothers and sisters, daughters and sons. Every loss, every death, would leave a terrible emptiness behind. How could Rhosmari face her young students, knowing what was coming to them? Could she really stand by and allow it to happen?

The thought was intolerable. Somehow, she had to find a way to stop her mother's scheme. But how? She had no authority or special influence that would make the Elders listen to her. She had no power to hold back an army.

But she might know someone who did.

Pulse quickening, she hurried to the window and peered out across the strait at the neighbouring islands. Most of their coves and inlets were lost in shadow, but here and there gleamed a distant star of light. And if she was not mistaken, one of those lights belonged to Lord Gwylan and Lady Arianllys. Determined to act before she lost her nerve, Rhosmari tugged on her shoes, wrapped a shawl about herself, and Leaped.

two

'I'm sorry to disturb you,' said Rhosmari, passing a hand over her rain-beaded hair. 'But I needed to talk to you and Lord Gwylan right away.'

'My dear, there is no need to apologise,' said Lady Arianllys, stepping back from the doorway to let Rhosmari in. Her dark hair tangled about her shoulders and her eyes were shadowed with weariness, yet her expression held only concern. 'I know you would not have come unless it was urgent.' She drew her dressing gown closer and called back over her shoulder, 'Gwylan?'

The door to the adjoining room creaked open, and Garan's father stepped out. He had a close-trimmed beard and his hair was more wheat than flax, but otherwise he resembled his son so closely that the two of them might have been twins. 'What is it?' he asked.

She had never seen Lord Gwylan look so bleak, not even when Garan left. Something must have gone badly wrong for him today – but there was no time to ask about it now. 'I have something important to tell you,' Rhosmari said, and went on to explain why she had come.

'I know my mother means well,' she finished, 'but I cannot sit by and see this happen to our people – and if there is any chance at all that you can prevent it—'

'Be at peace, Rhosmari,' Lady Arianllys told her. 'We understand your fears, and indeed share them. And yet...' She glanced at her husband. 'I fear there is little we can do.'

'But how can that be?' Rhosmari asked. 'My mother's scheme has not been approved yet. Surely Lord Gwylan could talk to the other Elders, and—'

'It is too late for that.' Gwylan's voice was heavy. 'As of today, I am no longer part of the Twelve.'

The breath stopped in Rhosmari's throat. She could manage only one hoarse word: 'Why?'

'Because,' he replied, 'in their eyes and the eyes of the people, I am no longer fit to rule. Or as your mother put it, how can I be trusted to govern the Green Isles if I could not govern my own son?'

Rhosmari took a shaky step backwards and sank into a chair. Lord Gwylan had long been the most moderate voice on the Council, and the only Elder she knew with the courage to stand up to Lady Celyn. No wonder her mother had looked so satisfied at supper. No wonder she had been confident that her plan would be approved...

'But we do not blame your mother,' said Lady Arianllys. 'For she only did what she believed was right and best for our people. And though the Elders' decision was painful, it was not unexpected: as soon as Garan left the *Gwerdonnau Llion*, Gwylan and I knew this day would come.'

'But it's so unfair,' Rhosmari said. 'You didn't help him. He didn't tell you anything...did he?'

'He hardly needed to,' said Gwylan. 'I read it in his face, the moment we Elders told Linden and Timothy we could not give them the magical help they sought. I looked down from the dais and saw my son standing there, and I knew that he was determined to take the Stone and free the faeries enslaved by the Empress, just as Rhys used it to free our people from tyranny a thousand years ago.'

Rhosmari drew in her breath. 'Then you agree with him? You think he was right to take the Stone?'

'That does not matter now,' said Arianllys. 'The Stone is gone, and the Children of Rhys are terrified. Something must be done to restore our people's confidence. But if your mother's plan is not the answer, then what is?'

'I don't know,' said Rhosmari. 'I thought...if I came to you...' She looked up pleadingly at the Lady Scholar. 'You haven't foreseen any of this? You don't know if my mother will succeed, or if we will get back the Stone, or...any of it?'

Arianllys was quiet a moment. Then she said, 'I have not seen anything that will help you. My visions come rarely, and they are seldom clear or certain.'

Rhosmari dropped her head into her hands. If Lord Gwylan could not stop her mother from carrying out her plan, and the greatest scholar and prophetess in the Green Isles had no wisdom to offer, then what hope was there?

Then a thought came to her, and she straightened up again. Perhaps all was not quite lost. After all, even if Lady Celyn did succeed in convincing the Elders, she would have to present their decision before the assembly and win the approval of the other Children of Rhys as well. And then the Elders would have to choose which faeries would serve in the army, and appoint commanders over them, and supply them all with weapons and provisions before sending them out on their journey. It might be a week, or even two, before all was ready.

So there was still time to find an alternative, a way of recovering the Stone without conflict or violence. It might not even be that difficult. Despite the rash things Garan had done, Rhosmari could not believe he was a traitor: he had only meant to help the faeries on the mainland, not to harm the Children of Rhys. Perhaps, if someone from the Green Isles were to go to him and tell him what the loss of the Stone had done to their people, he might realise his mistake and give it back.

But who could make such a journey? When Garan fled, he had taken all of his closest comrades with him; Rhosmari was the only one left outside his family who knew him well. His parents had already suffered enough on his account, and their wisdom and moderation were needed here. No one else knew the details of her mother's plan.

Which meant that there was only one person who could do it.

No.

Please, no. Not me.

She had longed to visit the mainland, but not like this. Not alone and unprepared, with nothing to protect her from the evils of which her mother had so often warned. Even if Rhosmari could find the courage to expose herself to such danger, it might take her days or weeks to accomplish her mission. And all the while she would be running against time, afraid that her mother's army might overtake her at any moment.

Yet what else could she do?

I do not desire evil, Garan had said to her once, *but it seems to me that to stand idle while evil is being done is no virtue either.* Rhosmari had not understood at the time, but now she did. She had to do this, no matter what the risk to herself, because to allow her people to go to war would be a great evil.

And because one young faery, travelling alone, might escape the Empress's notice where a troop of armed warriors could not…

Rhosmari closed her eyes, gathering courage. Then she stood up and said, 'I will go. I will find Garan, wherever he is, and ask him to give us back the Stone.'

Lady Arianllys caught her breath, and Lord Gwylan looked more grim than ever. Rhosmari tensed, afraid they would try to stop her – but then Arianllys moved forward, wrapping her arms about Rhosmari and holding her close.

'May Rhys and the Great Gardener watch over you,' she said, 'and bring you safely to your destination. And when you have found Garan…give him our love.'

Rhosmari dug through the chest at the foot of her bed, pushing past old shoes, half-finished journals and her medals from the Rhysian Games until she found her pack. She would need to dress warmly, for once she left the magical climate of the Green Isles there would be nothing to protect her from the harsh mainland weather. Yet there were no winter clothes in her wardrobe, so she could only bring her grandmother's cloak and a few extra pairs of stockings, and hope for the best.

She had none of the coins and papers that humans used for currency, but she had a pearl necklace that her father had given her. Surely it would fetch a decent price, if she could find someone willing to buy it. Lady Arianllys had supplied her with a map that showed the nearby towns on the mainland, and a small packet of food to see her through the first day of her journey. Apart from a comb and toothbrush Rhosmari could think of little else that she might need, for if all went well it should only take her a day or two to reach her destination.

And she knew, now, what that destination would be. According to Gwylan and Arianllys, Garan had gone to the Oakenwyld, where Linden and her forty or so sister faeries lived. Rhosmari remembered Linden saying that the Oak was close to the town of Aynsbridge, and that their human friends Paul and Peri McCormick – Timothy's guardians – lived behind the great tree in a house called Oakhaven. Surely, with that much information, the place should be easy to find.

Rhosmari closed up the pack and cinched it tight, all the while reminding herself not to think about what she was doing. It did not matter that she was leaving behind her home, her family, and the only life she had ever known. It was not important what Fioled and the other scholars would think when she did not appear at the House of Learning tomorrow, or whether Rhosmari's mother would guess what she had done. She dared not consider the perils that awaited her, or all the things that could go wrong. She must simply go, now, before it was too late.

Yet her feet seemed to have put down roots into the floor, and her chest felt so tight she could hardly breathe. Rhosmari gripped the bedpost as her knees buckled. Had she lost her wits, to believe that she could get away with this? Or even that it was necessary?

But I can't turn back now, she told herself. *No matter what happens, I have to try.*

Besides, Lord Gwylan and Lady Arianllys were waiting

for her. They had warned Rhosmari that it was too windy for her to fly across the strait, and that the waves were too treacherous for her to take a boat. Nor could she Leap, because magic could not transport her anywhere that she had not set foot before. But if she met them at a certain place when she had finished packing, they would show her a safe way to the mainland.

Rhosmari swung the pack up off the bed and hugged it in front of her, like a protective shield. She was ready now. Any moment—

'Rhosmari?'

The voice was her mother's, husky with sleep. The latch of her door began to lift, and with a stab of panic Rhosmari Leaped, throwing her mind across miles of land and water and then hurling her body after it.

She landed on the beach at Ynys y Porth, smallest and southernmost of all the Green Isles. The ocean breeze blew gently and the night air was mild, but as Rhosmari hurried to meet Gwylan and Arianllys, even her hooded cloak could not stop her shivering.

'My mother knows I'm gone,' she panted. 'She'll start looking for me any minute – and if she finds out you've helped me escape—'

But Lord Gwylan shook his head. 'She will not be quick to assume you have run away,' he said. 'She will only think that you have gone for a walk because you could not sleep.'

'But—'

'The path to the mainland is not far,' said Arianllys soothingly. 'You will be gone before Lady Celyn knows it. Let me show you.' She led them across the tide-damp sand. At the far end of the beach was a staircase, its steps so worn as to be almost invisible. They climbed to the top of the promontory, then descended on the other side into a pebbly cove Rhosmari had never seen before.

'Here is the way you will take,' Lady Arianllys said, touching the cliffside. A crumbling archway rippled into view, mottled with moss and lichen and sealed by a door of carved limestone. Arianllys laid her palm against its surface and the portal grated open, revealing another set of stairs leading downwards.

'This is Gruffydd's Way,' she said, 'a tunnel built centuries ago for the use of our human friends. It is so little used nowadays that few of our people even remember its existence. But though it is old and neglected it is still sound, and will take you safely under the ocean all the way to the mainland.'

Dread crawled up Rhosmari's spine, wrapping cold fingers around her throat. To climb down into absolute blackness, beneath the damp earth and an unfathomable weight of sea, feeling the walls press closer about her with every moment—

'No,' she faltered. 'Please. I can't do this.'

'You must,' said Gwylan. 'There is no other way for you

45

to leave the Green Isles without your mother and the other Elders knowing it.'

'Wait,' Arianllys said. 'Let me talk to her.' Then she turned to Rhosmari and said, 'May I ask you a personal question?'

Rhosmari managed a nod.

'Do you love my son?'

She was taken aback. Love? What did that have to do with anything? Certainly she had liked and respected Garan, and his appearance was not unpleasant – though he did have the poured-milk hair and pallid skin common among the Children of Rhys, both of which Rhosmari was glad to have escaped herself. She had seen no reason not to pledge herself to him, knowing that the alliance would benefit both their houses and likely make one or both of them Elders someday.

And yet, though Garan had always been gracious and kind to Rhosmari, he had never touched her, or shared with her the deeper thoughts of his heart. Nor had Rhosmari told him of her own private longings and fears. There had been no reason to believe that their marriage would be any different from the partnerships of most faeries – a practical arrangement that would produce two or three children and bring them respect within the community, but nothing more.

'Not like that,' she told Arianllys. 'I do care for him, but...'

'Then it was not for his sake that you chose to undertake this journey. But is there not someone in your thoughts that you would like to see again? A certain young human who lives near the Oakenwyld, perhaps?'

Heat flooded Rhosmari's cheeks. 'No!'

The Lady Scholar smiled gently. 'I apologise,' she said. 'I was unkind to test you so. Yet on the day when Linden and Timothy came before the Elders...Gwylan may have been watching Garan's face, but I was watching yours.'

'I don't understand,' said Rhosmari, struggling between embarrassment and confusion. 'Why are you asking—'

'Because in order to find the courage you need to travel Gruffydd's Way,' said Arianllys, 'you must fix your thoughts on something greater than your fears. And love gives great strength...but so does conviction.' She put a hand on Rhosmari's shoulder. 'If you truly believe that finding Garan and the Stone is the only way to save our people...'

'I know. I have to do this. It's just—' Rhosmari bit her lip, and glanced at the tunnel again.

'There is no need for fear,' Gwylan told her. 'No enemy or stranger can open Gruffydd's Way, only the Children of Rhys and those we deem worthy of our trust. On the mainland side, the entrance will be invisible and impenetrable even to you, unless you approach it at low tide and place your hand where you see this mark.' He pointed to a symbol carved beside the doorway, a circle bisected by a wavering line. 'Not even Garan and his companions know this secret, so guard it well. Are you ready?'

Rhosmari nodded.

'Then I wish you success on your journey, Celyn's daughter.' He touched his fingers to his forehead in respect, and stepped aside.

Lady Arianllys bent and kissed her. 'Take good care,' she whispered. 'For you are dear to me as my own child, even though you will never marry my son.'

'Is that a prophecy?' asked Rhosmari with a feeble attempt at humour, but Arianllys did not answer. She only turned towards her husband and buried her face against his chest. Was the Lady Scholar actually *crying*? But before Rhosmari could ask what was wrong, Gwylan raised his hand in farewell, and the two of them disappeared.

Rhosmari turned to face the cliffside. The tunnel gaped before her, wide as a sea serpent's throat and no less daunting. Even when she kindled a glow-spell and sent it floating through the archway, she could see little of what lay ahead. Only rough-hewn walls and uneven steps leading down into a blackness like spilled ink, too thick for her magic to penetrate.

She didn't want to go in there.

But she had to.

Rhosmari closed her eyes and whispered a prayer for courage. Then she hefted her pack, straightened her shoulders, and took her first step into Gruffydd's Way.

*

Shadows swarmed around Rhosmari, dragging at her feet
and tangling in her hair. Every step into deeper darkness
was an agonising effort of will. Her glow-spell hovered
beside her, but its scant radiance brought no comfort. At any
moment she might faint, and the light would sputter and
go out.

She did not belong here, trapped between water and
rock. She was a child of open skies and soft pastures, but this
tunnel had transformed her into a blind, crawling
earthworm. Her hand gripped the stair rail until the rough
stone scored her palm, but even pain could not distract her
from the bone-numbing cold. What madness had made
her believe that she could do this? She had not even reached
the bottom of the stair, and her legs shook as though she had
been running.

Perhaps it was not too late to turn back. She could Leap
home again, shove her pack into the back of the wardrobe
with her bow and quiver, and forget that tonight had ever
happened...

No. Only a fool and a coward would think such a thing,
and she was neither. She was the daughter of Lady Celyn,
and her people were counting on her. She would get
through this tunnel somehow, even if it took her all night—

Rhosmari!

Her stomach lurched as that familiar voice spoke into her
mind, faint but unmistakable. Faeries of the same blood, or

who had mutually agreed to the arrangement, could speak mind to mind across short distances – and now Lady Celyn was Calling her. If Rhosmari did not answer, it would be obvious that something was wrong...but if she did, her mother would know immediately where to find her. What was she going to do?

Then she realised the answer. Outside the tunnel, on the beach of Ynys y Porth, two great stones called the Sentinels marked the boundary between the Green Isles and the mortal realm. There were no Sentinels here, at least not as far as she could see, but still the border could not be far away. And once Rhosmari crossed that magical line, it would be difficult for Lady Celyn to stop her.

Answer me! The Call pierced her mind like an icy needle. Rhosmari pressed a hand to her ear, but she could not shut it out. How long would it be before Lady Celyn picked up one of Rhosmari's belongings and cast a tracking spell? Urgency gripped her, and she began to hurry down the steps as quickly as she could go.

At the foot of the stair her glow-spell beamed straight ahead, revealing curving walls that stretched out far into the distance. It was even colder here, but the tunnel widened with every step, and the tightness in Rhosmari's chest began to ease.

Where are you, daughter? Speak to me at once!

This time the Call was so clear, so penetrating, that Lady Celyn had to be nearby. Rhosmari broke into a run, racing down the tunnel as fast as her shaky legs would carry her. The pain in her head was intense, but she forced herself to ignore it. Where was the boundary? It had to be close, and yet—

There! She could not see it, but she sensed it: a glimmering skin of magic stretched across the tunnel some fifty paces ahead. Rhosmari was panting now and her sides had begun to cramp, but she kept running. Just forty paces left…now thirty…twenty…

A wave of heat rippled up Rhosmari's back. The air knotted around her, jerking her to a stop in mid-stride. She struggled, but the invisible net would not break. There was no escape – her mother was coming—

She was here.

'Fool of a girl!' snapped Lady Celyn. Loosed from its customary braids and wrappings, her hair haloed her face like a storm cloud. 'How dare you run off to see the human world, when I expressly forbade you to go?'

The accusation was so unexpected it made Rhosmari gasp. 'That's not what I was doing!'

'Indeed?' said her mother. 'Then why are you here?'

Rhosmari lifted her chin, determined not to show her fear. 'I am going to the mainland, to find Garan and get back the Stone.'

For an instant Lady Celyn looked startled. Then her eyes narrowed again. 'So,' she said. 'You have so little respect for your Elders, or your people—'

'That's not true! I only wanted to help!'

'I am not interested in your motives,' said her mother coldly. 'Whether you are arrogant or merely naive makes no difference. Either way, this folly ends now, and you are coming home with me.'

'Why?' Frustration seethed inside her. 'Why send an army after Garan, when a single faery might be enough? If you only wait a few more days, and give me the chance—'

'Enough!' Lady Celyn slashed her hand through the air. 'I have told you that the mainland is no place for you. Are you truly so incapable of seeing reason?'

Rhosmari wrestled against the net of spells again. There were gaps in the mesh big enough for her to thrust her hand through, but what good would that do her? Unless...

'I see you are determined,' said her mother. 'So be it.' She drew herself up, tall and pitiless as a goddess. 'You will come back to the house as my prisoner, and I will weave such spells as will keep you there, until you swear by your true name that you will never try to leave the Green Isles again.'

Horror gripped Rhosmari. 'You wouldn't.'

'I will do whatever I think necessary to protect you from yourself,' Celyn retorted. 'Your grandfather – my father – was killed by the humans on the mainland, and I will not allow my only daughter to share his fate. *Will not*, do you understand?'

Rhosmari sank back against the net, stunned by the

revelation. She knew what it was to lose a father, and Lady Celyn's words tore at her heart. To think that humans could be so evil, and cause such pain…

And yet what her mother wanted to do to her was evil, too.

'Then you are no different from the Empress,' Rhosmari said shakily, as she pulled herself upright again. 'For you want to force me to obey you, instead of allowing me to choose for myself what is right. And though you are my mother and I love you, I will not let you make me your slave.'

And with that she extinguished her glow-spell, plunging the tunnel into darkness.

It only took a moment for Lady Celyn to kindle her own light, but it was enough. In that instant Rhosmari willed herself small and darted free of her mother's web of spells as it collapsed. With a flurry of her new-grown wings she launched herself into the air, shooting down the tunnel like a loosed arrow – and as she flashed over the boundary to the mortal world, Lady Celyn's cry of protest cut off as though she had been choked.

Still Rhosmari dared not hesitate. On this side of the border her mother's powers were weaker, but so were her own. Her wings blurred as she urged them to greater and greater speed. Yet she was flying blind, and if the tunnel were to curve even a little, she would smash into the wall and knock herself senseless – or worse.

But no spell pursued her, nor could she hear Lady Celyn calling. And when at last Rhosmari slowed down and looked back the way she had come, she could not see the smallest spark of light. Unwilling even to set foot into the human world, her mother had gone.

Rhosmari glided to the floor of the tunnel and transformed herself back to her usual size. Her lungs burned and her eyes stung, as though she had been breathing smoke. But she wiped her face on her sleeve, kindled another light, and doggedly continued on.

Now that she had no choice but to go forward, Gruffydd's Way no longer seemed as terrible to Rhosmari as it had before. The tunnel was high and spacious, its walls so far apart that even the outspread wings of an albatross could not have touched both at the same time. The stones beneath her feet felt solid, and the roof showed no sign of collapsing. Still, every time she glimpsed a shining thread of water or felt the air grow clammy, she quickened her stride just in case.

How many hours had passed since she left the Green Isles? Without sun, moon or tides to tell her, Rhosmari had no idea. All she knew was that she had never walked so far in all her life. She had already broken her journey twice to eat some of the food Lady Arianllys had given her, for all that flying had given her a ferocious appetite. But now her stomach felt empty again.

She had half convinced herself that her mother had trapped her in some cunning illusion, and that she would wander through Gruffydd's Way forever, when the floor began to slant upwards. Only a few steps ahead lay the foot of a staircase, its broad steps rising into darkness. She had reached the mainland at last.

Rhosmari paused, surveying the ascent. This tunnel had been built for humans, not the smaller Children of Rhys; she would likely find the climb easier if she made herself human height. How tall had Timothy stood, when he visited them? Perhaps just a little shorter than that...

She knocked a fist against her forehead in frustration. Not Timothy again. Why had Lady Arianllys reminded her? She had done her best to put him out of her mind, especially once she realised that he and Linden were to blame for what Garan had done. And yet when he told how one of the Empress's servants had tried to steal his musical talent, Rhosmari had shivered like a plucked bowstring...

Enough of that, she told herself severely. Collecting her scattered thoughts, she counted stones up the tunnel wall until she reached a measurement that seemed reasonable to her, then grew little by little until she had matched it.

The stairs looked far less daunting now. Gratified, she began to climb.

Up and up Rhosmari went, the walls around her narrowing with every step – but she did not mind that much, not when she knew she would soon be free. The stillness in the tunnel broke into a rumble, then swelled to an echoing roar, but Rhosmari recognised the sound of waves crashing against rock, and welcomed it. Finally the stair twisted back on itself and stopped at a door of carved stone, identical to the one Lady Arianllys had opened for her hours ago. Her glow-spell picked out the outline of a wave-crossed circle; she touched it, and the door rasped open.

Never had the ocean breeze tasted so sweet, though its coldness took her breath away. She saw no moon, but her night vision revealed a great stretch of sand and foam-capped waves, with the shadowy bulk of an island in the distance. Rhosmari stepped out of the tunnel, and when she looked back, the exit to Gruffydd's Way had vanished. All that lay behind her now was a slanting cliffside, with tufts of grass and gorse springing here and there from the rock.

Her heart fluttered. What if she could not find the door again? But when she looked closer she glimpsed the familiar symbol, delicately etched into the rock. There was still a way home for her, and perhaps – if the Elders chose to be merciful – for Garan and his followers as well.

She tried not to think about the possibility that if she failed to bring back the Stone, the Elders might not let her return to the Green Isles either.

three

When at last the sun crept over the horizon, it unveiled a rugged and rolling landscape, divided into a patchwork of small fields dotted with sheep. There were no trees in sight, only a few wandering tangles of shrubbery. It had a wild beauty, but it made Rhosmari feel vulnerable, and for the first time she could remember, lonely.

But stranger things awaited her as she approached the town of St David's. Until today, she had only ever seen one human, but now they were everywhere. Driving in cars and riding bicycles, both amazing sights in themselves; strolling alone, in couples, in families; walking dogs that yapped and strained at their leashes when she passed by. Even at this early hour, the roads were busy with them, and every time one of them crossed her path it was an effort not to stare.

Never before had she seen such bulky figures, for though faeries might be lean or stocky they were almost never fat.

Nor had she realised what a shock it would be to look into the faces of the older humans and see wrinkles, florid spots, and hair streaked with white. Of course she knew that human lives were brief compared to those of faeries, their bodies far more vulnerable to sickness and decay. But it was one thing to read about it, another to see it firsthand.

Yet fragile as humans might be, they still had formidable powers. They used cold iron freely, working it into posts and railings, and on her way up from the cathedral Rhosmari almost put her hand on an iron gate before she realised the danger and snatched it away. Iron sapped faeries' strength and stopped them from doing magic – and in this hostile place she could not afford to be defenceless, even for a moment.

Especially now that she knew that humans had killed her grandfather.

How had it happened, and why? Only Lady Celyn could tell her, and there was no chance of asking her now. But despite Rhosmari's resolve to find Garan and the Stone, it made her queasy to think of it. Until today she had resented her mother for keeping her from the mainland – but now she understood just how dangerous the human world could be.

And yet it did not *look* dangerous. The streets of St David's were cosily narrow, lined with buildings of white plaster and grey stone. Bells tolled out from the ancient cathedral that gave the city its name. Rhosmari was already beginning to feel hungry again, and when she passed an open window and the smell of frying sausage drifted towards her, her stomach groaned with longing. She could only hope she would soon find someone to buy her necklace.

Fortunately, there was a jeweller's shop tucked away in a little corner of the High Street, not far from the city square. She waited until the man turned the sign in the window from CLOSED to OPEN – but even then she could not get past the door, for faeries could not enter a human dwelling without invitation. She was reduced to peering in the window and making hopeful gestures until the man came to let her in.

'What can I do for you?' The jeweller's voice was gruff, and he looked at her as though he did not like what he saw. But Rhosmari refused to let herself be daunted, for he held no weapon, and did not look quick or strong enough to do her any serious harm.

'I have a pearl necklace I'd like to sell,' she said.

As the pearls poured out across his counter, the man's brows shot up. He picked up the necklace in his big, calloused hands and examined it with a lens, then bared his teeth and rubbed the strand across them. When at last he laid the pearls down again, it was with almost reverent care – but then he shook his head.

'You've had your fun,' he said curtly. 'Now get out of my shop. I don't do business with thieves.'

If he had slapped her in the face, Rhosmari could not have been more shocked. 'I am not a thief!'

'I suppose you just found the pearls then, washed up on the shore? Or did you inherit them from your old aunty, the Queen of Sheba?' He snatched up the receiver beside him and began jabbing at it. 'I'm calling the police. They'll sort this out—'

She knew what that meant, and she knew it must not happen. In desperation Rhosmari flung up her hands, and magic enveloped the man in its sparkling glow.

At once the jeweller stopped, his angry look fading to bewilderment. 'Now who was I calling?' he murmured. He set the phone back down, blinking and rubbing one eye. 'Sorry to keep you waiting, miss. How can I help you?'

But by the time he finished speaking, Rhosmari and her pearls were gone.

Rhosmari hurried down the street, heart hammering with the nearness of her escape. Why had that jeweller refused to believe that the necklace was hers? Was it because she was young? Or was there something else about her appearance that made him suspicious?

She paused to consider her reflection in a shop window, but noticed nothing unusual. The only thing that might give her away as a faery were the points on her ears, but her thick, loosely clasped hair hid them in any case.

Well, she would just have to find another shop that sold

jewellery and try again. It was not a pleasant thought, but neither was the hollow feeling in her stomach, nor her growing conviction that someone from the Green Isles would come to arrest her at any moment. Shouldering her pack, Rhosmari set off again.

It took her several minutes of squinting at one window after another, but at last she found it: a tree-shaped rack of pins and necklaces, tucked between a stack of glazed pottery and a sculpture of a leaping dolphin. She knocked on the door, and waited.

'Was it stuck?' asked the woman, as she ushered Rhosmari in. 'That's a funny thing, it's never done that before.' But she spoke cheerfully, and her expression was kind. Heartened, Rhosmari showed her the necklace.

'Good heavens, that's a lovely piece,' said the woman. 'And antique, too. I don't know anyone in St David's who could give you the price of it. You'll be better to take it to Haverfordwest at least, if not Swansea or Cardiff—'

'I need the money now,' said Rhosmari. 'Please. I'll take whatever you can give me for it.'

The woman looked from the pearls to Rhosmari and back again, her brow creasing. 'You're in trouble, are you, dear?'

Rhosmari bristled, but the woman held up a hand. 'Don't worry. I don't mean to interfere. But it would help me to decide, if I knew why you needed the money so badly.'

'I have to get to London,' said Rhosmari. 'It's important. And urgent.'

'Do you have friends there? Relatives who can look after you?'

'Not in London,' Rhosmari told her. 'But…I know some people who live not far from there. In a place called Aynsbridge…'

A bird fluttered against the window as she spoke, distracting her. But by the time she glanced around, it was gone. She turned back to the woman and finished, 'That's where I have to go.'

Fortunately, those details were enough to put the shopkeeper at ease. She named a price that she could afford to pay, though she warned that it was far less than the necklace was worth, and assured Rhosmari that if she returned to the shop within six weeks she would give her the chance to buy it back again. Relieved, Rhosmari accepted the money, expressed her gratitude as best she could without actually saying *thank you* – for faeries did not say those sacred words unless it was a matter of life and death – and left the shop with a lighter heart.

She was crossing the square on her way towards the City Hall – the woman had told her she could catch a bus to Haverfordwest from there – when she heard it. *Cark*, came the rasping cry, and when Rhosmari looked up there were two ravens perched on the tall, circle-framed cross at the centre of the square.

There was nothing unusual about that, at first glance. But as their unblinking gaze met Rhosmari's, apprehension shivered through her. Those were not ordinary birds – they were faeries, male faeries, in raven shape.

Yet they were not members of the Council Guard, or anyone else she recognised. That ought to have reassured her, but she could not help feeling uneasy just the same. On their way to the Green Isles, Timothy and Linden had been pursued by two raven brothers who served the Empress. What if these were the same Blackwings, come to capture Rhosmari and take her to their mistress?

But no, she was being ridiculous. According to Linden, few of the mainland faeries had even heard of the Children of Rhys, and still fewer believed in their existence. There was no reason that Corbin and Byrne Blackwing should be interested in Rhosmari at all, let alone pursue her.

Just then a smaller bird flashed across the square, tiny as a flung stone, and in a shirr of black feathers the ravens launched themselves after it. In seconds all three of them had vanished, and Rhosmari was alone.

After that unsettling experience, Rhosmari did not linger in St David's even long enough to eat, let alone buy gloves for her cold-cramped hands. When the next bus left for Haverfordwest, she was on it.

Crowded by humans on both sides, nose wrinkling at the meaty pungency of their smell, she sat stiffly in the back of the bus as it skirted the coast and squeezed its way through the little towns of Solva and Newgale. But she soon forgot her discomfort, as every passing mile and every curve of the highway brought new and entrancing sights before her eyes. It amazed her that the human world could be so unpleasant in some ways, yet so beautiful in others.

At last the bus reached Haverfordwest railway station, and the door wheezed open to let them out. Most of the passengers headed straight inside, but Rhosmari hesitated. Her studies had taught her about the existence of trains and even a little of how they worked, but no faery she knew had ever ridden one.

Still, it was the fastest way to get where she was going. Rhosmari followed the last few humans into the station, watching and listening as they paid for their journeys. Then she stepped up and did likewise, and soon emerged onto the platform with ticket in hand. But apprehension had stolen away her hunger, and when a rich smell of meat and pastry wafted out of the nearby cafe she found herself edging away from it, nauseated.

As the crowd on the platform swelled from a few to many, the atmosphere became charged with expectation. But instead of gazing down the track like the rest of them, the human beside Rhosmari kept looking at the sky. Was it about to rain? Automatically she followed his gaze – and her heart jolted. Two ravens were flapping towards the platform, their wingbeats purposeful and sure.

And they were angling straight for her.

She must not panic. She must stay just where she was,

and behave as though she had no reason to fear. Even if they were the same ravens she had seen in St David's earlier, they might not mean any harm. Perhaps they only wanted to observe her a little more closely.

The ravens swooped lower, and Rhosmari braced herself for a confrontation – but then they veered away over the rooftops, out of her sight. Had she been mistaken? Had they just been ordinary birds after all?

A hand clamped around her arm, jerking her back beneath the station overhang. She cried out – but the sound went nowhere. Someone had cast a spell of silence over her, and there was nothing she could do to break it.

A lean body pressed against her back, and she smelled the sharp evergreen scent of an unfamiliar faery. His lips moved beside her ear, breathing an urgent whisper:

'*Help me.*'

Startled, Rhosmari twisted to face the stranger. He was a wiry-built male not much taller than herself, with sharp features and pale hair slanting across his forehead. There were grey shadows beneath his greyer eyes, and his cheeks looked hollow with hunger.

'Hide me from the Blackwings,' he begged. 'I will give you whatever you ask for, do anything in my power to repay you, but do not let them take me. *Please.*'

Rhosmari's insides went cold. So the ravens were the Empress's servants, after all. But were they only chasing this wild-eyed stranger, or did they want her as well? It was hard to believe that they would have followed her all the way from St David's to Haverfordwest merely by coincidence...

She was still trying to decide what to do when the Blackwings stepped onto the platform in human shape, twin brothers with raven hair and the menacing grace of veteran hunters. With a shared glance and a nod to each other, they began to walk in opposite directions, studying each of the passengers in turn.

There was no more time for hesitation. 'Stay close to me,' Rhosmari mouthed to the stranger, and cloaked them both in the most powerful invisibility glamour she could devise. The Blackwings' eyes slid towards them... Over them...

And past them, without so much as a pause. Rhosmari relaxed – then tensed again, struck by fresh anxiety. The Blackwings had already seen her standing on the platform when they flew in. Now that she had disappeared, how long would it be before they guessed she was hiding the stranger?

Distracted, she did not even hear the train approaching. But then came a metallic squeal, and the space beside the platform became a blur of carriages. The strange faery nudged her elbow, and she understood: they had to get on the train as soon as it stopped, and pray that the Blackwings did not follow.

The train slid to a halt, doors hissing open. The humans crowded forward, and Rhosmari and her companion crept invisibly after them. They slipped inside the carriage, pressing back against the wall.

Outside, the Blackwings paced the platform, unaware that their quarry had gone. But then the shorter of the two stopped, as though struck by realisation. His nostrils flared; he turned towards the train—

The door sang a wavering note and whirred shut, sealing the carriage. In seconds the train had glided away, leaving the station and the Blackwings behind.

The blonde faery let out his breath. 'I am in your debt. My name is Martin.'

Which was his common name, nothing more – faeries never gave away their true names if they could help it. But still, the introduction showed a measure of trust. 'I am called Rhosmari,' she said.

'A lovely name,' said Martin. 'It suits you.'

He spoke lightly, as though the words were mere courtesy. But the look in his eyes said otherwise, and Rhosmari had to drop her gaze.

'I am grateful beyond words,' Martin went on, 'for your willingness to help a stranger. Few faeries I know would be so generous.' He touched a button on the wall, and another door slid open to reveal a narrow-aisled compartment lined with seats. 'Are you hungry? Let me get you something to eat.'

'I have money,' said Rhosmari, but Martin shook his head.

'I told you,' he said. 'The debt is mine.' He gestured to the seats. 'Make yourself comfortable. I'll be back.'

Inside the compartment the air smelled stale, but at least it was warm. Rhosmari took a seat by the window, as far as she could get from the humans sharing the train with them, and let her pack slide to the floor at her feet. At first she was a little unnerved by the speed with which the countryside flashed by, but soon she began to find it comforting. Surely now it would be impossible for the Blackwings to catch up with them.

Soon Martin returned, holding two small loaves covered in filmy wrapping. He gave one to her and sat down, casually crossing one leg over the other, as though he had ridden a train many times before. Rhosmari unwrapped her loaf and pried off the top to find it stuffed with a generous portion of white meat, some surprisingly fresh-looking greens, and a scattering of dried berries. Where had it come from? She gave Martin a questioning look, but he had already bitten into his own loaf, and she was too famished to wait any longer. She spread her hands out in blessing and began to eat.

'Why did you do that?' asked Martin, and Rhosmari nearly dropped the bread before she remembered that this was not her mother's table.

'Do what?' she answered, when her mouth was clear. She knew there was nothing actually *wrong* with talking during a meal, but still she could not help feeling uncomfortable and even a little guilty.

'That gesture you made before you ate. I've never seen anyone do that before. What does it mean?'

How could she answer, without explaining that she was one of the Children of Rhys? 'It's a tradition,' she said at last, 'that my mother taught me. A way to show gratitude that we have something to eat.'

'Ah,' said Martin, but to her relief he did not press her further. They finished their meal in silence, and Rhosmari was just brushing the last crumbs from her skirt when the door at the end of the compartment opened and a brisk-looking man stepped in. 'Ticket, please,' he said to the woman on his right, and began working his way down the aisle towards them.

Martin reached into his jacket. Rhosmari stooped to look for her own ticket, but Martin was already holding out two cards for the man's inspection.

'But I—' she began, only to be silenced by Martin's warning look. As soon as the man handed back the tickets and moved on, Martin gave Rhosmari a conspiratorial smile and flicked the cards with a finger. At once they turned blank, and he tucked them back into his pocket.

So he had tricked the man? Rhosmari was speechless. She knew that male faeries had a special talent for changing the shapes of things, but she had not realised it could be used so deceitfully.

'Oh, come now,' said Martin. 'Don't look so shocked. You ate that sandwich I gave you readily enough.'

So he had stolen their dinner, too. Rhosmari felt as though she had swallowed a handful of dust. But what could she do? The food was gone now, and she had no idea where it had come from. She pressed her lips together and looked away.

Martin gave a short laugh. 'Are you really so virtuous? How it must gall you to serve the Empress. Or…do you?'

Rhosmari glanced at him warily. 'Do you?'

'What do you think?' He raised his brows at her. 'Would the Blackwings be trying to kill me if I did?'

'Kill you! Why?'

'Because the Empress commanded it,' he said. 'Why else? She ordered me to kill someone. I told her I would rather not. And when she tried to force my obedience and found she could no longer do so, she declared me a traitor and a spy.'

Rhosmari's fingers tightened on the arms of her seat. *Could no longer do so.* If Martin was free of the Empress's control, then he must have touched the Stone of Naming. But how, and when? Did she dare ask, or would that be giving too much away?

'I have a question,' said Martin. 'Why did you help me? Are you not afraid of what the Empress would do to you if she found out?'

'I have a question first,' said Rhosmari. 'How did *you* defy the Empress?'

Martin studied her closely, as though weighing her with his gaze. At last he said, 'Have you heard of the Stone of Naming?'

Even if she had been capable of lying, she could not have brought herself to do so. 'Yes.'

'Then you must also have heard about the Battle of Sanctuary, where Rob and his fellow rebels fought the Empress. You know Rob?'

'A little,' said Rhosmari cautiously. Rob was the one who had first told Linden and Timothy about the Stone of Naming, and urged them to look for it. Though if she remembered the story correctly – and after viewing the loreseed so many times, she ought to – Rob had not known where to find the Children of Rhys, and neither did any other faery on the mainland. Timothy had figured out that part all on his own...

No, she was not going to start thinking about Timothy again. In a firmer voice Rhosmari said, 'Go on.'

'I was at Sanctuary when the battle took place,' said Martin. 'After the Empress and her followers fled, Rob offered the Stone to anyone who wished to be free, and of course I accepted the offer. But I was not ready to join the rebellion, so I struck out on my own.' He gave a rueful shrug. 'You can see how well that succeeded.'

'She captured you?'

'In a sense. She believed that I was still loyal to her, and I decided to play along, thinking I would soon find another chance to escape. But when I refused to kill Rob, she realised her mistake...and I have been running from the Blackwings ever since.'

Rhosmari was silent, mulling over his words. So the Stone had last been seen in London, with Rob and the rebels. But that had been days or even weeks ago. Where was it now?

'I thought at first that if I could find the rebels again, I would be safe,' said Martin reflectively. 'And I heard a rumour that they had gone to a place called the Oak, so I decided to look for them there. But by the time I arrived...well.' He grimaced. 'You know the rest of that story.'

Apprehension flickered in Rhosmari's chest. 'What story?'

'About the Oak, and what happened to it.' He gave her a curious look. 'You really have not heard?'

Her pulse was racing now. If Garan had gone to the Oak to help Linden and her people, and then Rob had followed them there with the Stone... 'Tell me,' she said. 'Please.'

Martin spread his hands, as though to apologise for what he was about to say. 'The Empress attacked the Oak a few days ago, and burned it to the ground. A few of the rebels and Oakenfolk escaped, but many were captured, and the rest...are dead.'

four

'No!' The word tore out of Rhosmari before she could stop herself. 'The Oak destroyed? That can't be!'

'I understand,' said Martin. 'I could hardly believe it myself. With Rob and his rebels there, I would have expected more of a battle. But when I got to the Oakenwyld, it was already over.'

Rhosmari's hands were shaking. She pressed them against her thighs to still them. Had Garan been killed? Her fellow scholar Broch? Or Llwynog, whose common name meant *fox*, but who was so mild-mannered that everyone called him *Llinos*, a harmless little bird, instead? What of Linden, and her human friends? Timothy, and Paul, and Peri – had the Empress killed them too?

And what had become of the Stone of Naming?

Rhosmari squeezed her eyes shut, breathing hard. She could not afford to fall apart. She had to concentrate. She had to *think*.

'I've upset you,' said Martin. 'I apologise. But I thought every faery in Britain must have heard the news by now. Where have you been, not to know about all this?'

She shook her head, too distracted to answer. The Oak was gone, the rebels scattered. She had no idea where the Stone had gone, or whether she had any hope of finding it in time to forestall her mother's plan. Perhaps she should just give up now, and turn back?

But if she returned to the Green Isles empty-handed, that would only prove to everyone that Lady Celyn had been right, and the only way to retrieve the Stone was to send the Children of Rhys out in force...

'Well,' said Martin, 'I know at least one thing about you now: you do not serve the Empress. And I could almost swear that you have never belonged to her, unlikely as that seems.' He leaned closer. 'So why leave the safety of your Wyld, if you have managed to avoid the Empress until now?'

Rhosmari kept silent, but Martin persisted. 'You obviously wanted the Oakenfolk and the rebels to succeed. Was that why you were travelling this way? Were you hoping to join the rebellion, and fight with them?'

'Fight? No!' Of course she felt sorry for the Empress's slaves, and would like to see them freed. But only the Stone of Naming could do that, not violence and bloodshed.

Although, if she found the Stone and took it back to the Green Isles, the mainland faeries would never have the chance to use it...

Rhosmari rubbed wearily at the bridge of her nose. Why did everything have to be so complicated? 'No,' she repeated. 'I only wanted to find someone who left our Wyld to join the rebels, and ask him for – for help.'

'Ah, that makes more sense,' said Martin, settling into his seat again. 'I was finding it difficult to imagine you as a soldier. I have no love for fighting myself, particularly in what seems to be a losing cause.' His gaze flicked to the window. 'Yet I am not ready to surrender to the Empress, either. Perhaps…we can help each other.'

'How?' asked Rhosmari.

'We can look for the rebels together,' he said. 'I know Rob well enough to guess where he and his people would be most likely to hide. I know how to get almost anywhere in this country by train, which is a good way to stay ahead of the Blackwings, or anyone else who might follow us. And we each have magical skills that the other does not, so the two of us can protect each other better than either of us could do alone.'

He did have a point, Rhosmari had to admit. And he was in her debt, so he had good reason for wanting to help her. 'And once we find the rebels?' she asked.

'Then I'll go my own way,' said Martin. 'As I said, I have no interest in martyrdom. But if you need an escort back to your home Wyld…' He gave a shrug that was not quite indifferent. 'I would be glad to do that, too.'

Now she understood. He must be thinking that if he

helped Rhosmari, her people would give him refuge from the Empress. But the Elders would never allow a thief and a deceiver to set foot in the *Gwerdonnau Llion*, unless they were certain he had repented of his ways.

'All right,' she said at last, 'it's a bargain. But no more tricks. If we need food, or lodging, or transport, we pay for it honestly.'

'Then you'll have to pay for both of us,' said Martin. 'I have no money at all. But if it means so much to you…'

'It does.'

'Then I accept your terms.'

The train station at Cardiff was the noisiest, most confusing place Rhosmari had ever seen. Humans hurried in all directions, laughing and arguing and embracing one another, shouting into little boxes they held in their hands or bobbing their heads to rhythms that they alone could hear. Though most faeries – Rhosmari included – were chary of touch, she was grateful for Martin's steadying hand on her elbow as he steered her through the commotion.

'I know this city,' he said, as they emerged into the brightly lit hall at the end of the corridor, a place lined with booths selling food and merchandise and swarming with people of all colours and ages. 'I have friends here, and I know a place we can stay.'

His confidence surprised her. Faeries did not often speak

of having *friends*, even on the Green Isles. 'Where?' she asked.

'This way,' said Martin. He plunged through the crowd to the station entrance, dodged a pained-looking human couple with a trio of squabbling children, and led the way outside. 'Cardiff,' he announced with satisfaction, spreading his arms to the looming buildings and the darkening sky.

Rhosmari had never been in a large city before, and ordinarily she would have been fascinated. But right now she was too tired to do more than squint and nod.

'Come on,' said Martin. Unlike her, he was practically springing with energy – but then, he had slept on the train. Before Rhosmari could protest he caught her hand, fingers snaking through hers in a way that made her shiver, and dragged her towards the street.

As they came out onto the main road, Rhosmari winced and shielded her eyes. Everything hurt to look at: signs blazing above shop windows, streetlights glowering overhead, the headlamps of vehicles blinding her as they rumbled past. 'Is it far?' she asked. 'I—' Then a wave of smog assaulted her and she doubled up coughing, unable to finish the sentence.

'You'll get used to it,' Martin told her, looking more amused than sympathetic. 'And we've a few streets to go yet – but we'll be there soon enough.'

Minute after dreary minute they walked, while the night closed in and the air turned from cool to cold. Rhosmari was numb all over by the time they stopped, in front of a narrow door whose painted sign read BARDHOUSE THEATRE COMPANY. There was a button beside the doorway; Martin pressed it and waited.

'Shh,' warned a hoarse voice, as the door cracked open and a tousled head poked out. 'They've already started. If you want to audition, you'll have to—' The man straightened up, eyes rounding with surprise. 'Mad Martin! I thought we'd seen the last of you! Who's this, your girl?'

'Not so much, I'm afraid,' said Martin. 'We met on the train. Good to see you again, Toby. Mind if we come in and watch for a bit? I thought Rhosmari might enjoy—' his voice dropped into a mocking drawl— 'a *unique cultural experience.*'

'Oh, you'll have that here, all right,' sighed Toby, pushing his hands through his hair until it stood on end. 'I've never seen such a dismal lot of amateurs, and Lyn's been carving them up like Christmas geese. But if you're up for the punishment, I won't stop you. Watch the ladder—' and with that, he backed inside.

Rhosmari stared after him, weariness forgotten in the astonishment of discovering that Martin's friends were human. But she had little time to dwell on it, because Martin had already stepped over the threshold, and she had to follow.

They emerged into a narrow entryway, with a paper-littered study just visible to their right and a staircase heading upwards on the left. A battered stepladder stood to one side of the corridor, with a striped cat sleeping underneath. Martin slid past it without so much as a glance, but Rhosmari crouched to look at it more closely. There were no cats on the Green Isles, and this was her first encounter with one. Was it tame? Would it let her touch it?

'Come on,' Martin hissed over his shoulder, and reluctantly she rose and joined him. They stepped through a curtained arch into a deep, windowless room half lost in shadow. Rows of chairs filled the space from top to bottom, angling downwards to a starkly lit platform at the front. With a nod to their human guide, Martin slipped into a seat, and Rhosmari sat down beside him.

'What is this place?' she whispered. But Martin only pointed to the stage, where a drab-looking woman stood clutching a book to her chest. Her gaze was fixed on someone in the front row, her expression full of nervous hope as she asked, 'How was that?'

'It was bloody awful,' said a laconic female voice. 'Not this time, love.'

The woman wilted and slunk off the platform. 'Next,' said the bored-sounding woman, and a girl with frizzy brown hair scraped back into a knot climbed up to take her place. She gave a wavering smile, cleared her throat, and began:

'The quality of mercy is not strained; it droppeth as the

gentle rain from heaven upon the place beneath. It is twice blest: it blesseth him that gives and him that takes…'

Unlike the woman who had come before her, she held no book in her hands; she seemed to be reciting the speech from memory. Unfortunately, she was concentrating too hard on getting the words right to put much expression into them, and Rhosmari felt an unexpected flash of sympathy. She leaned forward in her seat, willing the girl to relax and not be afraid.

The result was startling. At once the girl stood taller and began to speak with more confidence, investing the speech with such passion that it almost seemed the words were her own. Her eyes shone and her gestures became eloquent as she urged her unseen hearer to consider her argument, examine his heart, and choose compassion over the letter of the law:

'I have spoke thus much, to mitigate the justice of thy plea; which if thou follow, this strict court of Venice must needs lay sentence 'gainst the merchant there.'

She finished with a little bow, then stepped back and waited. The stark lights picked out the freckles on her skin and the flush in her cheeks; she was breathing quickly, and Rhosmari felt her nervousness as though she were on trial herself.

'Well, now,' came the pronouncement from below. 'That was more like it.' With an energy that belied her languid tone, a short, steely-haired woman leaped up from her seat and seized the girl's hand in an approving shake. 'Good work, Lucy. Come back tomorrow. Next!'

'It seems you don't need me to teach you to appreciate theatre,' Martin murmured to Rhosmari as another human made his way onto the platform. 'But who would have thought an honest faery like yourself would take so readily to an art built on trickery and lies?'

'Lies?' Rhosmari was taken aback. 'But I thought that girl was giving a speech – an argument—'

'Of course she was. But in doing so, she was also playing the part of a woman disguised as a man, pretending to be a lawyer in a court that never existed,' said Martin, leaning back and lacing his fingers behind his head. 'That was from William Shakespeare's play *The Merchant of Venice*.'

A play. Rhosmari knew that humans sometimes put on disguises and acted out stories to amuse an audience, but she had never seen it done before. 'That's not a lie,' she protested. 'How can it be, when no one is really deceived?'

'Ah, but they *want* to be deceived,' Martin replied. 'And the closer an actor comes to making them believe that the emotions he pretends are real, the better they love him for it. Watch.' He nodded at the stage as a dark-eyed boy who moved like a candle flame stepped forward and began to speak:

'I am a Jew. Hath not a Jew eyes? Hath not a Jew hands, organs, dimensions, senses, affections, passions…?'

By the end of his speech, Rhosmari was blinking back

tears. The earnestness with which the young man delivered his lines, the pride and despair alternating upon his face, communicated his yearning for justice with a power that made her ache. When he spoke of wanting revenge on those who had wronged him, it made her uneasy – and yet she understood why he might feel that way. And when she glanced at Martin and saw how his eyes had narrowed and his hands tightened upon his knees, she realised that he too was moved and trying not to show it.

When the boy finished there was silence, tense as a held breath. Then—

'I knew it!' bellowed the woman in the front, spinning around to jab a finger at Martin. 'It's you! I should have known you were back the moment this rabble started performing like real actors. But what's the good of having a muse who won't stay put?' She strode up the aisle, seized Martin and gave him a resounding kiss on both cheeks.

'I haven't the slightest idea what you mean,' said Martin with dignity, scrubbing his lip-printed face.

'No, of course he doesn't,' said the woman, turning to Rhosmari. 'He only likes to hang about the smallest theatre in Cardiff because we're cheap. As if I don't know the *Tylwyth Teg* when I see one.' And with that startling pronouncement she barked back over her shoulder, 'Steven, I want you back. Tomorrow at seven.'

The boy's face blazed with a smile. He snapped his heels

together and bowed, then leaped off the platform and vanished through a door at the foot of the stage.

'Lyn has this delightful notion that I'm some sort of faery benefactor,' Martin told Rhosmari, so casual it made her blink. 'I wouldn't have thought she'd be going senile at her age, but you never know with these theatre people – ow!' He clutched his arm where the woman had pinched him. 'Careful, now. If you make me angry, I might put a curse on your box office receipts.'

'They couldn't be much worse than they are already,' retorted Lyn. 'Just ask Toby, he's been weeping over the books for weeks. Why do you think we're casting Shakespeare with spotty-faced adolescents and the cleaning woman's second cousin? We certainly can't afford anyone better.' She let out a sigh. 'But a few of them show promise, and those last two had a real gift. At least we'll have *something* to work with this season.' She eyed Martin critically. 'So how long are you going to hang about? A few days? A week?'

'It's worse than that, I'm afraid,' said Martin. 'Rhosmari and I are only here for the night. Do you think you could spare us a corner?'

'Oh, don't tell me you're skint again,' said Lyn. 'I thought your people had gold lining every pocket. You're a very disappointing sort of faery, you know.'

'Try Rhosmari,' said Martin. 'She's a much better one.'

Lyn looked Rhosmari up and down and snorted. 'Oh,

that's likely. All right then, both of you, come with me. I'm sure we can find a bed for you somewhere.'

'There you go,' said Lyn a few minutes later, flopping a mattress onto the floor of the study. 'Sorry about the paint stink, we're still cleaning up after the upstairs toilet flooded last week.'

'All part of our usual charming state of chaos,' added Toby, shoving a box under one of the desks. 'Though I'll get this office fixed up eventually, I promise. You never know when some random bloke and his girl will come through and want to use it as a hostel.' But he spoke cheerfully, with a nudge at Martin's side and a wink for Rhosmari. 'Right, Lyn, are we done for tonight? Sure these two aren't going to murder you in your sleep?'

'Reasonably,' said Lyn, in a dry tone. 'Off you go.'

Toby grinned and kissed her cheek, then sidestepped the ladder and disappeared. Lyn stood a moment, surveying the room – the two desks heaped with papers, the glass-fronted machine displaying dizzying patterns in the corner, the mattress taking up most of the floor – and said, 'Not exactly the Lanesborough, is it? But there's sheets and blankets in the cupboard under the stairs, and I can at least offer you a fry-up in the morning, if you bestir yourselves around eight or so. Not that you'll likely have a choice, with that fat lump crawling all over you,' and she jerked her head at the still-sleeping cat.

'Bless you, Lyn,' said Martin, without a trace of irony; it was the closest most faeries ever came to saying *thanks*, and Rhosmari was startled to hear it. 'We're in your debt.'

'That you are,' Lyn replied. 'I'm going upstairs to cuddle with Burbage – just knock if you need anything.' And with that she stalked up the staircase, flicking off the corridor lights behind her.

'Is Burbage the cat?' asked Rhosmari, when the woman had gone.

'Actually, I believe Burbage is her laptop computer,' replied Martin. 'The cat doesn't have a name, as far as I know.' He leaned back against the desk, hands splayed casually on the pale wood. 'And I've a feeling she's not quite sure what to make of you, either.'

Rhosmari glanced around the room, uncomfortable with his steady gaze. 'You seem to know her quite well. I thought the Empress didn't want her people being friendly with humans?'

'She doesn't,' said Martin. 'But even when I belonged to the Empress, just because she *could* control me didn't mean that she always did. And I was careful not to give her reason to think she might need to, either.' He pushed himself upright and walked out into the corridor, adding over his shoulder, 'You'll want some bedsheets?'

'Yes, please,' said Rhosmari.

Martin returned with an armful of linens, snapped out the bottom sheet and began fitting it over the mattress. It was a servant's task, yet he did it without self-consciousness – and with an ease that suggested he'd done it many times before.

'You still haven't told me how you met Lyn,' Rhosmari said, watching him. 'How did she guess you were a faery?'

'Lyn is remarkably perceptive that way,' said Martin. 'She doesn't trust her instincts enough to admit it's anything more than a joke, but she recognised what I was the moment I first walked into her theatre. I suspect there's faery blood in her somewhere.' He tucked in the top sheet and turned it down, adding, 'She would have recognised you too, if she let herself. But you didn't fit her idea of what a faery should look like, so she dismissed it.'

Rhosmari frowned. How could she look any more like what she was? It was true that her ancestors had come to Wales from a far-off country, so she was one of perhaps fifty faeries in all the Green Isles who did not share the bland colouring most common to the Children of Rhys. But why should that matter? She was no less magical than the others, and no less loyal to her homeland. It made no sense that anyone would compare her to Martin, and think she was not a true faery.

'In any case, Lyn is just one of several humans I've come to know since I discovered theatre,' Martin continued. 'Most of my acquaintances are in London, where there are hundreds of acting troupes, and a play is born every minute. But whenever the Empress gave me liberty to travel, I took the chance to broaden my horizons.' A little smile played along his lips. 'And I have to admit that of all the theatres I've visited, this little place is my favourite.'

Rhosmari gazed down at the mattress, now neatly made up with sheets and blankets. 'What I did earlier, when that girl was giving her speech...I didn't even realise that was possible. I know our people make humans more creative just by being near them, but I could *feel* the difference. And now I wonder if I did her more harm than good.'

'You wanted to help her,' said Martin. 'And you did. But the ability to deliver Portia's speech came from within her, not you. All you did was take away her nervousness and give her a chance to prove herself. And it is intoxicating to see your power affect them, isn't it?' He yawned, stretching both arms above his head and arching his back so far she could see his hipbones. 'Anyway, I'm going to sleep. Good night.'

Rhosmari tensed. Surely he didn't mean... Of course he had made up the bed, but he couldn't really think... And there was no way she would even consider... She would just have to tell him—

But before she could find the words, Martin turned and walked to the door. And then, with a last mocking glance over his shoulder that told her he knew exactly what she'd been thinking, he transformed himself into a tiny black and white bird and fluttered away.

five

'You'll be coming back next time you're in Cardiff,' said Lyn after breakfast the next morning, giving Martin a pointed look as she unlocked the front door. 'We're doing *Merchant* in June and *Much Ado* in August, and I'll want to see you at both.'

'You don't really need me, Lyn,' said Martin. 'You've got a couple of fine young actors there, and you'll bully the rest into genius yet. How do you know you're not part faery yourself?'

'Ha! With this old face? Not likely.' She stepped outside with them, into the wan grey light. The sky was rumpled with cloud, and the breeze smelled of dust and impending rain. 'So you'll be all right, then? I've a sense you're in some kind of trouble.' Her eyes flicked to Rhosmari. 'Or is it you that's the trouble?'

'Rhosmari is far too well-behaved to cause trouble for anyone,' replied Martin. 'Don't worry, we'll be fine.' He touched his fingers to his forehead. 'Peace and good fortune to you, Lyn. You won't regret your kindness.'

The human woman gave a tight smile. 'I'll hold you to that.' For one last moment her gaze lingered on Rhosmari, as though she were still not quite sure what to make of her. Then she shook her head, waved them both off, and went back inside.

By daylight, Cardiff looked more friendly to Rhosmari than it had the night before. It still felt strange to be surrounded by pavement and metal, and buildings so tall they made her feel dizzy to look at them. But here and there she glimpsed trees beginning to bud, and grassy spaces where gold and purple crocuses bloomed. And though the fumes of passing vehicles still tainted the air, there were more pleasant smells, too: the aroma of fresh bread wafting from a bakery, the dusky scent of coffee, a floral swirl of perfume as a group of young women hurried by.

'Did you sleep well?' Martin asked Rhosmari as they walked. 'I did. You'd be surprised how comfortable it is to sleep as a bird, as long as you don't have to worry about predators swooping down on you.'

'Like the Blackwings?' asked Rhosmari, glancing at the sky. Not that there was any point: the air was full of dark shapes, and even her faery senses could not have told a real bird from a false one at this distance.

'I doubt they'd eat me,' Martin said, as though he were

considering the possibility. 'Though they could certainly make my life unpleasant. But enough of that talk. We need to decide where to start looking for the rebels.'

'You don't think there are any here?'

'There might be, but I don't know of anyone specific – and even if I did, we don't have anything to track them with.' He stooped to peer at his reflection in a shop window, combed his hair smooth with his fingers, and straightened up again. 'Besides, Rob was born and raised in London. I doubt he'd take his followers into Wales, not when there are still places in England left to hide.'

'Then perhaps the rebels are in London?'

Martin appeared to consider this, but then he shook his head. 'I think not. The Empress might have lost Sanctuary, but many of the London faeries are still under her control, and the rebels would find it hard to establish a stronghold there. I suggest we go north, to somewhere like Birmingham or even as far as Manchester. There are strong Wylds in both those places, and if Rob is looking for allies it would make sense for him to try there first.'

He obviously had no doubt that Rob had escaped the battle. Rhosmari wished she could be half as sure about Garan and the other Children of Rhys who had gone with him. Garan and Broch had both done well in the Rhysian Games, and Llinos had served in the Council Guard, but none of them had ever experienced real warfare, any more than she had.

'And even if we don't find the rebels themselves,' Martin continued, 'we may meet some sympathisers who can point us in the right direction. Or at least tell us something about them.'

Rhosmari could not argue with that. Even bad news would be better than uncertainty. 'Then we'll go to the Wyld that's the farthest,' she said. 'If the Blackwings are still following us, it will take them longer to catch up with us there.'

'Wisely thought,' said Martin. 'Manchester it is. But before we go, I have a suggestion. Take a little of your money and buy a coat, instead of that old-fashioned cloak. It will make it harder for the Blackwings to pick you out from a distance, and you will likely find it warmer as well.'

At first she was tempted to argue with him: the cloak was warm enough, and surely it could not be *that* old-fashioned. But it was true that she had not seen anyone else on the mainland wearing one. Could that be why the jeweller in St David's had been suspicious of her? Had he thought she was too poor to afford a proper coat, let alone own a pearl necklace?

Embarrassed to think that she had made such a foolish error, Rhosmari swallowed her objections and followed Martin to a clothing shop not far from the railway station. They negotiated their way inside, and once she found a fitted jacket that matched the soft brown of her boots, she felt ready to give up her cloak without regret.

Martin seemed pleased with her choice – or perhaps he was just pleased with himself, because as Rhosmari was counting out her money he gave the girl behind the counter a smile that made her lower her eyes and turn pink.

'Did you put a charm on her?' asked Rhosmari as they left the shop. She did not mean to sound accusing, but the amount she had spent on the coat was less than she expected.

'Hardly,' said Martin. 'It's a second-hand shop, that's all. Beguiling's not one of my talents; I could have stopped time and stolen the coat more easily than I could have confused her into charging you the wrong price for it. Why are you so suspicious?' He leaned closer, his breath warming her ear, and murmured, 'Or…were you jealous?'

Rhosmari felt her face grow hot. Unable to think of a reply, she raised her chin and walked faster.

Martin laughed.

They left Cardiff by the next train, heading for Manchester. Rain streaked the windows of the carriage as they sped along, blurring Rhosmari's view of the countryside until she could see little more than her own shadowy reflection.

'Tell me more about the Empress,' she said to Martin, as she settled back into her seat. 'Where did she come from? Why is she so determined to bring all the faeries under her control?'

Martin shrugged. 'All I know is that she is powerful, and ruthless, and that she despises humans – although that may be more ironic than any of us guessed. She looks like a porcelain angel, all blonde curls and sweetness; but at the battle of Sanctuary I glimpsed her true face, and it was withered with age. Either her use of dark magic has corrupted her body, or...' He ran a finger thoughtfully across his chin. 'Or else she was once human herself.'

Rhosmari found that hard to believe. Surely the Empress would not find it so easy to hate humans if she had spent most of her life as one? 'She must be quite old, then,' she said. 'Does she think she can live forever? Or does she have some plan for carrying on her empire after she is gone?'

'She has several trusted lieutenants,' said Martin, 'who have served her for many years. And naturally, Corbin and Byrne Blackwing are among them. But there is another faery named Veronica who is even closer to her in spirit, and there are rumours that she has already begun to learn the secrets of the Empress's power. So if you were thinking that all we need to do is wait a few more years for the Empress to die...' He gave a thin smile. 'Then you would be wrong.'

Reluctantly, Rhosmari nodded. Of course the solution could not be so simple. She was beginning to understand why Garan had felt he had to help the mainland faeries in their struggle – though for the Children of Rhys's sake, she still wished that he had not.

'But enough of that gloomy talk,' said Martin. 'Tell me about the Wyld you came from.'

His expression held only curiosity, and she felt sure he

93

meant no harm. Yet how could she entrust a near-stranger with the secrets of the Children of Rhys? 'I...can't,' she said.

'Oh, come now, you must be able to tell me *something*. What about this countryman of yours, who left to join the rebellion? Why is it so important for you to find him again?'

Rhosmari bit her lip, torn between the temptation to confess everything and the fear of what might happen if she did. She longed to share her burden with someone. Yet Martin owed his own freedom to the Stone of Naming. What would he say if he knew – or even suspected – that she had come to take it away?

'I'm sorry,' she said at last. 'I'm grateful for all you've done for me. But I can't.'

Martin's jaw tightened, and she could see that she had offended him. But all he said was, 'Very well.'

The streets of Manchester were dreary with rain, and as Rhosmari followed Martin out of the train station she turned up the collar of her jacket. Humans passed by them on both sides; few gave Rhosmari a second glance, and those who did looked more approving than otherwise. She was glad to have taken Martin's advice, and left her cloak behind in Cardiff.

'Where are we going?' asked Rhosmari, when they had walked along the pavement for several minutes.

'Somewhere private,' Martin replied. It was the first time he had spoken in hours, but to her relief he did not sound angry, only preoccupied. 'Finding spells take concentration, and I don't want us to be interrupted.'

'Finding spell?' asked Rhosmari. 'Is that like a tracking spell?'

'Not exactly. For a tracking spell you have to be looking for a specific person, and you need something of theirs to use as a focus. With a finding spell, you're only seeing if there are other faeries nearby.'

She had never heard of such a thing before, but that was no great surprise; it made sense that separate groups of faeries would develop their own magical specialties. She would be willing to wager that Martin had never heard of loreseeds, either.

'The only thing is,' Martin went on, 'is that to cover an area this large, we'll have to cast the spell together. Ah. Here.' He grabbed Rhosmari's arm and whisked her into a narrow space between two buildings. 'Come behind these boxes, so no one can see us from the street. Are you ready?'

Rhosmari gave a cautious nod. She had never cast a spell in partnership with another faery before. Yet magic was in her blood, and instinct told her everything she needed to know. She faced Martin, and stretched out her hands to meet his.

She was not prepared for the caress of his thumb across her knuckles, nor the possessive way he twisted her hands upright and laced their fingers together. Blood surged into Rhosmari's cheeks, and she almost pulled away – but then she felt the magic beginning, and did not dare to break it.

Martin closed his eyes, drawing on their shared power and sending it outward. Hastily Rhosmari collected herself and did likewise, willing the spell to grow and expand. For a long time she felt nothing but a steady pulse of magic, rippling over the buildings around them and spreading in waves across the city. But then…'

'There they are,' murmured Martin as a starburst flared in Rhosmari's inner vision, followed quickly by another. 'Two of them at least. Let's see if we can find more.'

The stars glowed brighter, then winked out. An instant later they sparked back into Rhosmari's awareness again, closer and hotter than before.

'They've sensed us!' exclaimed Rhosmari, and snatched her hands away. But were the other faeries allies, or enemies? There was no way to tell. All she knew was that they were coming, and quickly.

'I'll mask our scent,' said Martin. 'You make us invisible. Don't move or speak until I tell you it's safe.'

They crouched behind the boxes, watching the mouth of the alley. Humans strolled past without even glancing in their direction. On the far side of the road, a lorry beeped its way into reverse. Rhosmari was beginning to wonder if she and Martin had been anxious for nothing, when a slender figure stepped off the pavement and headed down the alley towards them.

The faery was female, with skin the colour of old ivory

and a shining black waterfall of hair. She stopped just short of their hiding place, a frown creasing her brows. 'Where are you?' she asked in a lilting voice.

All at once Martin backed up against Rhosmari, pushing her deeper into the shadows. The muscles of his shoulders were tensed like steel. 'What is it?' she whispered – but then a second faery stepped up behind the first, and she almost cried out for joy. It was not just his ocean-breeze scent that thrilled her, it was the familiar lines of his face, with its mild expression that had always seemed so at odds with the spear he used to carry as one of the Council Guard.

'*Llinos*,' she mouthed, and leaped up to greet him – but Martin yanked her back down. His breath scorched her ear as he hissed, '*Don't move.*'

How dare he try to keep her away from her own people? For the first time in her life, Rhosmari was angry enough to fight. She dropped the invisibility glamour and struggled free of Martin's grip, crying out, 'Llwynog! *Llinos!*'

Martin swore. With a snatching gesture he summoned two of the crates stacked against the wall and sent them flying through the air, knocking Llinos and the female faery off their feet. Rhosmari made a strangled protest, but Martin had already cast a second spell, stunning both the newcomers unconscious. Then he clapped a hand over Rhosmari's mouth and dragged her to the back of the alley.

She kicked and writhed, but Martin did not slow his pace. He wrestled her through the narrow passage, across the short gap behind the buildings, then down another alley that opened onto the street. Rhosmari let her legs buckle, turning herself to dead weight in a last attempt to break free, but Martin was too strong. One hand still covering her mouth, he heaved her upright and pushed her against the wall.

'Are you insane?' he snapped, eyes blazing inches from her own. 'Those faeries belong to the Empress!'

Furious, Rhosmari shook her head, but Martin did not relent. 'No, I am not mistaken. The female is Lily, one of the Empress's oldest and most devoted servants. And the male...he's under the Empress's control as well. Didn't you see his eyes?'

Rhosmari's confidence faltered. His eyes? She had not thought to look closely at them. But Martin had to be wrong. Llinos could not be the Empress's servant... could he?

'There is a look that all the Empress's slaves have when they are carrying out her orders,' said Martin. 'And having been forced to obey her any number of times myself, I know it all too well. Whatever that male was to you once, you can't trust him now.' He added in a quieter voice, 'I'm sorry.'

A gasp burst from Rhosmari's lips as Martin took his hand away. She turned her face to the rough stone of the wall, shaken. To think of gentle Llinos controlled by the Empress, his will and conscience twisted into doing her bidding – she had never imagined such a thing was possible.

But if it could happen to Llinos, it could happen to Rhosmari, too.

'Please,' said Martin. His eyes were wild now, and he kept glancing at the sky as though fighting the urge to go there. 'Trust me this much, this once. We cannot let them capture us. We have to get away.'

Part of her still wanted to deny it. But Martin obviously believed she was in danger, for he had fought to rescue her – even though he could simply have turned himself into a bird and flown away. And now he was begging her to flee and she was standing there like a witless child, waiting for the tide to come in.

'You're right,' she managed to say. 'I'm sorry.'

Then Martin's hand locked around her wrist, and they took off running.

To Rhosmari it seemed that they fled through the streets at random, darting down laneways and shoving through clusters of baffled humans in a frantic effort to escape. But eventually they ended up back at the train station, and somehow Martin got them both inside, and before her whirling mind could take it all in they had scrambled onto another train, moments before it pulled away. She staggered down the aisle and collapsed into a seat, arms wrapped around her heaving sides.

Martin sat down next to her, looking grim. 'I was a fool to cast that finding spell,' he said. 'I should have guessed the danger. But I never imagined that when we met the Empress's servants, one of them would be someone you knew.'

Rhosmari's head throbbed with misery, and every breath stabbed at her heart. She had always known that the Empress's trick of stealing faeries' names was evil, always pitied those who had to live under her control. Yet she had seen it as a problem that afflicted the mainland faeries, not the Children of Rhys.

Now she knew better, and it terrified her. To imagine being trapped without power of escape, forced to do the very opposite of what her mind believed and her soul desired, bent wholly to the Empress's bidding—

'Rhosmari.' Martin laid a hand over her wrist, gently healing the bruises he had given her. 'Who was that male back there? Was he the one you were looking for?'

'His name…' She fought to push the words past the dry tightness in her throat. 'He was…'

And then her eyes welled up, and she turned her face blindly against Martin's shoulder as the train rattled out of the station, heading for Birmingham.

SIX

'No good,' panted Martin as he dropped out of his bird form and landed on the rooftop beside Rhosmari. 'They didn't know anything about the rebels, and I had to back off before they got suspicious.'

Nearly three days had gone by since they left Manchester, and in all that time they had found no other faeries who could help them in their quest. Afraid to cast another finding spell, they had been reduced to searching the streets of Birmingham using their wits and senses alone. Rhosmari's sense of smell was keener than Martin's, so she had been the first to pick up a trace of the elusive green fragrance that meant their fellow faeries were nearby. But when they finally succeeded in tracking the others down, Martin had advised her to stay well back and let him do the talking.

'None of the Empress's servants have seen us together yet,' he told her, 'not even the Blackwings, and I'd like to keep it that way. Besides, I know how to tell which faeries are safe to talk to and which ones aren't.' He arched a pale brow at her. 'Can you say the same?'

He was right, of course. More and more, Rhosmari was grateful for the way Martin looked out for her, how faithfully he was repaying her for saving his life. Though she still had not confided in him about her mission, it was not because she doubted his trustworthiness. It was only that she feared, now more than ever, that Martin would try to talk her out of taking the Stone back to the Green Isles…and that after seeing what had happened to Llinos, she might be tempted to agree with him.

So she had made herself small and flown up to crouch on the rooftop, straining to hear Martin's conversation with the two strange faeries as they stood on the street below. She had caught only the occasional word, but she could tell they were no less wary than he was, and not inclined to speak freely. Were they still under the Empress's power, and afraid that she would punish them if they disobeyed? Or were they like Martin, free but trying to remain neutral as long as they could?

Not that it mattered now. Martin had returned, and the other faeries were gone.

'It's getting late.' Martin glanced up at the sky, where a wan half-moon was creeping out between the clouds. 'But there's a theatre a few streets over, and they've got a performance of *My Fair Lady* starting in half an hour.' He held out his hand to her. 'Come with me.'

Rhosmari hesitated. It had been another long, worry-filled day, and she could not help being tempted by the distraction. But after paying for food, transportation, and two nights' lodging, her money was dwindling at an alarming rate.

As usual, Martin anticipated her objections. 'I met the stage manager earlier,' he said. 'He used to work with Lyn and Toby. All I have to do is stop by the back door and pick up our free tickets, so…'

He wiggled his fingers at her, and with a reluctant smile, Rhosmari took his hand.

'Here you are,' said Martin, handing Rhosmari her ticket as he rejoined her outside the theatre. 'Shall we?'

Together they joined the queue with the human theatregoers. As they neared the entrance, Rhosmari was glad to see a pair of humans holding the doors open – it was a clear invitation, and made it easy for even a faery to go in. At Martin's direction she gave one of them her ticket, and was perplexed when he ripped it in two and handed part of it back to her. Perhaps he would expect her to give him the other half on her way out, she thought, and tucked the torn card into her pocket.

They stepped through the doorway into a small, musty-smelling lobby. The place was full of humans, milling about and chatting about finances and the weather.

But faeries did not make idle conversation, so she and Martin waited in silence until the inner doors opened and they could go in.

'This way,' said Martin, glancing over his shoulder as he ushered her to a seat on the far side. At first Rhosmari was disappointed that they were so far away – everyone else seemed to be sitting closer to the stage. But when the lights dimmed and music swelled unexpectedly in the darkness, Rhosmari caught her breath. She had expected a story in words, but not one in melody as well, and it was all she could do to keep from squeezing Martin's arm in delight.

At first the actors seemed self-conscious, their speech stilted and their gestures artificial. But the more she focused on them, the more naturally they behaved, and when they burst into song and began to dance, Rhosmari's heart soared with pride. She had been almost afraid to go near humans after what her mother had told her, but surely her grandfather's death must have been an accident, or at least an aberration? Watching these gloriously creative beings, sharing with them in the joy of storytelling and song, it was hard to sympathise with Lady Celyn's mistrust of humans – let alone the Empress's hatred of them.

Yet the play itself puzzled her. Why were these two older men trying to make the young heroine into a different sort of person than she was? Why was she working so hard to behave like a haughty lady, instead of remaining her simple, warm-hearted self? She was still puzzling over it when the curtains closed on the first part of the story, and everyone filed out of the theatre while they waited for the second half to begin.

'What do you think?' Martin asked.

'The music is wonderful,' said Rhosmari, 'and I like the girl – Eliza. But I don't understand why those men want to change the way she speaks, just so they can trick other people into believing that she's wealthy instead of poor. It seems dishonest, and how is it going to help her?'

'You don't understand humans,' Martin told her. 'It's not just the cleverness of the trick that matters, or even the wager they're both hoping to win. It's that by passing a flower-seller off as a duchess, they're challenging the very assumptions that cause humans to judge and despise each other.'

'But that makes no sense,' said Rhosmari. 'Why would anyone despise Eliza? She hasn't done anything wrong.'

Martin shrugged. 'Humans make judgments based on all kinds of foolish things. The way other humans speak, the clothes they wear, the colour of their skin...but you must know that already. Looking as you do, you could hardly have gone far in this world without meeting someone who thinks less of you because of it.'

Looking as you do. Was he referring to the cloak she had left behind in Cardiff? But no – he had said more—

Her gaze drifted towards one of the mirrors on the wall. Reflected there she saw the dark ripples of her hair, clasped behind her neck and frizzed a little with neglect. She saw her brown-gold complexion, arched nostrils and generous lips – all the features she had inherited from her mother, the most beautiful and highly respected woman in all the Green Isles.

'That's ridiculous,' she said flatly.

'Oh, I agree,' said Martin. 'But for centuries humans have fought, oppressed, and even killed each other on account of such differences. So when you think about—' He stopped, frowning. 'What's wrong?'

Rhosmari stood frozen, no longer staring at her reflection but past it, into memory. *Why is it the right time for Fioled to go to the mainland, but not for me?* she had asked, and her mother had replied, *Because Fioled is not my daughter.*

Until now she had thought Lady Celyn was saying that her business was to protect her only child, not to tell other people what they should do with their children. But now Rhosmari understood what she had really meant: that no daughter of Lady Celyn's would ever be safe in the human world, any more than Celyn's father had been. *Killed by the humans…and I will not allow my only daughter to share his fate.*

So that was why Rhosmari's grandfather had died? Not because of anything he had done, but because of the way he *looked*?

Sickness scorched Rhosmari's throat. All at once the thought of staying in this place, among these people – these *humans* – was unbearable. Ignoring Martin's protest, she plunged through the crowd to the exit, and vanished out the door into the night.

When Martin found her, Rhosmari was sitting on a bench two streets away from the theatre, her knees huddled beneath her skirt and her collar turned up around her face. She did not look up as he approached.

'What are you doing here?' he demanded. 'You're going to miss the rest of the play.'

Rhosmari said nothing, only folded her arms closer to her chest as another group of humans strolled past. How could she explain herself to Martin, even if she wanted to? Her sense of injustice, of violation, of betrayal, went too deep for words. She was angry at her mother for not telling her exactly what humans were like, and she was angry at Martin for telling her. She was angry at humanity for being so cruel and ignorant, and she was angry at the part of her that still hoped, despite everything, that one particular human might be different...

'Rhosmari,' said Martin, 'tell me what's wrong.' He reached out, but she shied away and he dropped his hand. 'What can I do?'

She shook her head, wanting him to understand that this had nothing to do with him – but also wishing that he would leave her alone. If he pressed her any more she might lose her temper, and she did not want to add regret to the misery she felt already.

'So even now, you find me unworthy of your trust.' His voice was low and bitter. 'For days I have travelled with you, helped you, watched over you day and night. What else must I do to prove myself in your eyes? You act appalled at human prejudice, but it seems to me that you judge your fellow faeries no less harshly.'

Rhosmari's head jerked up. 'That's not true!'

'Isn't it? Then why have you never told me your history, as I have told you mine? You force me to guess at where you came from, why you are here, what it is you want – and even when I play your little game, you refuse to tell me whether or not I have won.'

He paced in front of her, fists clenched. 'Is it because I once served the Empress? I did not choose where to be born, nor to surrender myself to her power. Is it because I used a false ticket on the train? You may find it easy to be honest, coming from a Wyld that is prosperous and free. But I grew up on the streets of Brixton, and have had to struggle and bleed for everything I own.'

'Martin, I—' began Rhosmari, but at the same moment he winced and touched his ear.

'We have to get out of here,' he said, with a sharp glance at the darkened sky. Without waiting for a response, he seized Rhosmari by the shoulders, hauled her to her feet and gave her a shove. 'Now!'

Rhosmari stumbled on the pavement and nearly fell. Martin caught her, but the moment he set her upright he grabbed her hand and started to run. He yanked her through a cluster of young humans who swore and made gestures at them as they raced by, then around a corner to a side street. Rhosmari tried to shake free of his grip, but his fingers had locked around her wrist like a manacle, and the only way to make it hurt less was to run faster.

'Where…are we…going?' she panted, but then Martin stopped so suddenly that she ran into him. Two dark-haired, near-identical faeries blocked the pavement a few steps ahead, with smiling mouths and eyes full of mockery and menace.

'What a pleasant surprise,' said the first Blackwing. 'First the Empress sends us to hunt one faery, then another, and here we find both at once.'

'Indeed it is,' agreed his brother. 'It almost makes up for all those days of eating carrion.' He smacked his lips and laughed.

Martin pulled Rhosmari behind him. 'Get ready to run,' he whispered. Then he straightened up and faced the Blackwings. 'How did you find us?'

The taller Blackwing's eyebrows lifted. 'Do you *really* want me to answer that question, Martin? Though it would be amusing to see what you would make of it if I did.' His eyes slid to Rhosmari, glittering malice. 'You chose the wrong companion, girl. This one is a coward, and his only loyalty is to himself.'

'Your words are wasted, Corbin,' Martin said. 'She doesn't trust me anyway.' He dropped Rhosmari's hand and stepped aside. 'What if I offer you a bargain?' he asked, pointing to her. 'I'll hand her over without a fight, as long as you let me go.'

Rhosmari recoiled – and found that her legs would no longer move. Fear constricted her lungs as she tried to struggle free, but Martin's binding spell was too strong.

Now it was Corbin's turn to laugh. 'Do you see that, Byrne?' he said to his brother. 'He's done half our work for us. Ah, Martin. Do you even know which side you are on any more?' He spread his hands, magic rippling between them like a glowing chain. 'But we serve the Empress, not our own pleasure...and we have had enough of your *bargains*.' Then he whipped around, and flung the spell at Martin.

Martin leaped aside just in time. He darted behind Rhosmari, as though to use her as a shield. 'Count to twenty,' he whispered, with a touch that sent a shimmer of heat up her spine. 'Then run.'

And with that he flashed into his bird shape, and launched himself straight at the Blackwings.

Small as he was, Rhosmari had never seen anything move so fast. Corbin flung up his hands an instant too late: in a red flash of magic Martin's wing clipped the side of his head, and he collapsed to the pavement unconscious. The little bird zoomed around again, aiming for Byrne – but the other

Blackwing was not so easily caught off guard. He fired off a spell that sheared past Martin's wing and sent him spinning aside; then he transformed himself into a raven, and took off after him.

Martin fluttered upward, but his wingbeats looked uneven, and he was already losing speed. Byrne had nearly closed the distance between them when the two birds soared up over the rooftops, and were lost in the shadows of the night.

Rhosmari stood frozen on the pavement, the remaining Blackwing at her feet. Her chest ached, and her muscles felt like jelly – but she knew it would only be a few minutes before Corbin woke up again. She summoned all her reserves of magic, straining at her invisible bonds in a frantic attempt to break free.

Eighteen, whispered a voice in the back of her mind. *Nineteen. Twenty...*

And just like that, she could move again. Rhosmari took a step backwards, her gaze on Corbin's motionless body. Then she whirled and fled.

The sensible thing for Rhosmari to do, perhaps, would have been to take what little money she had left and leave Birmingham at once. But she had no idea where to go next, or what to do when she got there. And if Martin ever managed to escape from the Blackwings, it would be difficult for him to find her again.

She could not abandon him like that. Not now that she understood what he had done for her.

Rhosmari had never tried to Leap anywhere since she came to the mainland, for nearly every place she went was unfamiliar, and the rest were too crowded with people. But now in desperation she pictured the little hotel where she had been staying for the past two nights, and threw herself towards it. Landing on the doorstep, she dashed up the stairs to her room, locked the door, closed the window, and cast an aversion charm that would discourage anyone but Martin from touching either. Then she switched off all the lights, made herself invisible, and waited.

For two hours she huddled atop the narrow bed, acutely aware of the noises around her – every footstep on the stair or voice in the corridor, every thump or cough from the rooms on either side. The rumble of traffic on the nearby road seemed ominous as thunder, and whenever a shadow flickered past her window, she jumped.

At last, sheer exhaustion caught up with her, and Rhosmari had sunk into a feverish doze when she heard a tap at the window. Abruptly awake, she flung back the curtain and found Martin's tiny, heaving form crouched on the sill outside, one wing extended at an awkward angle. The feathers around his shoulder were clotted with blood.

Rhosmari slid the window open and gathered him in. She set the little bird down upon the edge of the bed, then stepped back as Martin transformed with a groan back into his faery self. He wore trousers but no shirt or jacket, and the wound on his shoulder was bleeding freely. Rhosmari clapped her hands to her mouth.

'Don't just stand there,' said Martin in a faint, irritable voice. 'I can't heal myself, you know.'

'I can't heal you either,' Rhosmari told him shakily. She had not seen so much blood since her father died, and its hot, metallic smell was making her queasy. But she had no talent for magical healing, even if she dared to try.

'Water,' Martin told her flatly, one hand pressed to his shoulder. 'Soap. Bandages. Go.'

Rhosmari hurried to the tiny sink. Obeying Martin's orders, she poured cupfuls of water over his shoulder and patted the wound with a soapy cloth until the worst of the mess was gone. Then she took the case off the pillow and tore it into strips to make a bandage. By the time she had wrapped the deep gash in several layers of cloth, the bleeding had slowed.

'Good. Yes,' said Martin, and then he eased himself onto his good side and lay still. Faeries usually appeared ageless, but the pain etched into his face made him look like a human of forty. Rhosmari pulled up a chair beside the bed.

'You shouldn't have done that,' she whispered. 'Byrne might have killed you.'

'Ha,' said Martin, though his laugh sounded feeble. 'What else should I have done? Flown off and left you there?'

'You could have.' And for a few horrible moments, she had believed that he would. Not until the binding spell he had put on her dissolved had she realised it had all been a ruse to make the Blackwings think she was helpless...and that he had risked his own life to give her a chance to escape.

Martin's eyes met hers, weary but unflinching. 'No,' he said. 'I couldn't.'

Rhosmari looked down at her hands, knotting and unknotting in her lap. 'I...was wrong not to confide in you,' she said. 'I was worried that...' She stopped and took a deep breath. 'I was worried about a lot of things. But I think you have a right to know.'

Martin did not answer, only watched her with his heavy-lidded gaze. The blood was seeping through the bandages on his shoulder, staining the white cloth dark. She had to look away before she could go on, 'You asked me about the Wyld I came from. Well, my home is a place we call the *Gwerdonnau Llion*, or the Green Isles of the Ocean...and my people are known as the Children of Rhys.'

seven

When Rhosmari had finished telling Martin her story, he was quiet so long that she feared he had fallen asleep. But then he said, 'So your people have never known war. Not even the oldest ones?'

'None that are still living,' she replied. 'The first generation of Rhys's followers were warriors, but their chieftains had abused the gift of their true names by—'

'Wait. They *gave* their names to these chieftains?' Martin's face contorted in disbelief. 'How could anyone be so stupid?'

'They did it out of loyalty,' said Rhosmari defensively, though deep down she agreed with him. 'In those days it was considered an insult, and an act of cowardice, for faeries not to give their true names when swearing fealty to their rulers. It was proof of their devotion, and of their faith in the good character of their lord or lady. But when the chieftains became greedy for power and began forcing their followers into battle after battle, that gift became a curse.'

'Until this Rhys showed up with his Stone of Naming, and led your people to a magical land where their chieftains could no longer find them,' said Martin. 'How convenient. So what is it like, this *Gwerdonnau Llion* of yours? It sounds peaceful, but a little dull.'

'Not at all,' Rhosmari said. 'We have as much to do as any faery on the mainland. We work and play and learn, we marry and raise children. And if we lack anything, we send out a party to visit the human world, and trade with them for whatever goods or knowledge we need.'

'So you can come and go from the Green Isles whenever you please?' asked Martin. 'And talk to any other faeries you wish, even if they are not of your people?'

Rhosmari hesitated.

Martin gave a thin smile. 'I didn't think so. You Children of Rhys may think yourselves rich, but you lack the most important thing of all – freedom. You talk about how Rhys and the Stone rescued your people from bondage, but it seems to me that you only left one form of slavery for another. Even if your Elders do not hold your true names, they still control you, as surely as the Empress controls the rest of us.'

'It's not like that,' said Rhosmari, but even to her own ears the objection sounded weak, and she could think of nothing else to say.

'This is not the first I have heard of your people, you know,' Martin said. 'Why do you think I went to Wales in the first place? I thought that if I could find the Children of Rhys, they might give me refuge from the Empress.'

So the news of Linden and Timothy's journey to the Green Isles had spread among the mainland faeries, and now they knew – roughly – where her people lived. Rhosmari's fists clenched in the folds of her skirt. How long would it be before the Empress knew as well? Or had she already questioned Llinos, and found out everything?

'But after what you have told me,' Martin continued, 'I think I will be better off here. And obviously your *betrothed*—' He put a slight edge on the word— 'felt the same, or he would not have left the Green Isles to join the rebellion.'

'But you must understand,' Rhosmari said, 'that what Garan did caused great trouble for our people? And that we need the Stone, too?'

Martin lay unmoving, his gaze distant. 'I am not much concerned with that,' he said at last. 'I have my freedom already. You can sort that out with the rebels when we find them.'

So he was not going to try to stop her, after all. Rhosmari exhaled, her tension draining away. If she had known it would end so well, she would have had this conversation with him days ago.

'Well,' said Martin. 'You should sleep.' He began to get

up, but Rhosmari stopped him with a hand to his chest. His skin felt so hot, she feared he might be feverish – but then, she was more than a little flushed herself.

'Lie down,' she said. 'You're still weak, and you need the bed more than I do. I'll sit up and watch, while you rest.'

Martin frowned, as though about to protest. But then he took her hand from his chest, raised it to his mouth and kissed it. 'As you will, lioness,' he said, and closed his eyes.

Rhosmari woke the next morning to the touch of sunlight on her face. She jumped up from her chair – only to stumble and almost collapse. Her foot had fallen asleep. She hopped over to the windowsill and leaned on it, flexing her toes to make the pins and needles go away.

'Sorry,' she whispered to Martin, who had opened his eyes and was regarding her blearily. 'I didn't mean to wake you.' Or doze off when she was supposed to be keeping watch, either. She could only hope he hadn't noticed that.

'No need to apologise,' he said, sitting up and swinging his legs around. 'I've rested long enough. It's time we were on our way.'

He moved more easily now, strength and energy returned. With a snap of his good arm he whisked the top sheet off the bed, and transformed it into a long-sleeved shirt. 'Byrne let something slip last night, when he was taunting me,' Martin added as he eased his bandaged arm into a sleeve. 'About knowing where the rebels are. And I'm pretty sure I know the place he was talking about.'

'Where?' asked Rhosmari.

'Waverley Hall, just south of London. It's a human house, but there's a wood nearby where the rebels could easily make camp.' He shrugged his way into the rest of the shirt and began to button it closed. 'I know it's a risk. It might even be a trap. But I think it's worth looking into.'

Could the rebels be that easy to find? After days of fruitless hunting and running from the Blackwings, Rhosmari could scarcely believe it. And yet her heart beat a little faster, just the same.

Martin muttered an oath. 'I can't get this button done,' he said, flapping his loose right cuff at her. 'Do you mind?'

They had to travel three hours by train, then another by bus, and finally take a meandering walk along a footpath before they reached the grounds of Waverley Hall. But when Rhosmari caught sight of the house, her weariness vanished. It was as big as the Hall of Judgment, a size to command respect, and its red-gold brick made it warm and welcoming, even to a faery raised among white cottages and the sound of the sea.

Yet as they walked up the drive, she noticed that the formal garden was not as well tended as it should have been. It was only March, so she knew not to expect many flowers, but still there was an unkempt look about it. Weeds had sprung up in the gravel, and the paths were littered with broken twigs and dead leaves.

'Stop,' said Martin. 'Can you smell them?'

Rhosmari inhaled, drawing deep of the fresh country air – and there it was, the tingling herbal scent that marked a faery presence. 'Yes,' she said, and broke into a smile.

'I thought so,' said Martin. 'The wood, then.' He started across the lawn, and with a glance around to be sure no one was watching, Rhosmari hurried after him.

It was odd, how quiet this place was. She would have expected there to be at least one or two humans about, for a house and garden of this size must take a lot of care. But when she ventured to say so, Martin only shrugged.

'Wealthy humans often go away for the winter,' he said. 'No doubt the owners will be back in a week or two.'

She was following Martin along the back of the house when a little dog crawled out from behind the shrubbery. It was barrel-shaped, with sandy fur and a deeply wrinkled face, and when Rhosmari bent closer, two anxious brown eyes gazed back at her.

'It's all right,' she said, and the dog waddled up and licked her fingers. Yet it was terribly thin for its round shape, its ribs showing through on both sides and its belly concave. She fingered the metal tag that hung from its collar and found it engraved with the dog's name: ISADORA.

'Martin?' she called, but he had already vanished around

the corner. She gave the dog an apologetic pat and hurried to catch up with him.

'Where were you?' he asked.

Rhosmari explained about the dog, but he showed no surprise. 'Dogs escape from their owners all the time,' he said. 'It likely broke its lead and ran off days ago, and only now decided it was hungry enough to come home.'

It was hard for Rhosmari to imagine such a squat little dog running anywhere. But Martin was walking again, and there seemed no point in arguing with him.

By the time they reached the edge of the wood, Rhosmari was tingling all over with anticipation – and anxiety. What if Garan was dead? Or, like Llinos, a slave of the Empress? At any moment one of the rebels would step out to greet them, and then she would know.

But no one came. And though she and Martin crossed the wood from one side to the other and back again, there was no sign of a faery presence. In fact, the scent of them seemed to be fading, not getting stronger.

'Stupid!' exclaimed Martin, startling her. 'I should have guessed. They're not here at all. They're in the house.'

'In there?' asked Rhosmari, frowning at Waverley Hall. The idea seemed ridiculous: even if the owners were in the habit of letting out rooms to strangers, the cost alone would make it impossible. After all, she had paid for only a few days' food and lodging, and she had hardly any money left... Did she even know how much she had?

Automatically Rhosmari slipped her hand into her skirt pocket. But when she pulled out the first bit of paper she found, it proved to be nothing but a narrow piece of card with one end torn. At first she was puzzled, and then she realised that it was her theatre ticket from last night. Except…that one had been blue, with the name of the play printed on it. And this was white, and blank.

'The Oakenfolk are friendly with humans,' said Martin, still looking at the house. 'Perhaps they know the people who live here, and struck some kind of bargain—'

'You lied to me.' Rhosmari spoke flatly, the card clutched in her hand. 'You're a faery, and you lied. How is that possible?'

'What?' Martin rounded on her. 'What are you talking about?'

'You told me the stage manager had given you the tickets. But the truth was, you never talked to him at all. That's why you picked the worst seats in the theatre, to make sure no one would challenge us for them. Because you *lied*,' and she flung the false ticket onto the ground between them.

Martin's brows crooked, as though she had troubled him. But when he spoke, his voice was cool. 'So? You needed a distraction; I gave it to you. And the play was all the better for our presence, so you might well say we paid for it. But if you are so offended by a bit of harmless trickery, then by all means go back to Birmingham and settle the account to your satisfaction.'

And with that he turned his back on her, and strode away.

Rhosmari stood alone beneath the slow-dripping trees, her anger receding as she realised that he had a point. They had helped the actors by being there. Perhaps it was not the straight bargain she would have preferred, but Martin had obviously wanted her to see the play, and she had forced his hand by being so anxious over money. Which of them had shown the more generous spirit?

And that reminded her of something Timothy had said to the Elders, when they refused to help any Oakenfolk who could not pass their test. *What good are your laws*, he had demanded, *if they only help people who are perfect already?* He had called the Children of Rhys self-righteous. And though Rhosmari still mistrusted humans in general, she was beginning to think that Timothy had been right.

'Wait!' she cried to Martin, but he did not look back. She ran to catch up with him. 'I'm sorry,' she panted. 'I was just…surprised.'

And she had been. In her experience, faeries could speak the truth in a misleading way, and some could even be sarcastic or facetious. But she had never guessed that any faery could lie outright. Perhaps Martin had learned it from his human friends… But that was not important now.

'I know you meant to be kind,' she said. 'And you have been. It was ungracious of me to accuse you, especially after you risked your life for me last night. Will you forgive me?'

For a moment Martin's face remained expressionless, and she feared he would refuse. But then he nodded, and took her hand, and they walked back to the house together.

'You should be the one to knock,' said Martin, as they climbed the front steps. 'If there are Children of Rhys among them, they will welcome you. Then I will wait until you convince them I can be trusted – that is, if you still think I can be.'

There was a bitter twist to his last words, and Rhosmari flushed. 'I trust you,' she said with deliberate firmness, and then she took hold of the brass ring upon the door and knocked.

At first there was no answer, and by the time the little dog came wheezing up the steps and collapsed beside her feet, Rhosmari was beginning to wonder if anyone had heard. She lifted the ring to knock again—

The door creaked open, revealing a frail-looking human woman with cropped white hair. The dog scrambled towards her, but she stopped it with her foot and said politely, 'Yes?'

'We're looking for our friends,' said Martin before Rhosmari could speak. 'May we come in?'

The woman frowned, and tilted her head to one side as though listening. Then she stepped back, motioning them to enter. 'Is that your dog outside?' asked Rhosmari, but their hostess had already shut the door.

'This way,' she said.

The inside of Waverley Hall was as grand as the outside, with sumptuous carpets, soaring ceilings, and gilt-framed paintings hanging everywhere. But here, as in the garden, there was evidence of neglect: dust filmed the mirrors, and muddy smears streaked the marble floor. They walked through the entrance hall, the slight echo of their footsteps the only sound, then down a broad passageway to the foot of a staircase.

'Up there in the study,' said the woman. 'The first set of double doors on your right.'

Rhosmari glanced at Martin, who nodded at her to go first. Perhaps he was still unsure of his welcome, but she need have no such worries – especially not if Garan was waiting for her, as she prayed he would be. Taking a deep breath, Rhosmari put her hand on the stair rail and began to climb.

On the wall to her right, as she ascended, hung a series of portraits: one richly dressed man after another, no doubt the former residents of the house. Each was marked with a brass plaque, which she could not help reading out of the corner of her eye: George Waverley, James Waverley, Philip Waverley—

She stopped, startled. For a moment, Philip Waverley's portrait had wavered, like a poorly maintained glamour. But when she touched the frame it felt solid, as no illusion could be…

'Go on,' said Martin impatiently from behind her. Embarrassed, Rhosmari hurried up the steps to the landing, then along the corridor to a handsome set of double doors. The right one was ajar, inviting her to enter; she pushed it open, and stepped in.

The room before her was dark and luxurious, with mahogany furnishings and windows draped in wine-coloured brocade. A great desk dominated the floor, with a wing-backed chair behind it. And in that chair sat a delicate-looking faery with honey-blonde curls and eyes like frosted steel, while standing in the shadows to either side—

No!

Frantic, Rhosmari tried to conjure an image of the wood outside the house, so she could Leap away. But her thoughts scattered, and her body refused to lose its substance. Choking off a cry, she whirled to flee.

Martin caught her before she could take more than a step. With a flick of a finger he spelled the doors closed behind them, then used his good arm to twist Rhosmari around so that she faced the Empress and the Blackwings once more.

'I think you'll find, Your Majesty,' he said, 'that I have won our wager.'

'Indeed you have,' replied the Empress, her gaze travelling over Rhosmari appreciatively. 'Well done. Heal him, Byrne.'

With a grudging air the shorter of the raven brothers

came around the desk and clapped his hand onto Martin's injured shoulder, hard enough to make the other faery hiss through his teeth. But when he took his hand away, the colour came back into Martin's face. He swung his newly healed arm in a circle and acknowledged Byrne with an ironic bow, before turning to the Empress and bowing to her as well.

'I apologise for this unpleasantness,' Martin murmured to Rhosmari. 'But given a choice between my freedom and yours, I'm sure you understand which one I prefer.'

Rhosmari could not bear to look at him. He had accused her of judging him unfairly, of not trusting him enough… and all the while he had been planning to betray her. Had anything he had told her about himself been true? Or had he been nothing more than an actor playing a part all along?

'I have been so looking forward to getting acquainted with you,' said the Empress, her voice silken and sweet. 'I know we will have a great deal to talk about. Oh, do not struggle – you will only hurt yourself, and there is nowhere for you to escape.' In a rustle of silk she rose from her chair and walked to where Rhosmari stood trembling in Martin's grip, then unsheathed a small dagger from her waist.

'This will only hurt a little,' she said.

eight

'Will you stay for dinner, Martin?' asked the Empress, as she sheathed the knife and returned to her seat. 'Or at least for tea – surely you can find time for that? This occasion must be celebrated.'

'Your Majesty is gracious,' replied Martin. 'But I have …other commitments.' His eyes slid away from Rhosmari's accusing gaze, ignoring the still-bleeding hand she cradled against her breast. 'I beg you will excuse me.'

'Martin,' said the Empress, still pleasantly but on a crisper note, 'I wish you the joy of your new freedom. But I think you may find that such independence is less fulfilling than you suppose.'

'I will take that risk, Your Majesty.' He bowed a final time, and disappeared.

Rhosmari was left alone in the centre of the carpet, facing the Empress. Her heart felt as though it were trying to climb out of her throat. But she reminded herself that she was the daughter of Lady Celyn, and kept her head high and her back straight, though beneath her flowing skirt her knees were trembling.

'Oh, child.' The Empress's face softened. 'The worst is over, I assure you. You are safe now.'

'Safe.' She forced the word out. 'How so?'

'Because you are with me,' the Empress told her. 'This estate is warded on every side, so no enemy can approach without my knowing it. You will have a comfortable bed to sleep in, and fresh clothes to wear, and food as fine as you could wish for – Sarah, our hostess, is a wonderful cook. And I will be glad of your company, for the days are long and lonely when my lieutenants are abroad.' She gave a little smile as she glanced from one Blackwing to another. 'I have been yearning for a chance to talk to one of the fabled Children of Rhys Corbin, bring a chair for our guest – Rhosmari, is it?'

The Empress knew Rhosmari's true name, a secret so precious that she had never spoken it aloud, let alone shared it with anyone. She could summon Rhosmari with a thought, and force her to do anything she wanted. But it seemed that she did not know everything about her – at least not yet. Biting her dry lips, Rhosmari sat down in the armchair Corbin Blackwing had provided for her, and willed herself to stay calm. Perhaps she could still prevent the Empress from finding out too much about the Green Isles, if she kept her answers brief and careful.

'You may go now,' the Empress said to the Blackwings. 'I shall see you at supper tonight.' She lifted a hand, and one after another the twins stooped to kiss it. Then they vanished.

'I apologise that I cannot give you quite so much liberty as Corbin and Byrne,' said the Empress to Rhosmari. 'You see, I dare not let you go until I am certain that you pose no threat to me. So...' She folded her hands together and rested her chin on them. 'You may not use magic anywhere within the bounds of this estate, except at my command. Nor can you step through any of the outer doors of the house, or climb out any of the windows, or leave it by any other means, unless I allow it.'

Until now, Rhosmari had thought that being controlled by the Empress would be an awful blank, an unknowing. She had expected to lose all sense of right and wrong, and have no desire but to do what she was told. But it was nothing like that at all. She still felt the same as she always had, yet when the Empress gave her an order, she was powerless to disobey.

And somehow, that was even worse.

'There,' said the Empress. 'Now, are you thirsty? I can have Sarah bring us some lemonade, if you like.'

So this was how it would begin. A long, torturous interrogation, with every answer dragged out of her by force. The Empress might think that she could disarm Rhosmari with her pleasant manner, but she would never forget what Linden and Timothy had said about her.

'How frightened you look!' The Empress's brows drew together in concern. 'Do you really think me so terrible? I assure you, it is not so. I take no pleasure in cruelty, and I abhor violence.'

'And yet you steal faeries' names,' said Rhosmari tightly, 'and force them to do your will. How is that not terrible?'

The Empress sighed. 'It is true,' she said. 'I do. And I have often wished that there were another way. Controlling my subjects is tiresome, and demeaning for both of us; I would be far happier if I never had to do it, and I try to do it as little as possible.'

Her eyes became distant, gazing into the shadows at the edge of the room. 'But I am only one faery, with a burden for my people's best interests that not all of them are quick to embrace or even understand. And too many times I have been betrayed, and had my trust and my confidence cruelly abused, by those I believed faithful. Can you blame me for wishing to be absolutely certain of my followers, and not merely hopeful of their obedience?'

'But I am not your follower,' Rhosmari said. 'I am not one of your people at all. You have no right—'

'Forgive me,' said the Empress, 'but I could not risk losing you before we had a chance to talk together. You have no idea how it alarmed me when I learned of the Stone of Naming, and found that your people had given it to Rob to help him in his rebellion. What else was I to think, but that the Children of Rhys had taken it upon themselves to overthrow my empire and set their own rulers up in my place?'

Shock hit Rhosmari like a cold wave, stealing her breath away. 'You mean – you actually believed – that we *wanted* to start a war?'

'I hoped not, but I had no way to be certain,' the Empress replied. 'Even my best sources could tell me little about your people's history, or what you were like. And all my attempts to find out where you lived, so I could send emissaries to you with an offer of peace, were in vain. So when Martin offered to buy his freedom by bringing me one of the Children of Rhys…' She spread her hands. 'How could I refuse?'

Rhosmari exhaled slowly. She still did not believe that the Empress's control of her people was justified, and Martin's deceit still sickened her. But if there was any possibility that all this was a misunderstanding, and that there was still a chance to make peace before her mother sent an army onto the mainland, then she had to try.

'We never meant to give the Stone of Naming to Rob,' she said. 'It was stolen from us and given to Linden and Timothy, who took it to the rebels. We have no desire to make war with you, or to overthrow your empire. All we want is to get back the Stone.'

The Empress's lips parted. 'Truly? Then I have no need to fear an invasion, or that your people plan to support the rebels against me?' She clasped her hands together. 'This is the best news I could have hoped for!'

'My people have sworn not to shed blood,' Rhosmari said. 'We would never willingly start a war with you. All we want is to live in peace in our own land.'

'You cannot imagine what a comfort this is to me,' said the Empress. 'So why did you come into my domain, then? Where were you going when Martin found you?'

'I was looking for the rebels,' said Rhosmari, 'because I had heard that they had the Stone, and I hoped I could talk them into giving it back.'

The Empress threw back her head and let out a peal of laughter. 'You really believed that they would?' she said. 'Pardon me if I sound ungracious, but only a child could be so naive. They will never give up the Stone, now that they know what it can do. Why should they?'

Rhosmari held her breath, fingers digging into the arms of her chair. So the Stone had not been lost in the battle of the Oak, or fallen into the Empress's hands. It was still with the rebels, wherever they were.

'If I believed you had any chance of succeeding in your quest,' the Empress continued, 'I would release you this very moment. I would be glad to see the Stone taken back to its rightful place, never to trouble me or my people again. But I fear all that will have to wait until I have dealt with this irksome rebellion.'

She rose from her chair, favouring Rhosmari with

a maternal smile. 'See how easy this was? And I did not have to compel you to answer even once. I hope we can have more such pleasant talks in future. But I am weary from all this excitement, and you must be as well. Why don't I call Sarah, and see about finding you a room?'

Rhosmari did not feel like answering when the bell rang for supper, but she had no other choice. She had spent most of the afternoon trying to make herself Leap back to the village or climb out the window, without success, and if the Empress had to summon her by name it would only make her humiliation worse.

She was halfway down the stair when some instinct made her glance to her left. There hung the same picture of Philip Waverley that had caught her eye before, but now the glamour that had hidden its true appearance was gone. Savage parallel slashes crossed the portrait like the claw-marks of some vengeful beast, tearing the canvas into strips and rendering the face unrecognisable.

Who had destroyed it? And why only that one, of all the paintings in the house? Rhosmari had no way to tell. But it reminded her that no matter how sweetly the Empress spoke or how graciously she behaved, she was still willing to use violence when it suited her – and was not above using deceit to hide it. Suppressing a shudder, Rhosmari descended the rest of the stairs, and made her way to the dining room.

Silver cutlery gleamed on white linen, and candlelight

washed the room in gold. The Empress sat at the head of the long table, with the two Blackwings at her right hand and a female with pale, feathery hair to her left. 'Ah, there you are,' she said as Rhosmari came in. 'Our honoured guest. Please, sit down.'

Rhosmari pulled out a chair at the other end, as far from the Empress as she could get without leaving the room. No sooner had she sat down than the side door opened and Sarah came in, staggering beneath the weight of a steaming soup tureen. Setting it down on the table, she began ladling out the contents with elaborate care.

'Bouillabaisse,' said the Empress. 'How splendid. Do you enjoy seafood, Rhosmari? Do your people eat it often?'

Rhosmari did not want to answer that question. She did not want to speak at all. She would rather eat a thousand silent meals at her mother's table, or even starve, than make dinner conversation with the woman who had enslaved Llinos, and had now stolen her own freedom as well.

Fortunately, the Empress did not seem offended by Rhosmari's silence. She turned instead to the female faery beside her. 'Tell me,' she said. 'How have you fared today?'

'I tracked down three renegades,' came the proud reply. 'They escaped, but not before I had taken their blood.' She reached into her jacket pocket, but the Empress stopped her with a shake of the head.

'Not at the table, Veronica,' she said. 'Think of our guest.'

Colour stained Veronica's high cheekbones, and the look

she shot Rhosmari was almost venomous as she crushed a handful of crackers into her soup. 'Of course, Your Majesty.'

All the while the elderly woman moved about the table, setting out baskets of crusty bread on each end and pouring glasses of wine and water. Rhosmari watched her, puzzled and a little disturbed. Humans did not have true names like faeries did; they could be confused and made forgetful by magic, but not easily controlled. And not even the most powerful faery could enter a human house without invitation, so this woman must have welcomed the Empress willingly. Did she not realise how much the Empress despised her kind, or did she not care?

'That will be all, Sarah,' said the Empress, and meekly the woman retreated, leaving the faeries alone.

'You have trained her well,' said Corbin, sipping his wine. 'I have not tasted such excellent food and drink in years. Still, does it not bother you to have her always shuffling around?'

'She cannot help her age,' replied the Empress. 'Indeed, I am impressed that she carries herself as well as she does. Rhosmari, you are not eating. Does the meal not please you?'

Rhosmari stared into her soup. Its savoury smell made her stomach cramp with hunger. But she still could not bring herself to eat.

'Or is it our conversation you find distasteful?' the

Empress continued. 'Are you fond of humans, perhaps?'

'I am not fond of humans,' Rhosmari said. 'I only think...' But then she trailed off, unable to finish the sentence. She was no longer sure what she thought.

'Perhaps you have heard that I believe all humans to be worthless,' said the Empress. 'It is not so. I have known humans who are gentle and good-hearted, and who cause no harm to anyone. But sadly, there are many others who are not so self-controlled, and they bring shame and trouble upon all the rest. Humanity needs to be tended like a garden, and the bad ones weeded out, or else they will destroy themselves and us as well.'

'I think we all know one human who could use some weeding,' said Byrne, and Veronica made a face into her wine glass. Rhosmari was wondering who they could be talking about when the Empress said with a little sigh, 'Ah, yes. Timothy.'

'Why?' The question leaped past Rhosmari's lips. 'What did he ever do to you, that you hate him so much? He's just a boy—'

'Ah, so you have met him,' said the Empress, unruffled. 'I wondered. A talented young man, not unattractive in his way, but regrettably prone to violence. Did he tell you, when he came to visit your people, that I had condemned him and his faery companion to death? It was not true. I sent the Blackwings after Timothy and Linden for the same reason I allowed Martin to go after you: because I wished to talk with them, and they would not come to me any other way.'

'I know that Veronica tried to steal his music,' said Rhosmari flatly.

'She was charmed by his guitar playing, and wanted to taste what it felt like to be so gifted. And she was viciously attacked for it. Did Timothy tell you that?' The Empress laid down her soup spoon and leaned forward, eyes holding Rhosmari's. 'Did he tell you how he and his friends repeatedly injured and abused my Blackwings, though they had done nothing to hurt any of them? Or did you know that at Sanctuary, Timothy knocked me down and attempted to strangle me, and so began the battle?'

'I— I can't believe—' Rhosmari stopped, flustered, and then tried again. 'There must have been a reason.'

'I offered Linden and her people a bargain,' the Empress told her. 'An opportunity for the Oakenfolk to get back the magic they had lost, and to live peacefully ever after under my protection. I assured her that I would not harm Timothy in any way, only erase his memories of the past few days so that he would not be tempted to meddle with my people again.' She touched her throat, her expression sorrowful. 'Ask yourself this: even if they did not wish to accept my offer, did that justify assaulting me and starting a war?'

There was more to the story. There had to be. And yet... Rhosmari put a hand to her forehead, her thoughts whirling. Could it be that the Empress was not so evil as she had been led to believe? That Timothy and Linden had misunderstood her, as Rhosmari herself had done?

No. Wait. She had not misunderstood one thing, at least. 'You captured Llinos,' she accused. 'You made him your slave, and then you sent him out to find other rebels and capture them as well. What excuse do you have for that?'

The Empress and her lieutenants all exchanged glances. Then the Empress turned back to Rhosmari and said, 'I beg your pardon. But who is Llinos?'

Disbelieving, Rhosmari darted her gaze from Corbin to Veronica to Byrne, then back to the Empress again. Their faces looked genuinely bewildered, without a hint of anger or guilt. 'He was with Lily.' she said. 'One of your most loyal servants?'

'Lily, loyal?' Veronica almost choked on her soup with laughter. 'After Rob, Lily was one of the first faeries to touch the Stone. She is as eager to overthrow the Empress and seize control of her realm as he is. And if this Llinos was with her, then you can be certain that he is one of the rebels as well.'

A chill crept up Rhosmari's spine. So Martin had lied to her even about that?

'Do not be unkind to her, Veronica,' chided the Empress. 'Can you not see that she is in shock? Obviously there has been a terrible misunderstanding.'

Rhosmari felt a sudden urge to say something that would throw the Empress off balance. If she could break through that charming veneer, even for an instant, she would know the truth. 'Martin told me that beneath the glamour you wear, you are old and wrinkled,' she said, and then for good measure, 'He thinks that you were once human.'

But the Empress's patient expression did not alter. 'He is right,' she said. 'In my youth I lost a magical contest with a rival, who thought the best way to humiliate me was to turn me into a human and send me away, helpless and friendless, into the world. It was many years before I had the chance to regain my powers and become a faery again, and in that time I learned such things about human cruelty as I hope you will never know.'

Her eyes turned wistful as she brushed her fingers down her cheek. 'Forgive me my vanity. Since my own beauty has been lost, I wear instead the face of my old mentor Snowdrop, the faery who first showed confidence in my abilities and taught me what it meant to be a queen. She died a long time ago, and to see her in the mirror now…is an inspiration to me.'

Rhosmari bowed her head, the last of her defiance fading. Slowly she unfolded the napkin from beside her plate and spread it out upon her lap; then she picked up her spoon, and began to eat.

'My dear, you look tired,' said the Empress the next morning when Rhosmari came down to breakfast. The Blackwings and Veronica had left the house early, so the two of them were alone. 'Did you not sleep well? Would another bedroom be more to your liking?'

Mechanically Rhosmari helped herself to a pastry, a shake of the head her only answer. She had lain awake half the night trying to think of ways to escape from the Empress, and the other half wondering if she ought to. Every time she thought of a reason not to trust the Empress, she was reminded of all the reasons she could not trust the rebels either.

Garan had stolen the Stone and disgraced his own family. Timothy had a disturbing taste for violence – among other things, she now remembered, he had admitted to hitting another boy at school for no good reason at all. And Linden had got all her information about the Empress from Rob, who had deceived and betrayed the Empress much as Martin had deceived and betrayed Rhosmari. There was no one she could be sure of, not any more.

But she had not forgotten that for all the hospitality the Empress had shown her, she was still a prisoner. Mustering her courage, Rhosmari looked straight at the Empress and asked, 'When will you let me go?'

'Go where?' asked the Empress. 'To the rebels? Surely you understand I cannot allow that. It would be folly to give you into the hands of my enemies.'

'Then—' Rhosmari's fingers clenched around her fork. 'Let me go home, instead. If I leave at once, there might still be time to convince the others not to come looking for the

Stone. They may be willing to talk to you instead, and come to an agreement—'

Then she stopped, struck by a new and unpleasant thought. What if the Children of Rhys joined forces with the Empress against the rebels? What would happen to Garan and his fellow exiles then?

'Others?' asked the Empress. 'You mean that more of the Children of Rhys have followed you into my domain?'

'Perhaps not yet,' Rhosmari said hastily. 'My – one of the Elders believed that it would take a large party of our people to convince the rebels to give up the Stone, but when I left nothing had been decided. So if you send me back right away—'

But the Empress shook her head. 'I need you here,' she said. 'You are my only source of knowledge about the Children of Rhys, and there is still so much I want to learn. If your people come looking for you, and some of them are willing to negotiate – then perhaps I could afford to spare you. But I need to be sure I can rely on the Children of Rhys not to interfere in my affairs.'

So she was not just a prisoner and a slave, she was a hostage. 'I see,' said Rhosmari. 'Please excuse me,' and with that she got up from the table and left the room.

The Empress retired to her study after breakfast, though with the double doors closed and only the occasional creak or rustle coming from within, it was impossible to know exactly what she was doing there. After a few minutes Rhosmari gave up listening and retreated to her bedroom. But, as the morning wore on she was startled out of her reverie by thumping noises and loud, wracking sobs coming from the direction of the stairs. She threw open her door to find two strange faeries marching into the study, dragging a wild-eyed, struggling female between them. But before she could ask what they were doing, the double doors slammed shut.

Rhosmari retreated and sat numbly on the end of her bed as the distant cries and pleas escalated to a shriek – then ended in abrupt silence. Rhosmari's stomach convulsed. What had the Empress done to the other faery? Had she turned her into a slave, or something even worse?

Dreading the answer, but determined to know it nonetheless, she watched the study doors closely for the next half-hour. But when the familiar sweet voice called, 'Rhosmari, would you come here, please?' and she rose to obey, she found no one in the study but herself and the Empress. The other faeries – or the two males at least – must have Leaped away.

'You should not spend so much time brooding in your room,' the Empress chided her. 'You have the freedom of the house; why not visit the library, or admire the paintings? There are some fine landscapes in the drawing room, and some excellent portraits as well.'

Like the one of Philip Waverley? Rhosmari wanted to ask,

but held her tongue. The violence with which the painting had been destroyed made her think it might be dangerous even to mention it. Especially after what she had just heard.

'You must have found all that commotion quite alarming,' said the Empress, as though she had guessed Rhosmari's thoughts. 'I apologise for subjecting you to it, but there are still a considerable number of renegade faeries who left my service after the Battle of Sanctuary, and who have little to do other than wander about and cause trouble. Many come quietly once they are found, having realised that they were happier and better cared for under my rule. But others are...not as reasonable.'

She twisted a ringlet of hair around her finger, her gaze distant. Then she straightened up and said, 'But never mind that. Go and explore the house, and see what you can find to amuse yourself, until I am ready to speak with you again.'

Put like that, it was an order. Hating her own unhesitating obedience, Rhosmari turned and left the study, shutting the doors behind her.

nine

Outside Waverley Hall the rain was falling, forming little puddles on the gravel and coaxing the lawn into a deeper shade of green. Rhosmari sat by the window in the library, gazing listlessly at the neglected garden. She had tried to read, but every book she chose seemed to be little more than a chronicle of human misery, and her eyes refused to focus on the pages for long in any case.

After a few minutes the little dog – Isadora – crept across the muddy gravel, thinner and filthier than ever. It turned appealing eyes to Rhosmari and lay down facing the window, chin resting between its stubby front paws. Why was it here? The Empress did not even seem to know that it existed, and Sarah had pushed it away from the door as though it were a nuisance...

Someone behind her drew in a sobbing breath. Startled, Rhosmari turned to find Sarah standing in the doorway – but as soon as their eyes met, the human woman clapped a hand to her mouth and fled. Wondering what could be wrong, Rhosmari followed her and found the elderly woman at the other end of the corridor, clutching her elbows and trembling.

'I'm sorry,' she quavered, as Rhosmari came up to her. 'Please don't tell her you saw me like this. I'm only an old woman who loves her little dog, and I can't help—' She broke off with a little sniff as her eyes welled up again.

So Isadora was Sarah's pet, after all. But if the dog was so dear to her, then why had she neglected it?

Please don't tell her, repeated Sarah's voice in her mind, and all at once Rhosmari thought she understood. 'Did the Empress tell you to shut Isadora out?' she asked. 'Did she order you to let her starve?'

Sarah wiped her eyes. 'I know I did wrong to look at her,' she said. 'It won't happen again. Please – have mercy—'

'I'm not going to hurt you,' Rhosmari told her. 'And I'm not going to tell the Empress.' *At least*, she added silently, *not if I can help it*. 'I only want to know why you're upset.'

'But you...you're one of *them*. Why would you care?' Sarah backed away from her, fumbling for the handle of the door. 'After all your people have done to me...to my dog...my beautiful house...'

'I had no part in any of that,' said Rhosmari. 'And I want no part of it, either. I'm a prisoner here, just as you are.'

'I don't believe you.'

How could Rhosmari prove her good faith? She glanced

back towards the library – and remembered the little dog still sitting patiently with her nose to the window, waiting for a mistress who would not, and perhaps even could not, come.

'Where do you keep Isadora's food?' she asked.

Carefully Rhosmari filled the dog's bowl and carried it to the front door. She could not step past the threshold, but she set the dish outside, and when she softly called 'Isadora!' the dog struggled up the steps to meet her. With a snort, it buried its nose in the bowl.

'You can't do this,' whispered Sarah from behind her. 'The Empress will find out, and then—'

But Rhosmari held up a hand for silence, and picked up the bowl again. Step by step, she coaxed the dog through the entrance hall and along the passageway to the kitchen, while the human woman followed anxiously behind.

'The Empress doesn't know everything,' Rhosmari said to her, when the kitchen door was shut. 'Does she ever come in here? Do any of the other faeries?'

The woman shook her head.

'Then I'll come down and feed Isadora whenever I get the chance,' Rhosmari told her. 'She doesn't deserve to starve, no matter what the Empress says, and if there's any trouble then I'll take responsibility for it.'

Sarah collapsed into a chair and buried her face in her hands, thin shoulders shaking. It was a long time before she composed herself enough to speak again. 'She was only trying to protect me,' she gasped. 'She's always been such a gentle thing, I'd never heard her growl at anyone before, let alone bite…'

'Why did you let the Empress into the house?' asked Rhosmari.

'She came to the door,' Sarah said thickly, 'asking if she might come in and look at the paintings. She'd heard we had a Wrenfield here, she said, the last portrait he ever painted, and she would dearly love to see it. And she seemed like such a nice young woman that I invited her in. But no sooner did I show her the painting than she—' She swallowed. 'She did *that* to it, with just a sweep of her hand.'

So the Empress had destroyed Philip Waverley's portrait herself. Rhosmari wondered what she had been trying to prove – or hide. 'Go on,' she said.

'After that everything went dark, and I got terribly confused,' said Sarah. 'I felt as though I were walking in a dream. Before I knew it I'd shown her upstairs to the best bedroom, and by the end of the day I'd turned away the groundskeeper and told the cleaning staff I didn't need them any more.' She pulled a crumpled tissue from her sleeve and dabbed her eyes with it. 'Then the Empress got angry with Isadora and told me not to feed her or let her in the house any more…and since then I've been all alone. With *her*.'

Isadora was nosing at the bottom of her dish; Rhosmari

refilled the bowl and sat down on the other side of the table. 'How long has it been?'

'Three weeks, but it feels like forever,' said Sarah wearily. 'At first I thought that if I could only walk to the village, or pick up the telephone…but it's impossible. I can't get past the end of the garden without turning back again, and whenever anyone rings or comes to the door all I can say is how fine I am and how nice the weather's been. The only one who comes here any more is the grocer's man, and he doesn't seem to notice anything wrong.'

No, of course he wouldn't, thought Rhosmari. The Empress must have put a glamour around the house, and perhaps an aversion charm to keep unwanted visitors away. But she had mentioned wards as well, and it was hard to believe that any faery, even a powerful one, could maintain so many spells at once.

'My husband died a year ago,' Sarah went on, 'and I never could have children. I should have sold the house after the funeral, only I couldn't bear to leave all those memories behind…and how could I have known something like this would— Oh!' She looked down, her eyes brimming again. Isadora had crept over to the table and laid her head at her mistress's feet.

'She's all I have now,' Sarah murmured. 'And I can't even touch her.'

Anger blazed inside Rhosmari at the Empress's cruelty. She stooped and lifted Isadora up onto the table, then took Sarah's hand in her own and placed it on the dog's head.

'Now you can,' she said.

'You had a pleasant afternoon, I hope?' asked the Empress as Rhosmari walked back into the study.

Seeing the Empress smile, with the memory of Isadora's suffering and Sarah's helpless tears fresh in her mind, it was all Rhosmari could do to hide her revulsion. But if she allowed her feelings to show, then the Empress would surely want to know what was wrong. So she could only bend her lips into an answering smile and hope that she had learned something, however small, from her visits to the theatre.

'Please sit down,' the Empress continued, motioning to the chair before her desk. 'I have been thinking some more about your people, and the things you have told me about them. They are sworn to peace, you say? For how long have they upheld this law, or tradition, or whatever you call it?'

'For a thousand years,' said Rhosmari.

'A thousand! They must be a mild-mannered folk indeed. Tell me, how many of your people are there?'

As a scholar, Rhosmari would never have thought to be glad she did *not* know something. But she was glad now. 'We don't keep count.'

'But surely you can estimate,' the Empress persisted. 'Are there fifty of you? A hundred?'

Rhosmari shifted a little, uncomfortable. 'I can't say.'

'I think you can,' said the Empress gently. 'And will.'

'About eight hundred,' said Rhosmari, and then wished she could bite off her tongue.

'Oh,' the Empress breathed. *'Oh*. That is…more than I expected.'

'Is it?' Rhosmari asked, hoping to get her off the subject. 'How many faeries are on the mainland?'

'Fewer than you might think,' the Empress replied distractedly. 'Our people are widely scattered, and we do not have many children.'

This had always been true of faeries, if the ancient histories Rhosmari had studied were reliable. In fact, it had once been common for faeries to adopt unwanted human children in order to bolster their numbers. Even the Children of Rhys had done so in the past, though Rhosmari could not remember it happening in her lifetime.

'Eight hundred,' murmured the Empress. 'To have allies so numerous would be a great advantage. But…' Her gaze focused on Rhosmari again. 'I must know more about your people, if I am to decide how best to approach them…and what they are capable of offering me.'

Rhosmari wanted to tell the Empress that the Elders would never make a bargain with her, that they would quickly see through her charming facade. But she had not thought that her mother would ever consider sending an army onto the mainland, either, and suddenly none of the things in which she had once put her confidence seemed certain any more. Her throat went dry as the Empress leaned towards her, eyes glittering.

'Tell me more about the Children of Rhys,' she commanded. 'Tell me everything.'

By the time the Empress let her go, Rhosmari felt sick with exhaustion – and shame. Long after she had left the study, she could hear the echo of that soft, relentless voice asking one question after another, while she babbled out all the secrets about her people and her homeland that she had been most desperate to hide.

There was very little now that the Empress did not know about the Green Isles, or the Children of Rhys, or about Rhosmari herself. She knew how upset the Rhysians had been over losing the Stone of Naming, why Rhosmari had been so alarmed by Lady Celyn's plan to get it back, and how she had escaped to the mainland through Gruffydd's Way to look for Garan and the Stone herself. The Empress also knew what a shock it had been to Rhosmari when she learned of the Oak's destruction (she had smiled at that point, which made Rhosmari loathe her even more) and when she had seen Llinos in Manchester (which the Empress seemed to find particularly interesting for some reason). And just when Rhosmari thought she had utterly humiliated herself and betrayed her people in every possible way, the Empress took her back to the beginning and made her go through it all again.

Rhosmari dropped into the chair beside her bedroom window, pushing the heels of her hands against her eyes. How could she have been deceived by the Empress, even for a moment? Let alone felt sorry for her, or believed they had anything in common? It was bad enough to feel that no one else was trustworthy, but now Rhosmari was beginning to think that she could not even trust herself.

At least one thing was clear to her, however: somehow, she must get word to her people and warn them about the Empress. No one could approach the Green Isles without the Elders' permission, and after what had happened with Timothy and Linden they would not be quick to welcome strangers again. Still, she wanted them to be prepared to refuse anything the Empress might offer – or better yet, not listen to her at all.

But how could she deliver a message to the Green Isles when she was trapped here in Waverley Hall, unable to use magic or even set foot outside the front door?

Even the moon's beaming face seemed to mock her, promising light when all she could see was darkness. Bitterly Rhosmari flung the curtains shut, and turned away.

Over the next few days Rhosmari's life settled into a kind of nightmarish routine. Every night she lay awake for hours, trying to think her way past the restrictions that bound her.

In the morning she would force down a few mouthfuls of breakfast with the Empress, then escape as quickly as possible. Some time before noon, or just after it, she would hear the screams of captured faeries being dragged into the study, never to come out again. When all was quiet, it was time to feed Isadora and exchange a few words with Sarah. Then she would wander about the house until supper, sit silently at the table listening to the Empress's lieutenants boast of their achievements and compete for their mistress's approval, and finally head back upstairs to begin the cycle all over again.

The worst of it was that after a while Rhosmari stopped caring. She knew the Empress was preparing something, or waiting for something to happen, so she could hunt down Rob and his remaining followers and put an end to their rebellion. But that hardly seemed relevant any more. Why should it be, when Rhosmari had no idea where the rebels were, let alone how to make contact with them? And if only a few of them had escaped the destruction of the Oak, how could they help her in any case?

But then one afternoon she started down the stairs to find Veronica bringing up her latest prisoner, and everything changed.

'Oh, look, Martin,' said Veronica. Playfully she clapped her hands to her captive's cheeks and tilted his head up toward Rhosmari. 'It's your little friend. Say hello.'

Martin made a croaking noise, like a bird trying to speak.

His hair hung limp over his eyes, and his clothing was rumpled and torn. Shaking her head, Rhosmari backed away.

'So disapproving, Rhosmari? I thought you would be pleased to see him like this. He deserves it, after all.' Veronica poked Martin in the shoulder, and he began to climb the stairs again. 'Just imagine,' she added in a confiding tone as Rhosmari edged aside to let them pass, 'all the interesting ways you could punish him for what he did to you! If I were you, I would have him begging for mercy.'

She twirled one finger, and Martin turned around and crumpled to his knees on the landing at Rhosmari's feet. 'Don't,' said Rhosmari, pressing back against the wall. 'Stop it.'

'Veronica,' said the Empress from the door of the study, 'stop playing with Martin and come here. You too, Rhosmari.' When they had all followed her into the room, she turned to Veronica and said, 'Release him.'

Veronica passed her hand over Martin's face, and his vacant look sharpened into fury. 'You broke our bargain,' he snapped at the Empress. 'We agreed—'

'We agreed that *if* you could deliver to me one of the Children of Rhys, I would let you go. And indeed, I was intrigued to know how you would manage it, so I chose to indulge you.' The Empress stopped behind her chair, resting one arm lightly along its high back. 'But you disappointed me, Martin. Instead of accomplishing the task on your own, you made a bargain with my Blackwings to help you carry it out. And since you could not have called on them without my leave, that makes Rhosmari's capture as much my doing as it was yours.'

Martin's eyes narrowed. 'You never said I had to do it alone.'

'And you never suggested that you planned to do it any other way,' said the Empress. 'So I think I have been quite generous to let you wander free as long as I did. Nevertheless, that is not the reason I brought you here.'

She walked back towards him and took his chin in her hand, like a mother rebuking a wilful child. 'I have heard some very distressing reports about your activities, Martin. Have I not warned you against spending too much time with humans? And what made you think I would tolerate you doing so, whether you were under my command or not?'

'The ability to play a role is a useful skill,' said Martin levelly, but Rhosmari could see he was shaken. 'And only the humans have it.'

'That is quite true,' agreed the Empress. 'And I have often made use of that talent myself. But I have never found it necessary to be friendly with humans, much less treat them as equals, in order to get it. Clearly you have lost sight of your position, and if I must take matters into my own hands to ensure you do not forget again, so be it.'

She nodded to Veronica, who seemed to take it as a dismissal and Leaped away, leaving Rhosmari, Martin and the Empress alone. The Empress let go of Martin's jaw and continued. 'Under ordinary circumstances, the penalty for your disobedience would be death. Yet you have rendered me good service in the past, so I am prepared to be merciful.' She reached for her dagger. 'Give me your hand.'

'Wait.' A muscle twitched in Martin's cheek; he looked close to panic. 'You don't have to do this. I can give you something else you want, and this time, I swear, I will do it on my own—'

'What else can you possibly do for me,' said the Empress, 'that the Blackwings or Veronica cannot do just as well, or better?'

'I can infiltrate the rebels for you.' He spoke quickly, flushed with eagerness. 'I can gain their confidence, learn their secrets – they will see that I am not under your control, and let me join them in the Oak—'

The Oak. Rhosmari's heart thudded against her ribs. So even that part of Martin's story had been a lie? Rob and his rebels, Garan and his men, the Oakenfolk, Timothy and the others – they were all still alive, still free, still together?

Joy surged up within her, and it took all the skills she had absorbed from her visits to the theatre not to exclaim aloud. But she managed to keep her expression neutral, right up to the point where the Empress turned to her and said, 'Strike him, Rhosmari.'

Immediately Rhosmari's arm whipped out, with the full force of her weight behind it. The blow connected with Martin's cheek, jarring the bones in her hand and stinging her palm like fire. He staggered back and almost fell, but as he righted himself one corner of his mouth turned up.

'You must have enjoyed that,' he said.

Rhosmari swallowed back the sickness in her throat. She had never struck another living being before. 'No,' she whispered, but even as her lips shaped the word she knew it was a lie.

'I have no interest in your offer,' the Empress told Martin. 'As far as the Oak is concerned, I have all the information I need. So one last time, before I lose my patience: *give me your hand.*'

Martin looked straight into her eyes, but he did not move.

'Or,' the Empress went on conversationally, 'I will have Rhosmari take control of your mind, and she will make you caper about the room like a clown until you die of exhaustion. Would you prefer that?'

Rhosmari's skin prickled with horror. *Don't let her do this*, she pleaded silently with Martin. *Just give her what she wants. Please...*

Martin's lips moved, shaping a curse or a prayer. Then he raised his clenched fist, unfolded it finger by finger, and turned his palm up to the Empress. Rhosmari turned away, not wanting to watch what happened next.

'What is your command, Your Imperial Majesty?' said Martin, when the Empress had finished. There was no mockery or insolence in his tone; he knew better than to openly defy her now that she held his name.

'You may join my other servants,' she told him, 'who are helping to rebuild my army. Capture as many renegades and rebels as you can find, and bring either them or a sample of their blood to me. But do not travel far. I want you within summoning distance.'

Martin nodded, flicked an unreadable look at Rhosmari, and Leaped out of the room. The Empress sighed and sat down, arranging her silken skirts. 'It is always so tedious forcing people to do what is best for them,' she said. 'Why can they not simply accept my judgment, even if they are too ignorant to appreciate it?'

Once, Rhosmari might have been tempted to sympathise. Now she only wanted to scream. 'Your Majesty,' she said unevenly, 'may I ask a question?'

'Of course,' said the Empress, with one of her indulgent smiles. 'What do you wish to know?'

'I am as much in your power as he is,' Rhosmari said. 'And I have done nothing to offend you. You already know everything I could tell you about the Children of Rhys. So why keep me here, and let him go?'

The Empress looked surprised, then amused. 'You mean you still have not guessed?' she asked. 'I know you are not accustomed to thinking like a soldier, but surely the answer is obvious. I need an army large enough to defeat the rebels and wipe them out completely. And once you have opened Gruffydd's Way for me and my followers, and led us to the Green Isles in secret…I will have that army.'

ten

Sitting alone in the blue bedroom, Rhosmari felt strangely insubstantial, as though someone had hollowed her out from the inside. Her bruised palm still throbbed, and she could not close her eyes without seeing Martin's head snapping back as she struck him. But that was nothing compared to the horror of what the Empress wanted her to do next to help her invade the Green Isles by stealth and treachery, and conquer the Children of Rhys.

How could she have been so blind to what the Empress was planning? Rhosmari had been so intent on saving her people from harm, it had never occurred to her that she herself could become the means of their destruction. But now, if she did not do something quickly, her people would be taken unawares, and turned into slaves of the Empress. Not just a few of them as she had once feared, but *all* of them.

She leaped up from her seat and went to the window,

staring out across the empty garden. Somewhere out there, the Oak was still alive and whole – and full of rebel faeries, Garan and his men included. If they knew what the Empress had in mind for Rhosmari, they would surely come and rescue her. But how could she get a message to them?

She could address it to the humans in the house, perhaps...but the Empress kept a close eye on Sarah's correspondence, and she could hardly be expected to overlook something marked for Oakhaven.

Could she coax a bird to the window, and tie a message to its leg? No, because she would still need to use magic to tell the bird where to go.

What if she... No, that wouldn't work either.

Rhosmari gripped the sill with both hands, fighting back panic. She *had* to find a way to contact the rebels. Any day now, or at any moment, the Empress might gather her forces and command Rhosmari to lead them to the Green Isles. Merciful Rhys, what was she going to do?

She was still gazing helplessly into the distance when Isadora came waddling up the gravel drive towards the kitchen. The little dog had begun to put on weight again, but she still needed regular meals to keep up her strength – and with everything that had happened today, Rhosmari had forgotten to feed her.

Well, at least she could do that much to thwart the Empress, if nothing else. But it was hard for Rhosmari to take much joy in saving a dog, knowing that the lives of hundreds of faeries were still in jeopardy…and that if the Empress conquered them, it would be her fault.

When Rhosmari came into the kitchen, she found Sarah hunched over the worktop, chopping vegetables. 'I'm so tired of making fancy meals,' the older woman said, wiping her hand across her brow. 'And the grocer's bill! It seems like every day I'm having to call for another delivery. If this keeps up I'll have nothing left to live on.'

She sounded so plaintive that, for a moment, Rhosmari almost told her about the Empress's plan. If it gave her no joy to know that the Empress would soon be leaving Waverley Hall, then at least it would be good news to Sarah. But she could not bring herself to share her burden with anyone, and she feared what might happen to Sarah if the Empress guessed that they had been talking together.

Quietly Rhosmari filled Isadora's bowl and set it out on the kitchen step. But as she watched the dog gobble down the meal, a new misgiving troubled her. How long would it be before the Empress noticed that the little dog had not yet died, and decided to investigate? And what would happen to Isadora then?

Rhosmari put a hand to her forehead. Every time she tried to help, all she seemed to do was make matters worse. Now she not only had to warn the Elders and get a message to the rebels, she had to find a way to save Isadora too…

Despairing, she turned to leave, and a picture on the far

wall caught her eye. It was a painting of Sarah at a slightly younger age, seated and smiling with her dog on her lap and a kindly-looking man standing behind her. Rhosmari had noticed the painting before, but never paid it close attention. Now something made her stop and consider it again.

By rights it ought to have disturbed her as much as Philip Waverley's ruined portrait, for it was impossible not to look at that peaceful scene without being reminded of how much Sarah had suffered since. But the bold, vigorous way the artist had used his brush upon the canvas, the glowing warmth of the colours he had chosen, made Rhosmari feel reassured and even a little comforted. It seemed to tell her of a better world that had been once, and perhaps would be again.

'That's a lovely thing, isn't it?' said Sarah, coming up behind her. 'The artist's quite well known in these parts, so I was surprised when he said he'd like to paint Richard and myself for free. I told him we'd be glad to pay, but he insisted, and by the time he was done we'd become quite good friends with him and his wife. It's a shame he has to use a wheelchair, but it doesn't seem to hold him back much…'

As she spoke, Rhosmari's eyes drifted to the bottom corner of the portrait, where the artist had scrawled his name. 'Yes, it's very good,' she said, and left.

But for the rest of that afternoon and evening, she was nagged by a sense that she had overlooked something important. It was not until nearly midnight, as she lay dry-eyed and sleepless in the light of the full moon, that she remembered the signature at the bottom of Sarah's portrait. *P. McCormick.*

Paul McCormick. Timothy's cousin, and the husband of Peri, who had once been a faery called Knife...

And their house was called Oakhaven, because the Oak was there.

Rhosmari sat up, gripping the mattress. Her brain had begun to work furiously, weaving connections from one idea to another. Paul McCormick. Isadora's need for protection. Sarah lamenting her grocery bill...

Excitement blazed through her, filling her with energy. She leaped out of bed and raced to the writing desk, switching on the little light above it. Then she pulled out a sheet of paper and began to write.

From Rhosmari daughter of Celyn, to Paul and Peri McCormick and the people of the Oak that is behind their house, greetings in the name of Rhys and the Great Gardener. I have been taken captive by the Empress and am being held prisoner by her at Waverley Hall, along with the house's human owner, Sarah...

Though her blood fizzed with eagerness, she knew she must not be hasty. She had to explain to the rebels, step by step, what they needed to do. First they would encounter the

Empress's wards, which would alert her the moment any faery or human crossed the estate's perimeter. And though the Empress spent most of her time at Waverley Hall alone, she always kept at least one or two of her lieutenants – and any number of lesser servants besides – within summoning distance. So it was crucial for the rebels to find a way to dismantle the wards before they approached, or they would find themselves in the midst of a battle.

And yet – Rhosmari's pen hovered over the page – even if they did reach the house without being seen, no faery could enter Waverley Hall without permission. And as long as the Empress was still the mistress of the house, the only guests she would allow Sarah to invite were her own...

But if Rhosmari kept thinking of all the ways in which her plan could fail, she would never have the courage to finish this letter at all. She kept writing, one line after another, until she had filled two pages in her precise, scholarly hand. Then she sketched a rough diagram of the interior of Waverley Hall, indicating where her bedroom and Sarah's, as well as the Empress's study and personal bedchamber, were located. Now for the conclusion:

The Empress plans for me to help her invade and conquer the Green Isles. If she succeeds in adding the Children of Rhys to her army, you will have no chance of resisting her. So I urge you to come quickly, for all our sakes.

When the letter was finished Rhosmari read it over again, afraid that she might have forgotten something – but no, it was good. With a shiver of anticipation she signed the page, folded it and tucked it into the box with the unused envelopes, where no one else would be likely to find it.

Now all she had to do was wait for morning.

When the first light of dawn crept through the curtains, Rhosmari woke at once, ready to carry out her plan. But her pulse beat erratically as she opened her bedroom door, and when she stepped out into the hallway she felt as though she were going to her own funeral. She carried the incriminating letter tucked into the waistband of her skirt, hidden from any casual glance, but that would not save her if the Empress became suspicious. It took all her courage to walk lightly past the study doors, and descend the stairs as though she were in no particular hurry at all.

Fortunately, the Empress must have been preoccupied, because Rhosmari made it safely to the bottom of the stairs, and after that it was an easy matter to find Sarah in the kitchen, preparing breakfast.

'Sarah,' she said breathlessly. 'I know how to get Isadora to a place where she'll be safe.'

The woman looked taken aback, and even once Rhosmari explained her plan, she hesitated so long that Rhosmari feared she might not go through with it. But at last she said, 'Yes. Yes, of course. It's the only way,' and hurried off to fetch Isadora's dog carrier.

Later that morning, Rhosmari watched from her bedroom window as the grocer's lorry came crunching up the drive and wheezed to a stop by the kitchen. As the driver unloaded Sarah's groceries and carried them into the house, Rhosmari clasped her hands together and mouthed a silent prayer. *Please let him be willing. Please don't let Sarah change her mind...*

The man stayed inside for what seemed a very long time, and Rhosmari began to feel nauseated with worry. But Sarah must have persisted, for in the end he went back outside with a bundle of banknotes in his pocket and Isadora's carrier under his arm. As he climbed into the lorry and drove away, Rhosmari held her breath. If the Empress had seen...if the wards alerted her that something was wrong...

But when the lorry reached the end of the drive and turned onto the road, she knew with a leap of her heart that she had guessed right: the Empress took little account of dogs – or humans. And when it was safe to go downstairs again, Sarah's tearful gratitude was all that Rhosmari could have wished for.

'You did it!' she whispered, clutching Rhosmari's hand in her soft, blue-veined ones. 'She's safe! Oh, thank you, thank you...'

Rhosmari was glad to see the old woman so relieved. Yet

to hear those sacred words, even from a human who did not know any better, made her squirm inside. She did not deserve to have Sarah so indebted to her. Especially since she had used Isadora's rescue as an opportunity to send her letter to the rebels, and not even told Sarah what she was doing...but then, that was for Sarah's own protection.

Or at least that was what Rhosmari told herself. But deeper down she knew the real reason: she did not dare to rely upon anyone now, even someone as well-meaning as Sarah. If the rebels came to rescue them, Sarah would share in her joy; but if not, Rhosmari would bear the disappointment, and the consequences, alone.

One day passed, and then another, and another. By the fourth day, Rhosmari had begun to lose hope. At the end of the fifth, she pressed her face into her pillow and wept. And on the sixth, when the Empress summoned Rhosmari and announced that they would leave for the Green Isles tomorrow, she could only bow her head in resignation. She had done her best, but she had failed. And now she could think of only one more way to thwart the Empress's plan.

That night, when the house was still, Rhosmari walked softly out of her bedroom and down the steps to the kitchen. She felt no fear, only a black and roaring emptiness, as she took Sarah's carving knife from the block and poised it against her heart. She would grip it with both hands, like so, and...

But the knife would not move, and neither would her body, no matter how much Rhosmari willed them to come together. She wrestled against herself until sweat broke out on her forehead, then dropped the knife with a clatter and reeled back, gasping and spent. When the Empress had told Rhosmari not to leave the house by any means, she had meant it. Even the door of death was closed to her now. Rhosmari stumbled back up to her bedroom, and fell into exhausted sleep.

When she woke it was mid-morning, and the sunlight slanting through the curtains seared her eyes like a brand. But her limbs felt too heavy to move, and what was the use of getting out of bed anyway? She rolled over and curled in upon herself, wishing she could go back to sleep and never wake up again.

Dimly she registered the sound of tyres crackling over gravel as a vehicle came up the drive. The grocer again, no doubt...but if it was his lorry, it did not make any of the usual noises. Nor did the muffled voice – no, voices – drifting up from the yard sound familiar. Rhosmari clambered out of bed and pressed her ear to the window, straining to make out their conversation. It sounded as though some human family had come by to see the estate, and Sarah was turning them away.

'No, we don't give tours any more,' she said. 'Waverley Hall is no longer open to the public. I'll have to ask you to— *Oh!*'

Ice shot through Rhosmari's veins. Someone was hurting Sarah! She whirled and dashed out into the corridor – only to collide with Martin, who seized her by both wrists and held her there.

'Cleverly done, my lioness,' he said, raising his voice as shouts and splintering noises resounded from the floor below. 'So you learned a few tricks from me after all.'

'What are you doing here?' Rhosmari demanded, struggling to see past him. 'What's going on?'

'What do you think?' he said. 'The Empress summoned me to keep an eye on you, because your rebel friends are attacking the house. Somehow they got past the wards – and now they've broken inside. How did they manage that, I wonder?'

Thumps and hoarse cries echoed from downstairs, followed by a crash of furniture being overturned. Rhosmari tried to twist free of Martin's grip, but he only said, 'The study, I think,' and began to drag her along with him.

'Timothy, don't you dare!' shouted a furious female voice from below, and Martin stopped. 'Aha,' he said. 'So that's how they did it. The Empress really must learn to stop underestimating humans.'

But even as he spoke footsteps pounded up the stairs, and a slim, dark-haired boy leaped up onto the landing, brandishing a fireplace poker like a sword. Cold iron ringed his fingers, braced his wrists, swung in cross-shape from a leather thong around his neck – an armour no faery spell could penetrate.

'Let her go, Martin,' he panted, levelling the poker.

A talented young human, the Empress had called Timothy, *but regrettably prone to violence*. Rhosmari knew it was true – and yet her heart at the sight of him, just the same.

Martin shoved Rhosmari behind him, so hard that she tripped and fell. Then with a gesture he spelled a vase off its pedestal, and hurled it at Timothy. Rhosmari cried out – but Timothy ducked and it shattered against the wall above him, showering him with china fragments. He shook the dust from his hair and advanced again.

A painting leaped off the wall behind Timothy, threatening to bludgeon him with its heavy frame. But he twisted sideways and it skimmed past him with a hand's width to spare. Martin was forced to dodge it, and Timothy sprang forward, closing the gap between them. 'I mean it,' he said. 'Let her *go*—' and he swung the poker at Martin, who leaned back just in time to avoid being hit.

Rhosmari scrambled backwards, glancing around for something she could use to help. She did not want to get in the middle of this fight; she did not want to fight at all. But she had seen the feral gleam in Martin's eyes and the answering glare in Timothy's, and she knew that if she did not intervene, someone was going to end up badly hurt...

Rhosmari! Leap to me at once!

The command exploded into her mind, obliterating every other thought. In a blink she left the corridor, and materialised in the Empress's study.

'So you too have betrayed me,' snapped the Empress. In her fury she had lost control of her glamour, and for the first time Rhosmari glimpsed her real face: grey-black hair threaded white at the temples, and features that had once been striking grown haggard with age. 'You will pay for this – but there is no time now. Take these.' She snatched up an armful of papers from the desk and thrust them at Rhosmari. 'Meet me in—'

The double doors crashed open and Timothy burst into the room, followed by a lean, ice-blonde woman who moved like a hunter. The woman's arm whipped out, hurling an iron horseshoe through the air – but before it could strike the Empress, she vanished.

Leap to the village and await me there! The Empress's last order rang out in Rhosmari's mind, and automatically she cast the spell to obey. But before she could fade Timothy lunged at her, and his iron-ringed fingers closed around her wrist.

Agony seared through her. The spell broke, all her magic extinguished in an instant. As Rhosmari's knees buckled, Timothy caught her in his arms – but then her cheek brushed the cross upon his chest, and everything went black.

eleven

Rhosmari woke at the touch of fingers sliding into her own, pressing something cool and hard against her palm. She closed her hand around it, feeling its smoothness, its rounded shape.

It was the Stone of Naming.

She gripped it fervently, willing its magic to work as she had never wished for anything in all her life. Light filled her mind, burning away the darkness, and the true name that the Empress had stolen vanished from Rhosmari's memory, erased as though it had never been.

Yet she felt no emptiness, no regret. No sooner was the old name gone than the new one took its place, but it did not feel like a replacement; it was as though she had been meant to bear that name all along, and she could not imagine anything more fitting or more beautiful.

And in that moment, Rhosmari swore to herself that she would face any peril, endure any torture, even fight to the death if she had to, rather than let anyone – *anyone* – find out her secret name again.

'Feeling better?' asked a voice, and slowly she opened her eyes.

She was lying on the sofa in the Empress's study. But it was not the Empress's any longer, for all the curtains had been flung back and the once-shadowed room was washed in light. Dust motes tumbled through the sunshine, winking like tiny jewels, and through the open window came a gentle breeze and the sound of a bird calling *hweet, hweet*.

And Timothy was standing there, watching her.

He was even taller than she remembered, his skin more tanned, his eyes greener. There was a smear of blood high on his forehead where something had cut him, and he was wearing the fireplace poker like a sword through his belt.

'Sorry about the iron,' he said, holding up his ring-circled fingers. 'But your magic should come back in an hour or so – and I figured you'd prefer a shock to going with the Empress.'

'Yes,' said Rhosmari, wincing as she sat up. Her wrist and cheek still tingled where the iron had touched her, and all her muscles ached. 'Is it over already? The Empress and her people – they're gone?'

Timothy nodded. 'And they won't be coming back, either. Sarah will make sure of that.'

So Sarah was all right, too. Rhosmari sent up a silent

prayer of gratitude. 'I didn't think you were coming,' she said to Timothy. 'The grocer told us he'd delivered Isadora, but then—'

'I know,' he replied. 'I'm sorry about that, too. But it took us days just to figure out how to get through the Empress's wards without setting them off. And then we had to make sure we took her by surprise, so she wouldn't have a chance to summon more than a few of her people before she had to run.' He picked a paperweight off the desk and rolled it between his hands. 'It would have been a lot harder without your letter, though. You're a very detail-oriented sort of person, aren't you?'

'I'm a scholar,' she said. 'We're trained to be specific.'

'And logical,' said Timothy. 'I like that in a faery.' He put the paperweight down, hitched a leg over the corner of the desk and sat there, a curious half-smile on his face. 'So what gave you the idea of writing to Paul and Peri? And how did you know how to find us?'

'Linden told us where you lived,' she said. 'When you and she came before the Elders.'

He looked surprised. 'You were there that day? I didn't see you.'

'I was sitting behind Broch,' she said, 'and I came down afterwards to talk to Garan. You must have forgotten.'

Timothy shook his head. 'I don't think so. Believe me, if I had seen you...' His mouth quirked. '...I would have remembered.'

Rhosmari put a hand to her unbound hair. She knew she must look ridiculous in her bare feet and rumpled nightgown, but did he have to mock her? Summoning dignity she stood up, still clutching the Stone of Naming, and said, 'Excuse me.' Then she walked back to her bedroom, dressed in her travelling clothes, and tucked the Stone into her skirt pocket.

When she opened the door again, Timothy was waiting. 'If you're feeling up to it, we should go down,' he said. 'Garan's anxious to see you.'

Garan. All at once Rhosmari's self-possession evaporated, and her mouth went dry. She had come all this way to find him – but what would she say to him now?

The ground floor of Waverley Hall was swarming with faeries, most of them strange to Rhosmari. They were busy mending the broken furniture, scorched curtains, and other damage that had happened during the battle, and few of them even looked up as she and Timothy came down the stairs. But she glimpsed Broch's long sardonic face among the crowd, and for a moment she thought she saw Llinos...

Then Garan came running across the entrance hall, whirled her around, and pulled her into a crushing embrace.

Rhosmari went rigid, staring over his shoulder as Timothy slipped away down the corridor and disappeared.

Fortunately, Garan did not seem offended by her lack of response. He loosed her to arm's length and looked her up and down, anxious. 'You are well?' he said.

If she had thought Timothy changed, Garan was even more so: he had clipped his sandy hair short and let his beard grow. It ought to have heightened his resemblance to his father, but oddly it did not. It only made him look older, and more like a leader.

'I am now,' she said. And with that she reached into her pocket, and took out the Stone of Naming.

When she left the Green Isles, Rhosmari would never have imagined that she could ever hold the Stone in her hand, knowing what it meant to her people, and yet choose to give it up. But that was before she had met the Empress, and experienced what it was like to be her slave. She would never forget the horror of knowing that her true name was no longer secret, or of becoming totally subject to another person's whims. Nor could she forget what a vast relief it had been to touch the Stone, and be made free.

She held it out to Garan, offered on her open palm. 'I came here looking for this,' she said. 'But I don't want it any more. The Children of Rhys don't need the Stone. Your people do.'

'We are still Children of Rhys, even in exile,' said Garan. 'But I am grateful for your sacrifice, Rhosmari.' Then, with a courtesy that reminded her painfully of Lady Arianllys, he inclined his head to her, took the Stone from her hand, and tucked it into the pouch at his belt.

'The prisoner's awake,' said a female faery with blunt dark hair, stomping up to Garan and jerking a thumb back over her shoulder. 'He wants to talk to Rhosmari.'

Rhosmari followed Garan and the stocky female through the passageway to the kitchen. A small cluster of faeries parted as they came in, and she found herself face to face with Martin. His hands were lashed behind him and there was an ugly bruise on his cheekbone, but his eyes met hers with the same cool arrogance as ever.

'Congratulations,' he said. 'You have your revenge. Would you like to hit me again, for old times' sake?'

Garan shot Rhosmari a startled glance, but she ignored it. 'What do you want, Martin?'

'You know the answer,' he replied. 'But it seems that freedom on my own terms is not an option at present. So untie my hands, and let me go back to the Empress.'

Rhosmari looked incredulously at the dark-haired faery, who shrugged and said, 'We offered to let him touch the Stone. He told us he wasn't interested.'

'But why?' Rhosmari asked Martin. 'After everything the Empress has done to you – why would you *choose* to serve her?'

His mouth twisted in a parody of a smile. 'I have already touched the Stone of Naming once,' he said. 'And what kind of freedom did it give me? Freedom to run in terror, without refuge or rest; freedom to beg, and starve, and live in squalor. At least if I belong to the Empress, I eat well and sleep sound.'

'You could join the rebels,' said Rhosmari, but Martin laughed.

'Go to the Oak and live like a squirrel in a tree? I know better than to imagine I could ever be content with such a life. And they have no more protection from the Empress than I do.' He raised his voice to address the room at large. 'You gain nothing by keeping me a prisoner. I can tell the Empress nothing about you that she does not know already, and she will offer neither bargain nor ransom for my sake. So either kill me, or let me go.'

Kill me. He spoke the words so lightly, as though he hardly cared what became of him any more. And Rhosmari remembered how she had stood in the kitchen only last night, holding a knife to her breast.

'Let him go,' she said.

'Who made you Queen?' retorted the faery who had escorted her to the kitchen. 'If you ask me, he ought to be nailed to a stump and left for the crows—'

'Peace, Thorn,' Garan said, his gaze on Rhosmari. 'She has the right to free him, if anyone does.'

'And we'll have the right to regret it,' said Thorn sourly, but she stepped up to Martin and loosened his bonds. Martin shook off the ropes and headed for the door, but Rhosmari called, 'Wait.'

He did not turn, but he paused. Rhosmari went on, 'You betrayed me once, and I was willing to forgive you for it. But by joining the Empress, you not only betray your fellow faeries, but Lyn and Toby and all the other humans you once called friends. I know you never cared for me, but can you say the same about them?'

Martin stood still for a moment, his face a cold mask. Then he pushed open the door and walked out.

'Well, that was all very special,' said Thorn. 'But who's going to break the news to Timothy? He seemed fairly pleased with himself after he knocked Martin out with that poker.'

'Can you blame me?' asked a voice unexpectedly from the pantry, and Timothy stepped out into the room. 'The first time I met him, he knifed me and took my wallet.'

So that was why Timothy had been so eager to fight Martin. Rhosmari should not have been surprised, let alone disappointed. Yet she was.

'Speaking of Knife,' Thorn said to Timothy, 'she's looking for you. And she's none too happy, either.'

'Yes, I know,' said Timothy. 'Why don't you go and tell her where I am? You like to do that.'

'Cheeky brat,' sniffed Thorn, but she went. The faeries who remained traded furtive glances and then hurried out after her, until only Rhosmari, Garan and Timothy were left.

'We must get Rhosmari back to the Oakenwyld,' said Garan to Timothy. 'It will be hours before the rest of us finish putting this house in order, and she will be safer there if the Empress should attack again.'

Timothy nodded. 'We can take her in the car, once Paul gets back.' He glanced out of the window. 'Oh good, that's him now.' He headed for the yard, and Rhosmari was about to follow, but Garan touched her arm.

'We will talk later, you and I,' he said.

The seriousness in his tone made Rhosmari uneasy. Did he just want to share information, or did he have something more personal in mind? But Garan had already walked away, and all she could do was watch him go.

When Rhosmari joined Timothy outside, a grey car was idling in the yard, with a blond and strikingly handsome man behind the wheel. He rolled down the window and said, 'Tim, could you find Peri and tell her I'm here?'

This must be Paul McCormick. Rhosmari bent towards the car to greet him – and saw the carrier strapped into the back seat. 'Isadora!' she exclaimed, and the dog yipped in reply.

Rhosmari was glad to take the carrier and reunite Isadora with her mistress, and once she was satisfied that both of them were resting comfortably, she bid Sarah goodbye and returned to the kitchen yard. She found Peri – the pale-haired woman who had thrown the horseshoe at the Empress – sitting beside Paul in the front of the car, and Timothy holding the back door open for her to join them.

'Hop in,' he said.

Rhosmari had never ridden in a vehicle so small before, much less with three humans. And yet, after nearly two weeks as a prisoner, she would have braved much worse to escape from Waverley Hall. She slid onto the back seat, and Timothy climbed in beside her.

'Will Sarah be safe now?' Rhosmari asked, as Paul turned the car around and headed for the main drive.

'If she follows my instructions, she will be,' Peri said. 'And I gave her one of my iron pendants, just to be sure. But I don't think Jasmine will come back in any case.'

'Jasmine?' asked Rhosmari.

'The Empress,' Timothy said. 'Remember the story Linden told your Elders, about the faery who stole the Oakenfolk's magic? Well, it turns out that she and this Empress are the same person.'

'And the first time she met Timothy, she nearly killed him,' said Peri. 'As did Martin, for that matter. So of course the first thing he does when we get to Waverley Hall is go haring off upstairs, so they can both have another chance to finish him off.'

She glared at Timothy over her shoulder. He bristled, and Rhosmari spoke up hastily before it could turn into a quarrel: 'The Empress told me that she had been human once.'

'She *told* you that?' asked Timothy.

But Peri did not seem surprised. 'Three times, actually,'

she said. 'From what Queen Amaryllis told me before she died, Jasmine was born human. She was adopted by the Oakenfolk as a child, but once she grew up, her Queen sent her back into the human world to learn about creativity. That was when she met a painter named Alfred Wrenfield, and fell in love with him.'

'In...love?' Rhosmari blinked, trying to digest this unexpected news. 'You mean she chose to stay with him, instead of going back to the Oak? Like you did with Paul?'

'Kind of,' said Timothy. 'Only with a lot more yelling and hitting.'

'One hundred per cent more, in fact,' put in Paul dryly. 'Just so we have that perfectly clear.'

Without a trace of self-consciousness, Peri leaned over and kissed her husband's cheek. Then she went on, 'Wrenfield could be selfish and unreliable, even cruel at times. But Jasmine's bond to him was too deep for her to even think about leaving, until he lost his temper and struck her.'

Rhosmari had never heard of such a thing before, but she had studied enough ancient faery lore to understand. A bond was a sacred covenant between faeries – or in this case, between faery and human. But if either party struck the other, all obligations between them were cancelled.

'Jasmine returned to the Oak angry and bitter,' Peri continued, 'and determined to keep her fellow faeries from suffering as she had done. Over the next few years she worked her way up to becoming Queen, and then she cast the spell that used up the Oakenfolk's magic and cut them off from the human world. But then Amaryllis came back from the outside world to challenge her...and I think you know the rest of the story.'

In my youth I lost a magical contest with a rival, the Empress had told her, *who thought the best way to humiliate me was to turn me into a human.* 'So that was why the Empress destroyed Philip Waverley's portrait,' said Rhosmari. 'Because Wrenfield had painted it.'

'Partly,' Peri said. 'But she had reason to hate Philip Waverley, too. His wife, Heather, was also a faery, but unlike Jasmine and Wrenfield, they were happy together. In fact, the two of them were so devoted to each other that even after Jasmine stole Heather's magic and trapped her in her faery form, she couldn't make her forget Philip or stop wanting to be with him.'

A bond stronger than magic itself? Rhosmari found that hard to believe. 'So Jasmine let her go?'

'Of course not,' said Paul without taking his eyes off the road. 'She had her executed.'

Rhosmari sank down in her seat, staring at the back of Paul's blond head. She had known the Empress could be harsh with faeries she deemed traitors, but she had not realised she was capable of outright murder.

'And then Philip died of a broken heart,' said Timothy. 'Which I didn't think ever actually happened. But they'd already had two children by that point, one of whom inherited Waverley Hall—'

'And became Sarah's great-grandfather,' Paul added. 'Or great-great-grandfather. Something of that sort.'

'And the other,' Peri finished, 'is Valerian, the present Queen of the Oak.'

Rhosmari pressed her fingers against her eyelids, her head swimming with all this new information. When she looked up again, the car was speeding between banks of trees and high hedgerows, and Waverley Hall was nowhere in sight.

'So the Empress really is old,' she said.

'She must be well over three hundred by now,' Peri said. 'I'm amazed she's even alive.'

'She's stronger than any faery I've ever seen,' Rhosmari murmured. 'The way she can maintain so many spells at once, and control her followers besides...' A chill ran through her, and she rubbed her arms. 'Whatever she did to get back her powers, it must have been terrible. She says she only wants what's best for her people, but how can she not see all the evil she's done?'

'I don't think she sees anything but her own ambitions,' said Peri. 'If she ever had a conscience, it's long gone by now.'

'Seared as with a hot iron,' Timothy said, in a distracted way that made Rhosmari think he must be quoting something.

'Yes, well,' said Paul. 'If we could defeat Jasmine by psychoanalysing her, she'd be dead a hundred times over. But here's what I'd really like to know, Tim – the next time we go up against her, are you going to dash off and play the hero again, or are you going to follow orders?'

Timothy gave Rhosmari a sidelong glance. Then he said, 'Follow orders. Probably.'

Paul looked at Peri, and his mouth twitched. Peri sighed. 'I know,' she said. 'Believe me, I know.'

Rhosmari had expected the Oak to be a large tree, to hold so many faeries. But as Paul's car turned the last corner and she saw it looming up against the sky, her eyes grew round. Never had she seen such a mighty breadth of trunk, or guessed that limbs could spread so wide and not crack under their own weight. Surely only magic could have kept a tree of that size alive and undamaged for so long.

'It'll be a couple of hours before Garan and the others get back from Waverley Hall,' said Paul, as he turned into the drive of a tall, peak-roofed house and brought the car to a stop. 'Would you like to go straight to the Oak, Rhosmari, or will you stay and have some lunch with us?'

Rhosmari hesitated. She had not eaten anything since last night, so she was quite hungry. And though her iron-blocked magic was beginning to come back, she did not feel quite ready to go into the Oak alone. But...

'Tell you what,' said Timothy. 'Come in and eat first, and

then I'll take you over to the Oak. I'll even come inside with you, if you like.'

'You can do that?' asked Rhosmari, but Timothy only looked smug.

'Timothy's a bit in love with the Oak, I think,' said Peri. 'Any chance to get in there will do. So don't think you're putting him to any trouble.' She opened the door and climbed out, adding over her shoulder, 'Or us, either.'

Rhosmari looked up at the house, then back at Timothy, who was regarding her hopefully. Why did it seem that every time she thought she knew what to expect from humans, they did something to throw her into confusion?

'All right,' she said. 'I'll come in.'

twelve

'Then something wet slapped my leg, so I looked behind me,' said Timothy, 'and there's Lydia in the bottom of the boat, struggling with this... *fish*.' He flung his arms so wide he would have knocked over the water jug if Peri hadn't caught it in time. 'I'm not even exaggerating, it must have been half as big as she was. How she managed to catch it, I'll never know. And then there's me, with this—'

He held his fingertips about a hand's width apart. Paul grinned, and Peri laughed. But Rhosmari was too distracted even to manage a smile.

Here she sat, eating the plainest meal of bread and meat and cheese, at a table so small that Timothy's knee bumped hers on one side and the wheel of Paul's chair boxed her in on the other. She was listening to three humans tell stories about places she had never been, people she had never met, and situations that had nothing to do with her – a kind of conversation that most faeries would find meaningless, if not rude. And now Timothy had just told them about a time when he had been made to look ridiculous by his little sister. How could she laugh without seeming to mock his failure?

But of course human ways were different from those of faeries; she had always known that, and no doubt she would get used to them in time. What troubled Rhosmari more was that in spite of the simple food, humble surroundings, and strange company, she was enjoying herself.

'So that's when I gave up fishing and decided to stick to the guitar.' Timothy pulled the fruit bowl towards him and helped himself to another handful of grapes.

'Well,' said Paul, 'we can't all be multi-talented.'

Timothy snorted. 'Says the professional artist with all the trophies for rowing and wheelchair rugby. Thanks a lot – oh, sorry.' This last was to Rhosmari, who had flinched at the careless use of *thanks*. 'For a minute I forgot you were a faery.'

'I suspect she might not take that as a compliment, Tim,' said Peri as she got up and began to clear the table. Timothy started to apologise again, but Peri interrupted, 'And if you keep digging that hole, you're going to fall into it. Why don't you take Rhosmari over to the Oak?'

'Right. Yes. I'd just better get rid of this...' Timothy shoved his hand into his right pocket, and slapped a tangle of iron and leather onto the table. 'Coming, Rhosmari?'

Compared to the neglected grounds of Waverley Hall, the

back garden at Oakhaven was a work of horticultural art, its lawn edged with neat flowerbeds and hedges squared to perfection. There were a few trees, too, some just beginning to bloom – but still, it was hard for anything to compare with the leafless majesty of the Oak. Seen close at hand, its bulk was even more daunting, and as Rhosmari followed Timothy out the glass door at the back of the house, she was glad that she would not have to enter the great tree alone.

But something still bothered her, and though she tried to put it from her mind her thoughts kept going back to it, like a tongue to a missing tooth.

'I know the Oakenwyld's not much like the Green Isles,' said Timothy. 'But the Oak itself is amazing, and…' He stopped, frowning at her. 'What's wrong?'

'Why are you being so kind to me?' Rhosmari hadn't meant to ask the question aloud, but it had grown too large to stay inside her. Only when it was out of her mouth did she realise how suspicious and even hostile she sounded.

'Does that mean you'd rather I wasn't? Or were you expecting me to be rude to you instead?'

Embarrassment flushed through her. 'I just wondered.'

Timothy stuck a hand behind his head and ruffled up his dark hair. 'Well,' he said. 'I read your letter. And I heard Garan telling the others about you. And I don't know quite how to say this, except…you reminded me of me.'

'I did? How?'

'I came here from Uganda a few months ago,' said

Timothy, his eyes distant. 'I'd lived there as long as I could remember, and my family and friends were there, and the church I grew up in, and everything was safe and warm and comfortable. Then I flew over here to go to school and it was cold and strange and I was all alone, and everybody I'd been counting on let me down, and whenever I tried to fix things it ended up in disaster. And that was *before* the Empress put a price on my head.'

He scuffed his shoe along the paving stones. 'Anyway, I was pretty miserable, and I figured that after all you'd been through, you must feel even worse. And I thought maybe I could make things easier for you, at least until Garan and the others got back.' He slanted a look at her, his grey-green eyes quizzical and a little sheepish. 'That's pretty much it.'

Rhosmari did not know what to say. She had never expected that a human would be able to understand how she felt. In fact, it seemed so unlikely that part of her feared Timothy might be another Martin, trying to manipulate her into trusting him.

'That's…generous of you,' she managed at last.

'I know,' said Timothy. 'I'm wonderful that way.' Then he grinned and she knew he was teasing her, though not unkindly. She gave a tentative smile in return, and together they followed the path to the end of the garden, where the afternoon sunlight faded into the shadow of the Oak.

'Here.' Timothy crouched and parted the grass around

the base of the great tree, revealing a dark hollow between two roots. "That's what they call the Queen's Gate. Have you ever made yourself small? Smaller than the Children of Rhys usually are, I mean.'

'Yes,' said Rhosmari. 'But what about you?'

'Oh, that's easy enough,' said Timothy, in a casual tone that belied his obvious pride. 'Queen Valerian made me a special charm, so I can visit the Oak whenever I like. Watch this.'

He pulled a wooden medallion out of his back pocket, looped the string around his neck – and shrank to Oakenfolk size, no taller than Rhosmari's hand was long. Not wanting to be left behind, she hastily cast a spell to do likewise. Her body tingled, wings sprouted from her shoulders, the world blurred and telescoped around her...

It was done. She stood face to face and eye to eye with Timothy, but now the ladybird crawling over her boot was the size of her fist, and the Oak had grown so huge that it blotted out the sky. Grass tangled around her legs, snagging the hem of her skirt; she stooped to brush herself free, and when she straightened up again Timothy had already vanished into the shadowy hole at their feet.

'Come on,' he called up to her. 'It's not deep.'

It looked deep enough to Rhosmari, who could barely make out his head and shoulders in the darkness. But then she saw a spidery lattice of roots woven into one side of the hole, forming a rough ladder. She turned around and climbed down it until she felt Timothy's hands at her waist, then let go and landed with a little jump at the bottom.

He released her and backed away, looking dazed. 'Er,' he said. 'Your wings...'

'Is there something wrong with them?' Rhosmari twisted her head back over her shoulder, trying to see. She had not actually looked at her wings before, for in Gruffydd's Way she had been too busy trying to escape from her mother to care. In the half-light they appeared to be partly black and partly blue, and shaped like a butterfly's, but that was all she could tell.

'No, not at all. They're...' He cleared his throat. 'Pretty amazing, actually.' Then he stooped and vanished into the darkness. Curious, Rhosmari followed. Tucked away into an alcove beneath the root stood a stout wooden door, wide enough for two faeries to enter side by side. Timothy hauled it open, and the two of them stepped over the threshold, into the heart of the Oak.

'So,' he said, 'what do you think?'

Rhosmari barely heard him: she was too busy gazing around in awe. There was no obvious reason this place should remind her of the Hall of Judgment, for instead of sandstone and marble it was shaped out of wood, with little decoration or ornament. It also had a huge staircase spiralling up through its centre, and a ceiling too high to see. But certainly the feeling the Oak gave her, of a place not only ancient but solemn and powerful, was the same. Light streamed in from window-slits all around, falling in a golden lattice upon the floor, and the air was rich with the smells of earth and woodsmoke, roasting meat, dried herbs...and faeries.

'Rob and Linden are around here somewhere,' said Timothy. 'They stayed behind with a few of the rebels to guard the Oak, while the rest of us went to—'

'You again!' snapped a voice from the passageway to their left, and a powerfully built faery woman shouldered out of a doorway, gripping a cleaver in one hand. 'Who let you in the door this time, human boy? What's it going to take to prove to you that you're not welcome here?'

'A majority vote might do it,' said Timothy. 'But apart from that, Mallow, you're just going to have to put up with me. Unless you're actually planning to use that knife you're holding.'

'It'd serve you right if I did,' snapped Mallow. 'Bad enough having the Oak overrun by hairy strangers, without adding humans to the lot. And who's this?' She cast a baleful eye over Rhosmari.

Rhosmari drew herself up, butterfly wings unfurling around her. 'I am Rhosmari daughter of Celyn of the Children of Rhys,' she said.

Mallow's indignant look dwindled into uncertainty. 'Is that so,' she said, lowering the cleaver. 'Well, in that case, you'd better get upstairs and see Valerian – but I'd send *him* back outside where he belongs, if I were you.' She jerked her chin at Timothy. 'I'm not the only one in the Oak who doesn't care for the stink of humans.'

'That's *Queen* Valerian to you,' Timothy called, but Mallow strode back through the archway and slammed the door behind her.

'Was that true, what she said?' asked Rhosmari as she and Timothy began to climb the spiral staircase. 'I thought the Oakenfolk had always been friendly with humans.' In fact, she had hoped they might help her overcome her distrust of them, but that did not seem so likely now.

'They were, until Jasmine got hold of them,' he replied. 'But once she stole their magic and altered their memories, most of them were too terrified to even look at us. It wasn't until almost two centuries later, when Knife – Peri, I mean – met Paul and fell in love with him, that the truth started to come out. And even then a lot of the Oakenfolk had a hard time accepting it.'

'What about the rebels?' Rhosmari asked. 'Surely they must feel differently, or they wouldn't have turned against the Empress?'

'Rob does,' Timothy said. 'And Lily – his second-in-command – respects humans as well, so the others follow their lead. But most of them still have mixed feelings about it, and even a few of Garan's people – your people – start to look uncomfortable when anybody talks about Peri and Paul.'

'That can't be right,' said Rhosmari, stung into defensiveness. 'My people don't despise humans; how could they? Many of our ancestors were born human. In past centuries we used to rescue sailors from shipwrecks, and some of them stayed with us—'

'By giving up their humanity and becoming faeries, yes,' interrupted Timothy. 'Nobody objects to that. But the Oakenfolk used to do the opposite – they sent faeries out to live in the human world for years or decades at a time, and some of them even married humans and gave birth to human children. That's the part nobody likes to talk about.'

He turned to her, his hand tightening on the stair rail. 'Be honest, Rhosmari. When Linden told your Elders about Knife becoming human to stay with Paul, weren't you shocked?'

Of course she had been. Until that moment, Rhosmari had never even imagined that faeries *could* fall in love with humans. After all, with plenty of both male and female faeries on their islands, the Rhysians had no need to look elsewhere for mates. And to Rhosmari, who had never visited the mainland, humans had always seemed as remote and untouchable as angels.

But then Timothy had stepped forward and begun to speak to the Elders, his voice husky with urgency. Her eyes had lingered on the dark feathers of his hair, the hint of golden warmth beneath his winter-paled skin, and she was fascinated; no one in all the Green Isles looked or spoke like that. Then her heart began to flutter, and warmth had bloomed in Rhosmari's cheeks as she felt, for the first time in her life, the kindling spark of attraction. At that moment she could no longer be shocked at the choice Peri had made; she was too busy being appalled at herself.

She looked away, her pulse beating in her throat, and said, 'A little.'

The stair ended at a circular landing, with a window-slit on one side and an archway draped with velvety curtains on the other. Timothy tugged a cord that dangled down the wall, and a chime rang out faintly on the other side. A voice called, 'Who is it?'

'It's Timothy, Your Majesty. And I've brought Rhosmari.'

'Rhosmari!' exclaimed the voice, and the curtain was swept aside. Before them stood a tall brown-haired faery with a glow-spell burning in her hand. Her face was a pale oval, her features serene rather than striking, and her dress was so simple that Rhosmari could easily have taken her for a servant, if not for the silver circlet she wore around her brow.

'You are welcome in the Oak,' said Queen Valerian. 'Please, come in.'

They had only taken a few steps into the passage when a door flew open and another faery scrambled out. She dropped a hasty curtsy, trying to smooth her tumbled ringlets and brush the wrinkles from her skirt at the same time. 'I'm so sorry, Your Majesty,' she blurted. 'I didn't mean to fall asleep—'

'Perhaps not,' said Valerian, 'but you needed it. There is no need to apologise, Wink. But if you feel well enough to join us, I would be glad to have you come.'

'Oh, yes, of course.' Visibly relieved, the red-headed faery fell in behind them. They passed through a doorway into a small audience chamber, generously lit by windows along one side. Three of the walls were lined with benches, while a low-backed chair stood on a dais at the far end. Walking up the crimson-dyed carpet, Queen Valerian sat down, and gestured to Rhosmari and the others to make themselves comfortable as well.

'I have just heard from Garan,' she said, 'and he and the others will be with us shortly. Then we can all hear what you have to tell us, Rhosmari—'

Just then Garan Leaped into the middle of the chamber, startling all of them. Rhosmari knew immediately that something must be wrong: it was considered rude among most faeries to appear suddenly in a room where others were present, unless it was an emergency.

'I beg pardon, Your Majesty,' he said, bowing to the Queen. 'But Mallow accosted me when I came in, and she insists on being present at our council. Do you wish us to refuse her entrance?'

The Queen lowered her eyes, as though the news

troubled her. But when she looked up again, her expression was resolute. 'No. Let her come.'

'As you wish, my Queen,' said Garan, and took his place along the wall by her side.

'Oh, Mallow,' sighed Wink. 'It never ends with her. Why can't she be more like Bluebell, and just accept it?'

Clearly there was more going on here than just a dispute over whether humans should be allowed in the Oak. But by now the other faeries had already begun to arrive, and there was no time to ask for an explanation.

They came in by ones and twos, rebels and Oakenfolk and Children of Rhys in turn, and made their bows or curtsys to the Queen before taking a seat. Together they made a strange company – especially when Linden in her homespun Oakenfolk garb arrived with a copper-haired rebel wearing a very human-looking sweatshirt and jeans, and Rhosmari's fellow scholar Broch sidled in between Lily and the stony-faced Thorn.

Mallow was one of the last to arrive, and she hardly bent her knee to Valerian at all; she only gave a grudging nod and then stood at the back of the room with arms folded and a sour expression on her face. The Empress would have punished her for such insolence; Lady Celyn would have had her thrown out. Queen Valerian, however, gave no sign of even noticing it. She waited until everyone was seated, and spread out her hands in a gesture of welcome.

'We have much to discuss today,' she said, 'especially now

that we have a visitor from the Green Isles among us. Will you please come to the front of the room, Rhosmari, and tell us how you came to be here?'

She had not been looking forward to this. But she must face it with dignity, all the same. 'Yes, Your Majesty,' said Rhosmari, and walked up the carpet to the dais.

Over the next few minutes Rhosmari related her story as briefly as she could without leaving out any important details. She told the assembled faeries why she had left the Green Isles, and what she had hoped to achieve by finding Garan and the Stone. She explained how Martin had deceived her into trusting him, only to betray her to the Empress, and finally she shared with them the things she had learned about the Empress while under her control – including her plan to invade the Green Isles and conquer the Children of Rhys.

'If you had not rescued me from Waverley Hall,' Rhosmari concluded, 'I might even now be leading the Empress's army into the *Gwerdonnau Llion*. I owe you all my deepest gratitude. So when I return home, I promise to do everything I can to convince the Elders that you should keep the Stone of Naming, and that we must not hinder your struggle against the Empress in any way.'

She spoke the last words firmly, sure that the faeries of the Oak would be glad to hear of her change of heart. But there was only an awkward silence. Several of the faeries traded apprehensive glances, while Timothy studied the toes of his shoes and would not meet her gaze.

'So you are the only faery outside the Green Isles who knows how to open this underground passage?' asked the male rebel sitting beside Linden, who she now realised must be Rob. 'And the Empress cannot enter it without your help, is that correct?'

Only the Children of Rhys, Lord Gwylan had told her, *and those we have deemed worthy of our trust.* And even Garan and his men did not know about the symbol that marked the entrance to Gruffydd's Way. 'Yes,' said Rhosmari, hoping that would reassure him. But still none of the faeries looked happy.

'Well, at least now we know why the Empress hasn't attacked us yet,' said Thorn. 'She's trying to put together an army we can't possibly defeat.'

'She might yet do so,' said Lily in her musical voice. 'Surely she has far more slaves than we have allies, even now.'

'Yet she was ready to invade the Green Isles and conquer its people before she turned her attention to us,' said Rob. 'Does that not suggest anything to you?'

'No, but apparently it does to you,' Thorn said dryly. 'Go on.'

'We have been sitting here all this while, waiting for the Empress to attack,' Rob said. 'And yet today when our forces confronted her, she fled from us almost at once.

Clearly she is not ready to face us in open battle – so why wait for her any longer?' He rose from the bench, eyes gleaming with feral light. 'Why not muster our forces and strike against her instead?'

'Have you cracked your nut?' demanded Thorn. 'Catching Jasmine by surprise at Waverley Hall, when we knew she could only call a few of her followers into the house before we took over – that was one thing. But taking on her whole army? We'd be squashed like so many beetles.'

'Once, I would have agreed with you,' Rob said. 'But consider this. Nearly two hundred faeries broke away from the Empress's control at Sanctuary, and with the help of the Stone we have freed still more of her followers since. True, some preferred to flee rather than join us, and that made it possible for the Empress to hunt them down and bring them back under her control. But even so, it takes time to rebuild an army.'

He began to pace around the chamber, his voice quickening with urgency. 'Why was she so eager to conquer the Children of Rhys? Because her own forces were still too weak and scattered for her to be sure of defeating us without them. She has not forgotten her pledge to destroy the Oak; she simply *cannot do it*.' He stopped and looked around at them all. 'And that means that attacking her now may be our best chance of defeating her.'

Rhosmari sat motionless, scarcely daring to draw breath. Surely it was wrong to provoke a battle, no matter how evil the enemy. But the way Rob spoke…it almost made her *want* to believe that he was right.

Thorn, however, seemed unmoved. 'That's a pretty slim hook to catch a minnow on,' she said. 'I'd like a bit more proof of the Empress being weak before I go charging off to fight her, if it's all the same to you.'

Beside her, Broch's mouth twitched as though he were repressing a smile, and the others in the room relaxed, Rob's spell over them broken. 'I agree,' said Garan. 'It would be rash to attack the Empress without being sure of her reasons for wanting to invade the Green Isles. Clearly she believed that conquering the Children of Rhys would be easy, and that adding so many faeries to her army would make her invincible. But that does not prove she had no hope of defeating us without them.'

'So what do you think we should do, then?' spoke up Mallow from the back of the room. 'Sit here in the pot and wait for the water to boil? That doesn't seem like much of a plan to me.'

'We should continue doing just as we have been,' Garan replied. 'Training our people to defend themselves, and strengthening the Oak against attack. But most of all we need to continue searching for other faeries who wish to be free of the Empress, and offering them the Stone. The greater our numbers, the longer the Empress will hesitate to attack us, and every faery we set free is one less soldier for her to command.'

'And where do you plan to put all these faeries?' Mallow demanded. 'The Oak's nearly full up as it is.'

'True,' said Garan. 'But our scouting parties have found the remnants of an old Wyld not far away, which could be resettled if need be. However, since you seem to have little faith in our suggestions about how to deal with the Empress, I can only suppose that you have an idea you think better. Why not share it with us?'

'All right,' said Mallow. 'How's this? I say we surrender.'

thirteen

Shouts of protest rang out from every side of the council chamber, loud enough to make Rhosmari wince. But Valerian held up a hand for silence.

'Continue, Mallow,' said the Queen. 'What makes you say that we should give ourselves up to the Empress?'

Mallow looked flustered. 'Well,' she muttered, 'it's not like she goes around killing people just for the fun of it, is it? She just wants to keep the humans in their place, and stop faeries being too friendly with them. What's the problem with that?'

'You do not know the Empress,' said Rob in a voice that was quiet but not in the least gentle. 'You did not grow up by her side, serving her every day from the time you were a child. You do not know what it is to be a slave, to live in constant fear, to be unable to choose your own companions or make your own destiny. You have not seen the Empress's cruelty towards humans who had done her no harm, or towards faeries who dared to befriend them. But I have. I have seen her deceive, and murder, and work sorceries more foul than your mind can begin to comprehend, and I swear to you that I would rather die than serve her again.'

Yes, thought Rhosmari fervently, gripping the bench to keep herself from standing up and shouting it. How Mallow could suggest, could even think of such a thing—'

'Well, that's very noble of you,' said Mallow. 'But not all of us are so convinced there's such a thing as a fate worse than death. I say we do whatever it takes to save our own necks, and let the humans worry about themselves. Who's to say the Empress might not reconsider if we offered her a decent bargain?'

And with that the room erupted, as several faeries leaped up at once to argue with her. Voices rose in pitch and passion as more joined in on every side. Some agreed with Rob's plan to attack the Empress, and some with Garan's more cautious stance; a few even seemed to think Mallow's point of view had some merit. Meanwhile Timothy watched the debate with set mouth and smouldering eyes, until Rhosmari felt sure he would leap up and shout them all down at any moment.

She cast an appealing look at Valerian, hoping she would call the room to order, but the Queen only sat listening, hands folded in her lap. Didn't she care that her people were becoming angry with one another?

'And here's another thing,' called out a square-built rebel

whose dark hair bore a single dramatic streak of white. 'If we're going to keep sending the Stone out of the Oak, why does it always have to be Garan or one of his people who carries it? What makes them better than the rest of us?'

Thorn half-started out of her seat, but Broch put a hand on her arm as the room went abruptly quiet. All eyes were on Queen Valerian, and no wonder: she had risen from her throne with a sizzling ball of blue flame in one hand, lifted as though she were about to hurl it down.

'I agreed to hold this meeting,' she said in her calm, deliberate voice, 'because some of you believed that your views were not being heard, and that they deserved a public audience. But I suspected that such a large gathering would not end well, and indeed this has proved it.'

Her grey eyes rested on each of them in turn, grave and a little sad. 'I will not rule you as a tyrant, but neither will I allow you to tear the Oak apart with your quarrelling. If any one of you does not trust me to act wisely and in your best interests, then I invite you to leave now, and join the Empress.'

Mallow looked sullenly at the floor, but she did not move. Neither did anyone else.

'If you wish to remain,' Valerian continued, lowering the flaming sphere, 'there are some things you will have to accept. One is that under no condition will I abandon Knife, Paul and Timothy to the Empress. Nor will I ever agree that their lives are less important than our own. Indeed, I regard them as vital allies in our struggle, deserving of both our gratitude and our respect.'

At that, Linden moved a little closer to Timothy and squeezed his hand. He gave a half-smile, but he did not look particularly comforted.

'Secondly, I want you to know that I regard all who live within this Wyld – rebels, Children of Rhys and Oakenfolk alike – as equal citizens of the Oak, and I will not permit either favouritism or prejudice. Some of you seem to believe that I have given the Stone of Naming into the care of Garan and his men as a privilege, but that is not so: carrying the Stone is a solemn and fearful responsibility, which only a fool would covet. Because the Stone is our only real surety against the Empress's power, and if it should ever be lost, then we will be lost as well.'

She paused as though waiting for an objection, but the faeries remained subdued, their eyes downcast. 'And lastly,' Queen Valerian continued, 'each of you will always be free to approach me with your concerns, and I will consider what you have to say. But I will choose my own advisors, and I will make my own decisions, and anyone who attempts to undermine my authority will face the consequences. We may not know precisely when the Empress plans to attack us or what she is waiting for, but it is certain that she *will* attack us when she is ready – and when that day comes we must be united, or we will fall.'

Until now Rhosmari had been wondering if Valerian

might be too tolerant to make a good ruler. But now, looking into those steely eyes, she knew she had been mistaken. For all her unassuming manner, the Queen's silence throughout the meeting had not been timidity, but deliberate forbearance.

'You are all dismissed,' said the Queen, and the spell-globe in her hand dissolved in a shower of sparks. 'Except for Garan, Rob and Thorn – I would speak to you three alone.'

'Are all your gatherings like this?' Rhosmari asked as she followed Linden and Timothy out of the chamber, raising her voice to be heard over the clamour of the other faeries around them.

Linden exchanged a glance with Timothy. 'Like what?'

'So…disorderly.' She knew she might be giving insult by saying it, but she could think of no better word. 'So full of arguments and divisions.'

'I hope not,' said Linden, with a frankness that put Rhosmari at ease. 'We don't usually have so many people all together at once, especially not with Mallow there to stir things up.'

'And it's not as though the Children of Rhys don't like to argue,' Timothy said. 'When Linden and I came before your Elders, there seemed to be plenty of debate going on about what to do with us, and it wasn't all friendly, either.'

'Yes, I know,' said Rhosmari patiently, though it was

hard not to be insulted at the reminder that Timothy had not even noticed her that day. 'Of course my people disagree at times. But still, we all recognise that the final authority belongs to the Elders, and that it is our duty to accept whatever they decide.'

'Even if that means sending an armed party over to the mainland to take back the Stone of Naming by force?' asked Timothy as they came out onto the landing. 'No offence, but you don't seem to have found that particular decision so easy to accept.'

Anger flared inside her. 'That was different. What my mother wanted to do was *wrong*. The Children of Rhys are sworn to live in peace with everyone, humans and faeries alike. If we break that vow, we destroy one of our most sacred traditions.' Rhosmari stepped aside to let a pair of male rebels go down the stairs, then turned to Timothy again. 'And then what's to keep us from breaking any other laws we find inconvenient? How can we live honourably with one another, how can we set an example for our fellow faeries, unless we stay true to our principles, whatever the cost?'

'I'm not saying I agree with your mother. But I'm not sure I agree with you, either,' said Timothy. 'Is that really what Rhys commanded you to do – never fight anyone, even in your own defence? Even if not fighting means becoming the slaves of someone who will force you to break that law and probably all the other ones, too?'

Rhosmari opened her mouth, then shut it again. It was true that Rhys had urged his followers to forsake violence, but there had been centuries of scholarly debate over exactly what that meant. After the shock of her father's death, Rhosmari herself preferred to be cautious; even competing in the Rhysian Games had made her uncomfortable at times. But others she knew – including Garan – believed that it was lawful to fight so long as the cause was just, and not a matter of selfish greed or personal vengeance. Could Rhosmari really say with authority that she was right, and Garan and the others were wrong?

'I don't know,' she said at last. 'I don't want to see anyone hurt, no matter how wicked they may be. But I don't want to stand by and watch innocent people suffer, either. I just think...what if there's a solution that doesn't involve fighting? Some way to stop the Empress that doesn't put so many lives in danger?'

'If you could find one,' said Linden, 'we'd all be glad to hear it. Or at least I know I would. I don't like the idea of people being killed, either.' She gave Rhosmari an encouraging smile, and Rhosmari smiled back.

'I should go,' said Timothy. 'Paul and Peri will be waiting to hear from me. But...' He turned to Rhosmari, serious and intent. 'If you need anything, or if you – I don't know, you just want to get away from the Oak – then you're welcome at the house. Any time.'

Rhosmari nodded her appreciation of the offer, but as he

galloped away down the Spiral Stair she could not help wondering why he had made it. She would only be here for a day or two, after all, and then she would be returning to the Green Isles.

Homesickness rose within her at the thought, and tired though she was, she wished she could leave at once. Having to answer to her mother and the Elders would not be pleasant, but at least now she could be sure they would not send her away. Even if they felt that she deserved to be exiled for what she had done – and Rhosmari doubted that, for she had shed no blood and committed no violence – it would be far safer to imprison her on the Green Isles than to risk having her fall back into the Empress's hands.

'Come with me,' said Linden. 'I'll take you to see Bluebell.'

Bluebell. She had heard that name earlier. 'Who is that?' asked Rhosmari.

'She's our Chief Housekeeper.' Linden led the way down the staircase. 'She'll find you a place to stay.'

'Was she at the council?'

'Bluebell? Goodness, no.' Linden gave a rueful laugh. 'She never wants anything to do with politics nowadays. Why do you ask?'

'Only that Wink said she wished Mallow could be more like her. I wondered what she meant.'

'Oh, that,' Linden said. 'Well, it's a bit complicated, but Bluebell used to be Queen Amaryllis's attendant. And she could be a little haughty about it at times, but no one thought much of that...until Amaryllis died. Then it turned out that Bluebell believed she was the rightful heir to the throne. Can you imagine?'

'Well...perhaps I can,' said Rhosmari. 'It might not be the way things are done in the Oak, but there is an old tradition that the faery queen's heir should serve as one of her attendants. Could Bluebell have been thinking of that?'

'I think it was mostly Mallow who talked her into believing it,' said Linden. 'But in any case it was all very unpleasant for a while, with Mallow and Bluebell trying to convince everyone that Valerian had tricked Queen Amaryllis into choosing her, and that she wasn't fit to hold the throne anyway because she was half human. Fortunately, most of the Oakenfolk were sensible enough to see that Valerian was a much better leader. And when Rob and Garan came to the Oak with their followers, they both recognised Valerian as Queen straightaway and paid no attention to Bluebell at all. So nothing came of that.'

Except for Mallow continuing to challenge the new Queen's policies at every turn, apparently. After seeing how she had behaved at the council, Rhosmari had to wonder at Valerian's patience with her.

'But afterwards,' Linden went on, 'Bluebell was so humiliated that she locked herself in her room for three days, and then she came out and apologised. And she's been loyal to Queen Valerian ever since... Here we are.' She turned off the stair onto a walkway, which led them across to a landing ringed with doors. Walking up to the third door on the left, she rapped and called, 'Bluebell, are you there?'

They waited, but no answer came. Linden was just about to knock again when Garan spoke up behind them: 'Rhosmari?'

Surprised, she turned and saw him coming along the walkway towards her. His manner was formal, his expression as sober as she had ever seen it.

'I need to speak with you in private,' he said. 'Perhaps we should go outside.'

The sky over the Oakenwyld was untroubled by cloud, and the breeze that blew across the garden was mild. But as Garan led Rhosmari out onto the grass, she sensed something ominous in the air. It was a feeling that had been creeping up on her ever since she delivered her report to the council, and it had grown along with her body when she and Garan left the Oak and changed back to their customary size. And when he turned to her and she saw the pity in his face, her heart skipped a beat.

'What is it?' she asked.

He reached for her hand, which did nothing to reassure her. 'Rhosmari,' he said, 'you cannot go back to the *Gwerdonnau Llion*.'

'What?' She stared at him. 'What do you mean, *cannot*?'

'You are the Empress's only hope of reaching the Green Isles. And now that she has set her heart on conquering the Children of Rhys, she will do whatever it takes to recapture you. Do you really believe that you can leave the Oak and set out on your own, and have even the slightest chance of reaching Wales in safety?'

'I could Leap—'

'Martin knows every place where you have set foot,' Garan said. 'As does the Empress herself. If you had ten times the power, then perhaps you could Leap all the way from here to St David's at this very moment, before she has a chance to send any of her people there. But the furthest you can Leap from here is Waverley Hall, and from there you could not even reach Cardiff by magic, let alone the Green Isles.'

He took her other hand in his own, his voice lowering to earnestness. 'We did not make this decision lightly, Rhosmari. It grieves my heart to think of you having to remain here against your will. But we cannot afford to lose you to the Empress again. For all our sakes, we dare not even take the risk.'

Rhosmari snatched her hands away. 'So you plan to make me your prisoner,' she said in a shaky voice. 'Trap me here in the Oak while you wait for the Empress to attack, because you are too cowardly to let me go – and when she does attack, and she defeats you, she will capture me anyway. And then the Green Isles will fall to her, without hope and without warning, and it will be *your* fault.'

'It is not cowardice, Rhosmari.' Garan spoke quietly, but there was no apology in his tone. 'To give you safe conduct, we would have to send our whole army with you and leave the Oak defenceless – and even then we could not be sure of protecting you from the Empress. Keeping you here is the best chance we have.'

Rhosmari put her hands to her temples. She felt as though the ground had given way beneath her and left her tumbling through a dark void, helpless and alone. As Garan went on, his words seemed to be coming to her from miles away:

'Do you think that knowing the Green Isles are in danger gives me any pleasure? If I knew any way to warn our people against the Empress, I would. But we have no means of communicating with the Elders at this distance. And even if we did, I fear they would not listen.'

No enemy can hurt us here. She had said that to her students at the House of Learning, believing it was true. And then she herself had made it into a lie, and now Garan was telling her there was no way to undo it.

'I am sorry, Rhosmari,' he said. 'I never wanted to have to tell you this. Until the council, I thought you understood it already. I even thought...' He stopped. 'Well. This is not the time.'

She raised her head, eyes burning but dry. 'Not the time for what?'

'When I heard you had come all this way to find me,' he said, 'I thought perhaps you were giving me a chance to make amends. I wronged you, Rhosmari, and I know you were disappointed, when I asked to break off our betrothal.' He moved closer, his sea-green gaze holding hers. 'I want you to know that if it brings you any comfort, if in any way it could make all that you have suffered a little easier, I am willing to fulfil the vows I made to you, and make you my wife.'

She was startled. 'You mean…now?'

'Well, not right away,' Garan replied, a little uncomfortably. 'You are only sixteen, after all. But in two or three years' time, if we are still alive…'

Rhosmari let out a disbelieving laugh. 'And what would be the use of that? You don't love me. You told me as much, before you went away.'

'Does that matter to you?' He gave her a puzzled look. 'I didn't think you cared how either of us felt, so long as we could live peacefully together.'

Her fingers crept to her wrist, where Martin's fingers had bruised her and Timothy's rings had burned. Both of them had hurt her, but one had been trying to keep her prisoner, while the other had been trying to set her free.

'Yes,' she told him quietly. 'It matters.'

Rhosmari sat at the foot of the Oak, hugging her knees as she gazed wearily across the lawn. Hedges rose on either side of the garden, blending into an old stone wall closer to the house, and in front of her stood the house itself, blocking out the sun and the sky.

The Oakenwyld was even smaller than Waverley Hall had been. And yet this was about to become her whole world.

Garan had told her she would be safe in the garden, for it and the neighbouring fields were under constant watch and ward, and the Empress's servants could not approach from any direction without being seen. But he had still tried to coax her back inside the tree with him, so that Bluebell could show her to a room – and Rhosmari was not ready for that. Not when it might be weeks or months, perhaps even years, before she returned to her homeland again.

She tore a handful of grass out of the lawn and scattered it to the wind, watching the blades flutter and spiral away. No wonder everyone at the council had looked uncomfortable when she spoke of going back to the Green Isles. No wonder Timothy had felt sorry for her, and—

Wait. What had he offered her, exactly? *If you need anything, or if you just…want to get away from the Oak…*

He had known what Garan was going to tell her. Could he have meant those words more literally than she realised? After all, he had told her himself that he knew what it was like to be alone in a strange country, and longing for home.

Rhosmari got slowly to her feet, eyes fixed on the house. She could not go there right now, at least not discreetly. But later tonight, when everyone was asleep…

Yes. She would do it. If Timothy understood – really understood – how she felt, then he would want to help her. And since he was human, and creative by nature, he might well be able to think of a way to get her safely to the Green Isles even though all the faeries in the Oak could not.

Just thinking about it eased the ache in her chest a little. Hope renewed, Rhosmari made herself small again, and climbed back down the root ladder into the Oak.

'Have you seen Bluebell?' Rhosmari asked a passing rebel on her way in, but he shook his head. She went back to the Spiral Stair and met three more faeries coming down, but they couldn't help her either. Rhosmari climbed all the way up to Bluebell's door and knocked again, but there was still no answer, so at last she gave up and followed the rest of the faeries down to dinner.

She had forced herself to finish her mug of hot chicory despite its bitterness, and was scraping the last bit of mashed roots from her plate when Holly, one of the faeries she had met on the stair, stopped by her table. 'Are you still looking for Bluebell?' she asked. 'Because I saw her pass by the dining hall just a little while ago.'

She paused with a meaningful look, and belatedly Rhosmari realised that the other faery was waiting for her to bargain. Linden had spoken to her so freely, she had forgotten that the other faeries might be a little less charitable about giving out information.

'I have nothing to offer you at present,' Rhosmari replied, choosing her words carefully. 'But if there is something I can do for you at a later time, I will be glad to hear of it.'

Holly sighed. 'Oh, very well. I saw Bluebell going down the East Root corridor. Probably to one of the storerooms. If you hurry, you might still catch her.'

'I appreciate your help,' said Rhosmari. Hurriedly she pushed her cup and plate aside, and set off to find Bluebell.

As she headed away from the core of the Oak the air in the passage grew damp and earthy-smelling, the ceiling webbed with thin roots. The lamps flickered wanly, giving off more shadows than light. The old fear of closed-in places crept up on her, and she was just about to turn back when she heard someone talking.

'...should never have come here. I have nothing to discuss with you. I don't even want to be seen with you any more.'

The female faery's tone was high-pitched and a little lofty, but it also sounded fearful. It came from behind a closed door to Rhosmari's right, and her first impulse was to go in. She reached for the handle.

'You're being ridiculous,' said a flat voice, and Rhosmari jerked her hand back. 'All I'm asking is for you to stop fussing and listen. Haven't I always looked out for you? I wouldn't bring this up if I didn't think it was worth your while.'

'I've already told you I'm not interested. Now let me go.'

'You're not going anywhere until I'm done,' retorted Mallow. 'Don't you care what Valerian's doing to us? It's not just a matter of bringing more faeries to the Oak or getting our magic back, not any more. She's going to force us all to fight the Empress, and like as not get us all killed, just so we can protect her precious pet *humans*.'

'That's her right. She's the Queen.'

'Queen of the Oak, maybe, and there's nothing much we can do about that. But I was at the council this afternoon, and I heard Garan say that he and his men found an old Wyld not far from here, just waiting to be fixed up and resettled. Why should we stay here and wait for the Empress to kill us, when we could strike out on our own and make peace with her? I know a good few Oakenfolk, and some of the rebels too, who don't much care for Valerian's human-loving ways. We could start a whole new colony, Bluebell – and you could be our ruler. Think about it—'

'No, I will not!' Bluebell's voice rose so sharply that Rhosmari flinched. 'I don't want to rule some dried-up old elm tree in the middle of a swamp. I've lived in the Oak all my life and I don't want to go anywhere else, and I've already told you I want nothing more to do with you. So leave me alone, or I'll— I'll—'

'Or what?' asked Mallow, with menacing softness. 'You'll tell Valerian? Is that how weak you've become? She's nothing compared to Queen Amaryllis, and you of all people know it. I can't believe it doesn't sicken you every day to go creeping around the Oak obeying her orders, when you should be the one giving them.'

Rhosmari had heard enough. She put her hand firmly on the latch, and pushed the door open.

fourteen

Bluebell was a small faery compared to Mallow, with hair coiled regally atop her head and a high-waisted gown falling in gauzy layers to her feet. At the sight of Rhosmari, her cheeks turned white as sea foam. But Mallow only glared at her and said, 'Do you mind? We're busy.'

'No, Mallow,' Bluebell said tremulously before Rhosmari could answer. 'You and I are *done*.' Gathering up her skirts, she swept past the other faery and out into the corridor, tossing back over her shoulder, 'And don't ever talk to me again.'

Rhosmari could think of nothing to add to that. She held Mallow's insolent stare a moment, then followed Bluebell back out into the passage.

'I'm sorry to have startled you,' she said as she caught up with the Chief Housekeeper, 'but Linden told me I should talk to you about getting a room?'

Bluebell turned to her, looking distracted. 'Oh, I see,' she said. 'Yes, of course. Let me just check my ledger first.'

She left Rhosmari waiting on the second landing of the stair, and returned a few minutes later with a ring of ancient-looking metal keys. Unlocking a door, she showed her into a tiny room with only one window. The only furniture in it was a narrow bed that sagged visibly in the middle, and the air was thick with dust.

'I'm afraid this is the best I can do,' Bluebell said. 'I'll have it cleaned, of course.'

'It's all right,' said Rhosmari. She did not care much for luxuries, and if all went well she would not be spending long here anyway. But as Bluebell turned to go she added, 'I don't mean to intrude. But I couldn't help hearing what Mallow said to you.'

'Is that so?' the other faery asked with a little sniff, and all at once Rhosmari could see the haughtiness Linden had spoken of – the spark of pride that had once made Bluebell think herself fit to be Queen. 'Well, it's all empty talk and bluster. Nothing will come of it. Not now that Mallow knows I want nothing to do with her and her schemes.'

'I hope you're right,' said Rhosmari. After all, even if she did not feel very kindly towards the Oak and its people right now, she did not want to see them vulnerable to the Empress. 'But it sounds as though you're not the first person Mallow has talked to about this. If she succeeds in convincing even a few other faeries to leave the Oak, that will put all the rest in danger. And if the Queen finds out that we knew what Mallow was planning, and said nothing…'

Bluebell's eyes widened. 'You mean…she will think that I was protecting Mallow? That I am as disloyal as she is?' She pulled her shawl tighter about her shoulders, as though the idea chilled her. 'I see now. You're right. I must go and talk to Valerian at once. Will you come with me? I don't want there to be any doubt that I'm telling the truth.'

Her haughty air had vanished; she looked anxious now, and Rhosmari felt sorry for her.

'Of course,' she said. 'I'll be glad to come.'

Rhosmari stood by the window in her lonely room, watching the half moon sail through waves of cloud and listening to the sounds of the night. Earlier that evening she and Bluebell had gone up to see Queen Valerian, who had given her full attention to hearing their story. Afterwards she had questioned them both for some time, drawing out every detail, before expressing her gratitude and letting them go. And though the Queen had not said how she intended to deal with the situation, Rhosmari could tell that she was deeply troubled by Mallow's behaviour, and would not allow her to continue spreading treachery for long.

Knowing that she had done something to help the Oak made Rhosmari feel a little better, but not enough to make her happy with the thought of being trapped here indefinitely. She waited until the great tree had gone quiet and only the occasional murmur echoed in the corridor outside her room; then she focused her thoughts on the humans' house, and Leaped.

Without Timothy's invitation, she could never have got further than the veranda. But she landed easily just inside the glass door, and from there it was not difficult to pick her way through the darkened sitting room and down the corridor.

Murmurs came from behind a closed door to her left, and she paused, listening. One male voice, one female: that must be Paul and Peri. So Timothy's room had to be upstairs. But across from the foot of the staircase stood a pair of glass doors, with light still glowing faintly through them – and when she glanced inside there was Timothy, seated at a desk with his eyes on a luminous screen. Gathering courage, Rhosmari tapped on the glass.

Timothy spun around in his chair. 'Rhosmari?' he said incredulously, and got up to let her in.

'I needed to talk to you,' she said. 'I hope it's not too late.'

'No, it's not.' He waited for her to sit down on the sofa before climbing back into his own seat, one foot casually hooked behind the other knee. 'So what's going on?'

'Garan told me this afternoon,' she said, pushing the words past the lump in her throat, 'that I can't go back to the Green Isles.'

Timothy grimaced. 'Yeah,' he said. 'I suspected that.'

'Can you help?' She did not mean the question to sound

so abrupt, but it came out before she could soften it. 'Please?'

'Help?' He crooked one dark brow at her. 'You mean…talk to them? Tell them to let you go?'

She shook her head. 'I know better than to think they will change their minds. But you – you ran away before, and you managed to avoid the Empress and all her servants, and find your way safely to the Green Isles. If you could just tell me, or show me, what to do…'

Timothy watched her for a long moment in the bluish-white light of the screen, his gaze travelling over her face from eyes to lips and back again. At last he said, 'You said the Blackwings found you and Martin in Birmingham. Did you ever find out how? Did they ever take something from you, or did you leave something behind, that they could use to track you down?'

'Never.' She spoke emphatically. 'I know better than that. Martin must have—' All at once she stopped, chilled by memory. Martin had been communicating with the Blackwings, certainly. But even so, he could not have been certain that he and Rhosmari would always stay together; he would have wanted to make sure they could track Rhosmari even if she was on her own. And just before they left Cardiff, he had done exactly that.

'My cloak,' she whispered. 'They have my cloak.'

Timothy nodded. 'So now they know exactly where you are. And they always will, no matter where you go – or how.'

'But they can't move faster than a car,' she said, knowing

that she was grasping at sand but unwilling to give up yet. 'You could take me—'

'I can't drive. And even if I could, I wouldn't.'

'Timothy—'

'If it was just you taking the risk, or even just you and me, that would be different. But this isn't about one or two lives, Rhosmari. The freedom of the Green Isles, of the Oak, maybe of all the faeries on the mainland, depends on you staying away from the Empress.'

'Don't you see that's exactly what I'm trying to do?' pleaded Rhosmari. 'If I can only get to the Green Isles, she can't touch me there. But here—'

'I know!' His voice rose in frustration, and he made a face before lowering it again. 'I know you'd be safer there, and I'd be glad to take you, *if* I thought we had a chance of making it. But Garan and the others are right. You have to stay.'

'I see. Well, then, I'm sorry I interrupted you.' She spoke bitterly, not troubling to hide her disappointment. Pushing herself up off the sofa, she walked to the door before turning back for the parting shot: 'But I thought you would understand.'

'Rhosmari, wait!' Timothy scrambled to his feet, but he had only taken two steps before his leg slipped out from under him. He crashed to the floor, muttered a curse, and grabbed at the chair to pull himself up again – but before he could speak, Rhosmari had Leaped away.

*

'Rhosmari? Are you there?'

The soft voice came from just outside her door, breaking into her troubled dreams. Blearily Rhosmari lifted her head from the mattress, to find that it was morning. 'Yes?' she mumbled.

'It's Linden. I just wanted to see if you were all right, since you didn't come down to breakfast.'

Her temples throbbed, and she felt as though someone had rubbed ash into her eyes. Rhosmari climbed off the bed, pulled her thick hair back into its clasp, and opened the door.

'Oh,' said Linden. 'I didn't mean to wake you. Would you like me to go away?'

There was no anger left in Rhosmari any more, only resignation. 'It's all right,' she said, stepping back to let Linden in.

The other girl moved cautiously into the room – then stopped short. '*This* is the room Bluebell gave you?' she said. 'I am so sorry. I'll see what I can do about getting you a better one.'

'It doesn't matter,' Rhosmari replied, sitting down on the edge of the bed. 'What can I do for you?'

Linden hesitated, then sat down beside her. 'Rob told me Garan had talked to you. About staying here. Are you…going to be all right?'

'I'll be fine,' said Rhosmari, getting up again and opening

the window for some fresh air. From here she could just see the back of the house, where Timothy and Peri were sparring on the veranda. Both were wearing light shirts and trousers, and neither carried a weapon – but as Peri dodged Timothy's swing and whirled behind him to slash the side of her hand across his shoulder, Rhosmari was appalled at the speed and ruthlessness with which the human woman moved. No wonder the other faeries called her Knife.

Linden came over to see where she was looking, and sucked in her breath as Timothy staggered. 'He pushes himself so hard,' she said softly. 'I wish he wouldn't.'

'Pushes himself?' asked Rhosmari. To her it looked more like Peri was pushing Timothy, and that relentlessly. But she had barely framed the thought before Timothy ducked under Peri's swing and poked her in the ribs, forcing a laugh out of her that echoed across the garden. Then the two of them broke off their mock fight and headed back into the house.

'The Empress nearly killed him at Sanctuary,' said Linden. 'Blasted him with all her power – if he hadn't been carrying iron, he'd have been dead for certain. And for days afterwards, he kept having these spasms where he'd drop things, or his legs would go numb. I think he still has them sometimes, though he doesn't like to talk about it.'

So that was why he had fallen last night. Rhosmari had thought it a harmless accident, but now guilt crawled over her. No wonder Timothy had gone into Waverley Hall wearing so much iron. No wonder Peri had been upset when he dashed upstairs to rescue Rhosmari from Martin and the Empress all by himself. How much courage must that have taken for him to face someone – indeed two people – who had hurt him so badly?

'He's trapped here too, you know,' said Linden, turning earnest hazel eyes to Rhosmari. 'Peri and Paul had to get permission to take him out of school, because the first day he tried to go back the Empress sent someone to kill him. If Lily hadn't gone along to keep an eye on him...' She gave a little shudder.

So the house had become Timothy's prison, just as the Oak was hers. Once again, Rhosmari had misjudged him – and now she owed him an apology. But perhaps, after she had so callously abandoned him last night, he would not want to speak to her again?

'Anyway,' Linden went on in a brisker tone, 'if you're ready to come out, I could show you around the Oak a bit. So you know where everything is, like the baths, and the kitchen, and the library—'

'You have a library?' The last of Rhosmari's fatigue vanished. If she had books to study, then at least she would not be idle. And if she looked carefully enough, perhaps she would even learn something that would help them against the Empress. 'Are there any histories of the Oak I could look at? Any books that mention Jasmine, and what she was like when she lived here?'

Linden blinked. 'Well, yes, we have a few of those. Not a lot, but—'

'Is the library far? Would you take me?'

'It's just at the foot of the Spiral Stair,' said Linden. 'Meet me on the landing when you're dressed, and I'll show you.'

'This is everything we have about Jasmine,' said Campion, pushing a stack of volumes across the table. The Librarian had quickly recognised a kindred spirit in Rhosmari, and the two of them had struck up a conversation about faery history while Linden crept apologetically away and finally slipped out the door. 'But are you sure you really want to read them all? I could summarise the information for you.'

'I appreciate that,' Rhosmari said as she pulled the topmost book off the pile, 'but I'd like to search through them myself. Do you have any loreseeds to go with these?'

Campion looked mystified, but also intrigued. 'No, what are those?'

'Living records of an event,' Rhosmari explained, 'from one person's point of view. They can still be misleading in some ways, and open to interpretation – but they're very useful if you want to get a sense of how something really looked and sounded at the time it happened.'

'Do you know how they're made?' Campion leaned forward, eyes lit with fascination. 'Could you show me how they work?'

'I'd be glad to,' said Rhosmari. 'Perhaps later, after I've had a chance to go through these?'

'Oh – yes, of course.' With ill-concealed disappointment the Librarian straightened up again. 'Well, if you have any questions, or need anything, just ring the bell. I'll be next door in the archive.'

Left alone in the library's musty, windowless silence, Rhosmari leafed through the first of the books Campion had given her. *Snowdrop the Queen* appeared to be a biography of the woman the Empress had called her mentor. Next came *A Restored History of the Oakenfolk* and *After the Sundering*, both by the late Queen Amaryllis, and finally three well-worn diaries that had belonged to Heather, the faery who had married Philip Waverley and borne him two children.

As she began to read, time vanished and the world around her slipped away. She pored over one passage after another, mulling over the details and making notes whenever she found something that might be useful. So far she had not learned much about the Empress that she did not know already, but...

'Found anything interesting?'

Rhosmari nearly dropped her book. 'Timothy! What brings you here?'

'Looking for you,' he said. He spoke easily, as though their quarrel last night had never happened. 'Paul and Peri and I were about to have tea, and I thought you might like to join us.'

Was it that late already? Somehow she had missed the noon meal and not even noticed. 'That's kind of you,' she said haltingly. 'But I owe you an apology—'

He held up a hand. 'No need. Yesterday was hard on all of us, but you especially. I don't blame you for being...' He stopped. 'OK, maybe *human* isn't the word I want to use here. But you know what I mean.'

'I think so,' said Rhosmari, unable to keep from smiling at the rueful look on his face.

'Good. Let's leave it at that.' He looked over her shoulder. 'Is that one of Heather's diaries you're reading? What for?'

So he had read them, too. 'I'm trying to understand Jasmine,' she said. 'If I can figure out how she thinks, then perhaps we'll be able to figure out a way to stop her.'

'That would be brilliant,' Timothy said. 'Though right now I'd settle for just knowing when she's going to attack.' He leaned against the edge of the table. 'I'd like to believe Rob's right about the Empress being weak, or at least not having quite as many followers as she claims. But Queen Valerian seems to think, and Peri and I do too, that the Empress is waiting for something. Or at least she was, before she got hold of this idea of invading the Green Isles...and now that she's lost you, she's gone back to waiting again.'

'Perhaps, but she can't wait much longer,' Rhosmari said. 'If she doesn't stop Garan and the others from using the Stone, it won't be long before they've freed more slaves than she can command.'

'Good point.' Timothy stood up again. 'So it has to be something pretty big, to make her hold off this long. We should probably talk this over with Peri – but that brings me back to tea. Are you coming?'

Rhosmari closed the diary and put it back on the top of the pile. 'Do you know,' she said. 'I think I will.'

As Rhosmari followed Timothy out into the garden, the sky was blue from one horizon to the other, and the sun was blazing through the branches of the Oak. The air felt so warm, the breeze so light, that if the meadow on the other side of the hedge had been water instead of grass, she could almost have imagined herself back on the Green Isles...

No, she was not going to think about that. But it was certainly a pleasant spring day. With a glance at Timothy's open collar and rolled-up sleeves, she slipped out of her jacket and laid it by the foot of the Oak. Then she walked with him across the lawn, where a number of faeries had gathered around Rob, Garan and Thorn for their daily lessons in combat.

By the rose hedge on their left, Rob was showing his onlookers various offensive and defensive spells. To their right, Thorn was telling a nervous-looking faery girl how to shoot a bow. 'Straighten your arm,' she said. 'Tighten those back muscles...and stop sticking your thumb out like that, you'll poke yourself in the eye.'

In the middle of the lawn some of the rebels and Children

of Rhys were sparring, the clack of wooden swords competing with the sweeter sounds of rustling grass and birdsong. Since all of the faeries had remained small, there was plenty of room for everyone; and between the tall hedge border that surrounded their training ground and the open meadows to either side, no passing human would be likely to notice them. Though judging by the ripple of power Rhosmari sensed around the edges of the garden, the whole area was protected by glamour anyway.

'I hope you can find a way to defeat Jasmine without fighting,' said Timothy. 'But just in case you can't, I'm thinking it might be a good idea if you learned to defend yourself.'

He spoke mildly, but annoyance flickered inside Rhosmari all the same. 'I already know how to do that,' she said.

'Really?'

'Yes.'

'So…how, exactly? I mean, what's your speciality?'

Of course he would ask about that – the last thing she wanted anyone to know. 'Does it matter? I competed in the Rhysian Games each year, like everyone else. And I did well enough.'

'Then you wouldn't mind giving me a demonstration?'

There was a gleam in his eye she did not like; it reminded her of the way Rob had looked when he suggested they attack the Empress. 'Fight you, you mean?' she asked. 'No.'

'Then fight somebody else. You don't have to hurt them. Just show me what you can do.'

She did not reply.

'Look, if you're shy about it—'

'I'm not *shy*.' She spoke flatly, her hands curling tight at her sides. 'I just don't want to. Why can't you just believe me? Why do you need proof?'

'I'm not asking for proof. All I want is a bit of evidence. You were the one who said you didn't believe in fighting, remember – can you blame me?'

He was baiting her. Trying to goad her into betraying herself. 'All right,' she said. 'If you won't take my word for it, then maybe you'll take someone else's.' She strode over to where Garan stood by the garden shed with bow in hand, showing the Oakenfolk how to aim at a target. 'Garan,' she interrupted him, 'do I or do I not know how to defend myself?'

For a moment Garan only looked baffled. Then his gaze shifted to Timothy, and his expression turned blank. 'That is not for me to judge,' he said.

Rhosmari stared at him, speechless at this unexpected betrayal. Then she snatched the bow out of his hands, nocked an arrow to the string, and fired it straight into the centre of the target, forty paces away.

'Judge that,' she snapped, and stalked off back to the Oak.

Back at the table in the library, Rhosmari buried her face in the crook of her arm. Now that her anger had subsided, she could only berate herself for being so foolish. What did it matter if Timothy thought her weak, or untrained, or even cowardly? It would have been better to let him despise her, to let him and most of the others go on believing that she was a scholar and nothing more.

But now that she had fired that arrow, she might as well have come to the Oak fully armed and bedecked with all her prizes from the Rhysian Games. No one who had seen Rhosmari shoot would be content to let her stay out of battle: an archer of her skill was too great an asset for any army to lose.

Yet she still could not bring herself to fire a bow at any living being, even in a cause she believed was just. To deliberately shed blood, she would have to ignore everything her father's death had taught her – and worse, it would mean giving up all hope of seeing her homeland and her people again…

'Rhosmari.'

The voice was Garan's. She sat up abruptly and pulled the books towards her as he went on, 'I did not mean to distress you. I know you have no love of battle, but you are such a skilled archer, and I thought…perhaps you wanted to show Timothy what you could do.'

'Why would I want that?' She spoke coolly, to deny the humiliation rushing through her.

'Because you wanted to be rid of him, perhaps? Ever

since he rescued you at Waverley Hall, he appears to have appointed himself your protector. And though I have tried to tell him you are well looked after here, he insists on seeking you out. I know you may scoff at my saying so, but...I believe Timothy is attracted to you.'

Rhosmari could not look at him for fear she might laugh, or weep. She opened a book and began leafing through it. 'Whatever makes you think so?'

He made a little, disbelieving sound. 'Rhosmari...you're holding that book upside down.'

Heat flooded her face. She snapped the book shut – and at that same moment, a thunderous bang resounded from the corridor outside. A chorus of screams followed, then a second crash, bringing both Garan and Rhosmari to their feet. They dashed out of the library together, but as they came through the door Garan flung out an arm to bar Rhosmari's path. Straight in front of them, Mallow stood with her back against the Queen's Gate, brandishing her cleaver at Llinos and an exasperated-looking Broch.

'Don't you touch me,' she panted.

'We are here to arrest you in Queen Valerian's name,' Llinos told her, quiet but adamant. 'You cannot escape justice, Mallow. If you have done no wrong, you have nothing to fear; but if you resist, we will have to restrain you.'

Mallow's scullions huddled in the corridor nearby, some open-mouthed and others sobbing. By the time a pale but determined Holly had come out of the kitchen and shepherded the lot of them back inside, Broch had disarmed Mallow and was lashing the Chief Cook's hands behind her back. 'More trouble than you're worth, aren't you?' he muttered, then dodged as she turned her head and spat.

'Peace, Mallow,' said Garan sternly. 'You have already dishonoured yourself enough.'

'*Dishonoured.* Think yourself so lordly, don't you?' she sneered back at him. 'Or should I say *kingly*? I've seen how you look at Valerian. There's more than one way to gain a throne.'

Startled, Rhosmari glanced at Garan – but he shook his head. 'You have the tongue of an adder, Mallow,' he said. 'But Valerian is five times my age, or more. Compared to her, I am a mere child – and I am not a fool.' He nodded at Llinos and Broch. 'Take her to the Queen. I will follow.'

The male faeries began to lead Mallow up the stairs, but when the Chief Cook saw Rhosmari, she planted her heels. 'You! You'll be sorry, you nasty little spy. When I get hold of you, I'll—'

Broch snapped his fingers, cutting off the sentence before Mallow could finish it. Yet her mouth continued to move despite the silencing spell, soundlessly vowing revenge.

Sick at heart, Rhosmari turned away.

fifteen

'Rhosmari!'

It was little more than a whisper in the darkness, but she recognised Timothy's voice at once. She threw back the covers and hurried to the window, to find his enormous grey-green eye peering in at her.

'What is it?' she asked, resisting the impulse to cringe. 'And who told you where to find me?'

'Linden. She told us your room's terrible. So Peri sent me to offer you the guest bedroom in the house. And to let you know you're welcome to sleep there as long as you like.'

Rhosmari looked behind her at the cramped little chamber, bare as a prison cell and no more welcoming. She scratched the place on her shoulder where the straw mattress always pricked her, and thought about Mallow locked up in the storeroom only two floors below.

'All right,' she said. 'I'll get my things.'

Once she had made herself presentable again, it was an easy Leap to the stone veranda behind the house, where Peri was waiting by the glass door to let her in. 'You'll be upstairs at the far end of the corridor, next to the bathroom,' she said. 'And you can have breakfast with us in the morning or go back to the Oak, whichever you prefer.'

Rhosmari glanced around for Timothy, but he had disappeared again. 'I'm grateful for your hospitality,' she told Peri with a little curtsy, and headed off to her new room.

That night Rhosmari slept as she had not slept in weeks, a deep and dreamless slumber. She woke naturally at daybreak, refreshed but also hungry – so she was glad to accept Peri's offer of joining the humans for breakfast. Timothy was already at the table, dressed but still sleepy-looking, with his hair sticking up on one side. 'Orange juice?' he asked as she came in, then tried to cover an enormous yawn with his elbow.

'Yes, please,' said Rhosmari, as Paul slid a plateful of scrambled eggs onto the table, pivoted the wheelchair expertly and rolled back to Peri for the bacon. The kitchen was pleasantly quiet compared to the clamour of the dining hall at the Oak – almost as quiet as breakfast in her mother's house would have been, but much more relaxed. For some time there were no sounds but the clink of cutlery and the crunch of buttered toast, until Paul spoke:

'I've been curious about something, Rhosmari. At what

age do faeries usually get married on the Green Isles? Because Garan looks like he might be old enough, but you seem pretty young to be betrothed.'

'We were betrothed when I was fourteen, actually,' said Rhosmari, watching Timothy pour more juice into his glass. 'But we're not any more.'

A splash of orange hit the tablecloth. Timothy hastily righted the jug and began dabbing up the spill with his paper napkin. 'Really,' he said. 'I'm…er…sorry to hear it.'

Paul and Peri exchanged glances, and both their mouths twitched. But all Paul said was, 'Right. Well, I'm going into town this morning. Does anyone need anything?'

Rhosmari spent the rest of that day in the Oak's library, studying the books Campion had given her. Among other things, she discovered that Queen Snowdrop, Jasmine's predecessor, had died under suspicious circumstances – so suspicious, in fact, that it was obvious Jasmine had murdered her in order to take the throne. And yet the Empress called Snowdrop her mentor, and was now wearing her face…which made Rhosmari more convinced than ever that the woman was not entirely sane.

And yet for everything she had learned about Jasmine, she had not found out what she really needed to know. When would the Empress attack the Oak, and how? Where did she get her remarkable powers, and was there any way to stop her from using them? She was no closer to answering those questions than she had been before.

'You should talk to Rob,' Campion told her, after the two of them had discussed the problem for a while. 'He was the Empress's court musician; he knows her as well as anybody. Maybe he'll be able to tell you something.'

So Rhosmari decided to join Rob and the others at supper, hoping that would give her a chance to talk to him. But when she came into the dining hall, she immediately noticed that something was wrong. Several faeries were absent from the tables – including Mags, the rebel who had complained about not being allowed to carry the Stone – and those that remained had separated into distinct groups. One corner was made up entirely of Oakenfolk, while their newest allies from the outlying Wylds had gathered along the back of the room. Even the rebels and the Children of Rhys seemed reluctant to mingle.

'The Empress won't even need to attack the Oak at this rate,' Rob said bitterly, stabbing a piece of squirrel meat off the platter. 'Not now that we have traitors and deserters doing her work for her. How can we make an army out of faeries who won't even eat at the same table?'

Linden sighed. 'Mallow must have done even more damage than we thought. I've tried to convince the Oakenfolk that we all need to work together, but some of them won't even look at me any more, let alone listen to me.'

'And we still don't know what the Empress is up to,' said

Campion, tilting her goblet and swirling the dregs of her honey wine around. Grateful for the opening, Rhosmari spoke up:

'Rob, I've been studying Jasmine's history, trying to find out how her mind works and where she got so much power. What can you tell me about her?'

'Her ways are devious,' Rob said, 'and I do not even pretend to understand them. Every time I thought I knew her, she proved me wrong.'

'But you must have learned something from your time with her,' Rhosmari persisted. 'Please. Even the smallest detail could make a difference.'

Rob was silent, his fork poised over his plate. Then he laid it down and said in a low, emotionless voice. 'The Empress took me into her service when I was only a child, and I was the nearest thing she had to a son. She offered me privileges and power such as she offered to no one else, and I had good reason to believe that if the Empress ever chose an heir, she would choose me.'

There was an audible intake of breath from the other faeries at the table. But Rob continued as though he had not heard: 'I travelled with her wherever she went, making music at her command – she had black moods sometimes, and she would call me to play my guitar for her until the shadow passed.' He looked down at his calloused fingers. 'Sometimes she would keep me playing all night, and then send me away without a word of praise. But at other times she would speak to me as though I were the only one she had ever loved.'

And then you betrayed her, thought Rhosmari. *And made her more unbalanced than ever.* Not that she blamed Rob for turning against the Empress, any more than she blamed herself for it. But it seemed that every time one of the Empress's followers abandoned her, she tightened her grip on the others.

'But in all the time I spent with her,' Rob said, 'she gave no hint that her power was less than absolute. If there were Wylds that had escaped her influence, she never spoke of them. If she ever faced resistance, she dealt with it alone. So I cannot tell you what she knows about leading an army against her enemies, or what strategies she might use to assure herself of victory. Nor did she share with me any of the deeper secrets of her power…save one, of which I will not speak. But it would not help you to know it.'

Rhosmari was about to ask how he could be sure – but then Rob lifted his gaze to meet hers, cold and dark as an undersea abyss, and she shut her mouth again.

'I have just had news from Telor,' said Garan after a moment, breaking the uncomfortable silence. 'He and Lily had success on their latest journey, and freed another twenty faeries with the Stone. They should be back at the Oak tonight, and the others will follow— Ah, there you are, Bluebell.' He craned his neck back as the Chief Housekeeper passed by their table. 'How is our prisoner?'

Bluebell looked bleak. 'She refuses to eat,' she said, holding up an untouched tray. 'Holly told me as much, but I thought perhaps Mallow only wanted attention... I was mistaken.'

Rhosmari had not seen Mallow since her arrest, but from what she had heard, the Chief Cook was being treated as fairly as any traitor could expect. She had been imprisoned in the same storeroom where she had once cornered Bluebell, the door reinforced with a stout lock and a warding spell to keep her from getting out. She had regular meals and some simple tasks to keep her occupied, and Llinos and Broch came twice a day to take her for a walk in the fresh air. But first Mallow had ignored the chores, then she had refused to leave the storeroom, and now it seemed she had decided to reject her meals as well.

Was it mere stubbornness that drove Mallow, or did she have some more sinister motive? Rhosmari did not know, but looking at Bluebell's drawn face she had to wonder who was more unhappy; the faery in the prison, or the one who had put her there.

Garan must have noticed it too, because he reached out to touch Bluebell's arm. 'You did right,' he said. 'Don't be discouraged. She may not be willing to repent now, but in time she may yet realise her fault and ask for pardon.'

Bluebell shifted away from him. 'You don't know Mallow,' she said. Then she hurried back to the kitchen with the tray, her faded gown sweeping the floor behind her.

Over the next few days Rhosmari spoke to everyone she could think of who might be able to tell her more about the Empress, including Lily and several more rebels whose names she barely knew. But none of them had any more ideas about her than Rhosmari did.

Meanwhile the Oak's preparations for war went on, with faeries stationed at the lookouts night and day, and Timothy bringing over bits of steel and other safe metals from the house to be transformed into swords and daggers. Thorn supervised the making of bowstrings and arrows, and Wink and her helpers sewed arm guards and gloves for the archers. But Garan must have explained to the other faeries that Rhosmari would only shoot for sport, because no one approached her to ask if she would take part in the fighting.

She spent her evenings and nights in the humans' house, occasionally joining them for supper as well as breakfast, and more than once staying up late into the night talking with Timothy. He told her the whole story of how he and Linden had first encountered the Empress, in more detail than she had ever heard it before – and with a disarming frankness about the impulsive, selfish, even unkind things he had said and done along the way. He obviously had a great deal of respect for Linden for putting up with him – but then, Rhosmari could tell that she had great respect for Timothy, too. And after spending time with both of them, she knew better than to suspect Timothy of being dishonest like Martin. Especially after the night she and Timothy had a long talk about faery theology, and discovered that they had even more in common than either of them had suspected.

Yet as much as she appreciated those peaceful evenings, Rhosmari felt certain that they would soon come to an end. And it frustrated her that all the other faeries were doing their part to keep the Oakenwyld safe, and she had not learned anything that would help them. The atmosphere in the Oak grew tenser every moment, nerves and tempers strained with constant expectation of attack – and yet day after day passed without incident, like a form of slow torture. Was the Empress hoping to drive them all mad? Was she waiting until they gave up and relaxed their vigilance, so she could strike when they were least prepared?

No, that was too passive for Jasmine: there had to be more to her plan than that. Surely there must be something Rhosmari had overlooked, or failed to consider. She could not bear to give up her search for answers, and leave the faeries of the Oakenwyld to fight what might well prove to be a losing battle. Especially knowing what the Empress would do to them all if she won...

A wave of nausea came over her, as it always did when she thought of losing her name again. To become once more a slave, a pawn, a tool in the Empress's hand or anyone else's – it would not happen. It *must* not. She would throw herself off the top of the Oak, or into the river, first.

Seeing her restlessness, Campion suggested that Rhosmari might find something in the Queen's personal library, and Valerian readily granted her permission to look there. But when Rhosmari searched the shelves, she could find nothing that might be useful except a small assortment of books on magic. She pulled one out and carried it to the table, but more out of duty than hope. After all, the Oakenfolk had not even used magic for almost two hundred years, so how much could they know about it?

Yet when she began to read, Rhosmari soon realised how wrong her assumptions had been. The Oakenfolk had some fascinating lore regarding the use of magical power, unlike anything she had read before. As a Wyld without any male faeries, they had found ways to cast spells that were normally difficult or even impossible for females – such as healing, or permanent transformation. Could that be how Jasmine had risen to power so quickly? Had her Oakenfolk heritage given her skills that other faeries would never expect her to possess?

'Are you getting along all right?' asked Wink as she came in, carrying a well-laden tray. 'I thought you might like something to eat while you study.'

'That's...very thoughtful of you,' said Rhosmari, concealing her surprise with difficulty. From what she had seen, Wink was no one's servant but the Queen's, and even Valerian seemed to hold her in high regard. Why was she waiting on Rhosmari? Even in the Green Isles, no one would do such a thing without being asked – or rewarded.

Wink poured her a cup of tea and then sat down beside her, blue eyes bright with curiosity. 'Have you found out anything that might help us against Jasmine? That is what you're looking for, isn't it?'

'Yes, it is,' said Rhosmari. 'But no, I haven't found anything like that. At least, not yet.' She paused for a bite of honey cake before going on. 'I'm impressed by some of the things I've been reading about your people's magic, though. I had no idea you could do such unusual spells.'

'Well, it wasn't really *us*,' said Wink. 'I mean, usually it was just the Queen who did them, because she was the only one with magic. And even she didn't do them except when she had to, because it was so exhausting.' Her face clouded with memory. 'I remember how after Amaryllis turned Knife into a human, she was weak for days afterwards...and I don't think her power was ever quite as strong after that.'

Rhosmari frowned. 'But Jasmine used a transformation spell on the Oakenfolk, didn't she, when she cast what you call the Sundering? Surely that must have been far more difficult, and yet—'

'She wasn't drained afterwards, no,' said Wink. 'But that was because she mostly used *our* magic to cast the spell, instead of just her own. And she did it by moonlight, so of course...'

Rhosmari froze, her teacup halfway to her mouth. 'What did you say?'

'I said that she mostly used—'

'No, not that. I mean, yes, that too, but the last part. What about moonlight?'

Wink picked up the book Rhosmari had been reading and flipped ahead a few pages. 'It's right here, see? Deep magic – that's what we call the kinds of spells you're talking about, the really hard ones – is much more easily performed by moonlight. On the night Amaryllis changed Knife into a human there wasn't much of a moon at all, so of course the spell took a lot out of her. But when Jasmine cast the Sundering, the moon was full.'

At the full moon. Both Amaryllis and Heather had used those words in their writings, when describing what Jasmine had done to the Oakenfolk. But only now did Rhosmari realise how important that detail might be. She put down her cup so quickly that tea slopped onto the table, and stood up.

'I have to talk to Queen Valerian,' she said. 'Right away.'

Within the hour, the Oak was on full alert. Queen Valerian needed no persuasion from Rhosmari to recognise the danger, for tonight would be the first full moon since the Empress's defeat at Waverley Hall. This was what Jasmine had been waiting for – the time when her powers would be at their height, and she could cast a spell so great and terrible that it would devastate the rebellion completely. It not only fit with her personality and her behaviour in the past, it made sense of everything she had done up to now. Rhosmari could only hope that before the Empress could carry out her plan, the faeries of the Oak would find a way to stop her.

Thorn, Rob and Garan assembled their troops by the foot of the Spiral Stair – the largest open space in the Oak – and explained to all the faeries what was expected of them. Those unwilling or unable to fight would be dispatched to reinforce the wards around the great tree, so that it could withstand any assault the Empress and her followers might make against it. Other faeries would cast their most powerful glamours, aversions and silencing spells over the Oakenwyld, so that no unwitting passerby could stumble into the battle. Then the rest would form companies and march outside to defend the Oak, the garden and the surrounding meadows against the enemy.

After the assembly dispersed, Rhosmari joined Campion, Wink and Linden for a private meeting in the library. It had not been easy for Rhosmari to decide how to help the faeries of the Oak, and harder still to volunteer to do it. But now, with Queen Valerian's blessing on her venture and an empty loreseed sitting on the table between them, she explained to the other faeries what she meant to do.

'Whether we win or lose,' she said, 'someone needs to be a witness to what really happened in this battle. The Empress and her followers can say whatever they like, but if you have this—' She touched the loreseed gently— 'then you will always have a record of the truth.'

'Like Heather's diaries!' Wink exclaimed, and Campion added, 'Only better.'

'Lorecasting takes concentration,' Rhosmari went on, 'and unless you've viewed a lot of loreseeds yourself, it's hard to know what goes into making a good one. That's why I've offered to make this one for you – but I'll need all of your help in order to do it.'

Briefly she sketched out the plan that she and Queen Valerian had agreed upon. They would all go out upon the West Knot Branch, which was the best vantage point from which to view the battle. Campion would stand with Rhosmari while she cast the loreseed, so she could learn how to do it herself. Wink, who had a special talent for invisibility, would keep them all safely hidden; and Linden would keep her eyes open for any details – or potential threats – that Rhosmari might otherwise miss.

Rhosmari explained all of this in the calm, clear voice she used with her students, but her insides writhed with every word. She knew her father would be proud of her for carrying on his legacy, but he was also the one who had taught her what death looked like, and what it meant to grieve. Could she really stand outside the Oak for hours on end, watching people she knew being hurt or even killed, and not break down or turn away? And if she could, what would that say about the kind of person she had become?

'Lorecasting,' Linden repeated wonderingly, as the two of them walked out of the library after the meeting. 'I'd never heard of such a thing. Did your people invent it, or—'

'Watch out!' screamed a voice from the passage behind them, and the two girls jumped back as a comet of blazing light scorched past. Dazzled, Rhosmari flung up an arm to shield her eyes as the spell exploded—

A hand clamped down on her shoulder, spinning her around and shoving her back into the shadows. 'Don't move,' Rob said tersely. 'Don't let her see you. Stay with her, Linden.' Then he transformed himself into a fox and took off running, dodging one spell after another as he raced towards the danger.

'He said *her*,' whispered Linden, clutching Rhosmari's arm. 'It couldn't be—?'

Several more faeries sprinted past and plunged into the corridor, Broch and Llinos among them. Shouts and cries echoed in the distance, followed by a muffled explosion and several more blinding flashes. Then, at last, silence.

Rob was the first to emerge from the smoke. He looked tired, his face streaked with dirt and his mouth a bitter line. 'She got away,' he said.

'Who did?' asked Linden, rushing to him. 'Who was it?'

He gathered her into the circle of his arm, dropping his face against her hair. 'Mallow. Who else?'

Rhosmari drew a sharp breath. 'But her cell was locked and warded. Wasn't it?'

'It was.' Rob straightened up, letting go of Linden with obvious reluctance. 'Or it should have been, unless someone was careless. Where's Garan? He was in charge of making sure the wards were maintained – he should know whose responsibility it was today.'

'I'll find him,' said Rhosmari, and hurried up the Stair.

'Garan?'

Rhosmari knocked several times upon his door, but there was no answer. She tried the handle, expecting to find it locked – but it swung wide, to reveal a tousle-haired Garan struggling to his feet. His eyelids were heavy, his expression dazed.

'Are you all right?' she asked, catching him as he swayed.

'I...yes, I believe so,' he murmured. 'I only sat down for a moment...at least I thought I did... I must have fallen asleep.'

No harm had come to him then, just simple exhaustion. And no wonder, after all the pressure he had been under. 'Mallow has escaped,' she said. 'Rob needs to know who was responsible for warding her cell today.'

'Escaped?' Garan stood up, instantly alert. 'But that cannot be. Lily renewed those wards this morning; I watched her do it myself. Mallow could never have broken out of her cell, unless...'

His face drained of colour, and he clutched at his belt pouch. Rhosmari tensed, but then Garan sighed and held up the white pebble they both recognised as the Stone of Naming. 'For a moment I feared…but it must have been a dream. What was I saying?'

'Mallow could never have escaped alone,' said Rhosmari. 'You think someone helped her?'

'I fear as much,' said Garan. 'Perhaps one of the kitchen workers, someone foolish enough to be bullied or bribed into letting her out. But there is no time to look into that now. I must go and tell Queen Valerian at once.' He stepped away from her, then hesitated and turned back.

'What is it?' asked Rhosmari.

Garan took her hands. 'I know how you feel about violence,' he said in a low voice. 'But you are one of the best archers we have. If you could think of yourself as fighting to save lives, and not of killing…I would be honoured to have you in my company.'

He had his mother's eyes, and Rhosmari felt a lump rise in her throat as she remembered how Lady Arianllys had wept when they parted. Garan had left his family and his homeland behind to fight the Empress, and now he would never see either of them again.

But if Rhosmari did as he asked, she would never be able to return to the Green Isles either. 'I can't,' she replied softly. 'I'm sorry.'

Garan nodded, resigned. Rubbing his temples, he walked towards the door.

'Garan,' said Rhosmari. 'Are you sure you're well?'

'Well enough,' he replied in a distracted tone, and vanished.

After hearing of Mallow's escape, Queen Valerian sent out a search party, but they returned empty-handed. Finally Thorn, Rob and Garan dismissed all the faeries to their rooms and ordered them to rest until nightfall.

Rhosmari went back to her old room and lay down, but she could not sleep. Her mind churned with worries and unanswered questions. Why had Mallow fought so hard to escape? What was her plan? Had she struck out on her own, or had she gone over to the Empress?

And why was it so hot? Rhosmari shifted restlessly on the crunching mattress, flinging the covers away from her. A breeze stirred the curtain at her window, but its coolness barely touched the stagnant air inside. She longed for the sea winds that freshened the Green Isles.

But that was not all she longed for. She missed the smells of sand and seaweed, the slap of waves upon rock, the distant cries of kittiwakes and gannets. She wondered what Lord Gwylan was doing now that he was no longer among the Elders, and if Lady Arianllys had seen any more visions, and whether Fioled would still get to visit the mainland. She wished she could have said goodbye to her students before she left.

She missed her mother.

Until now Rhosmari had not allowed herself the luxury

of weeping for her homeland. She had been afraid that if she started she might never stop. Once her initial shock and anger at being trapped in the Oak had passed, she had forced herself to accept her fate, and reject the temptation to run away. Even though a treacherous little part of her whispered that it might be worth giving herself up to the Empress, just to see the Green Isles again…

And now the tears came, soaking hot into her pillow. Despite all Rhosmari's efforts to make herself a part of the Oak, it was not her home, and these were not her people. Even Garan had become a stranger to her; he was occupied with other things. And the last person who had taken her in his arms and comforted her was Martin.

Yet just as her grief threatened to overwhelm her, Rhosmari was distracted by the sound of music. The shivering notes of plucked strings, lifted and borne to her on the wind from somewhere not close, but not very far away.

She sat up, wiping her eyes on the sheet. Was that Rob playing? But though she knew he was a skilled musician, he had not touched an instrument in all the time she had known him. In fact, she had seen no musical instruments anywhere in the Oak.

Rhosmari slipped off the bed and went to the window. It was hard to see with so many branches in the way, but she could just make out the back of the house and the slim young man seated on the veranda, cradling a guitar.

Timothy. Of course. How could she have forgotten?

He played well and fluidly, pausing only now and then to alter a note or repeat a phrase. And the music itself was unlike any she had heard before – melancholy one moment and quickening to hopefulness the next, slipping into a confident rhythm that made her fingers twitch before slowing to a hesitant and almost questioning pace. At times it seemed more like a speech than a song, the words of some foreign tongue that she had no way to interpret. And yet it soothed her, reassuring her that she was not alone.

The afternoon light was fading, the blue sky deepening to marine. Soon it would be nightfall, and who knew what would happen then? Rhosmari took her hair out of its clasp, combed it with her fingers, and twisted it back again. She ran her hands over her rumpled blouse and skirt, tightened her belt, straightened her shoulders. Then she Leaped to the veranda, where Timothy was sitting.

As soon as she became solid she staggered and almost fell, weakness rushing over her. Someone had planted cold iron all around the house. Bars of it lay beneath every threshold, nails were hammered into every window sash and sill. To keep the Empress from attacking Oakhaven with magic, Peri had turned the house into a place that no faery, Rhosmari included, would find it easy to go near. And when Timothy exclaimed and jumped up to help her, she could feel the numbing power of the iron cross radiating from beneath his shirt. She flinched and jerked away.

'Sorry about that,' said Timothy, pulling the necklace off

and stuffing it into his pocket. 'Thorn told us what you'd found out about the Empress, and Peri thought we should be prepared. We didn't expect to see you again today.'

'I understand,' said Rhosmari, breathing slowly to quell her dizziness. 'I just... I wanted to talk to you and the others. Before anything happens.'

'Well, we probably shouldn't talk here,' said Timothy, with a wary glance at the sky. He reached under the threshold of the glass door, pulled out an iron poker and cast it aside. 'Do you think it'll be any better if you come in?'

'I...I'm not sure.' Mustering her courage, Rhosmari stepped over the threshold – and immediately felt better. The iron was meant to keep hostile faeries out, but she was here by invitation, and inside the house the effect was much less unpleasant.

'Right,' said Timothy. 'I'll just get my guitar and fix up that door again, and then we'll go and find Peri.'

sixteen

They found Peri in the upstairs bedroom, peering out between the half-drawn curtains with an antique spyglass. With a pile of schoolbooks on the nightstand and a heap of unwashed clothing in the corner, it was easy to tell this room normally belonged to Timothy. But now the bed was littered with maps and scribbled diagrams, while an alarming assortment of weapons stood propped against the wall, a crossbow and a long hunting knife among them.

'Spotted anything yet?' asked Timothy, as he and Rhosmari came in.

Peri lowered the spyglass with a frustrated huff of breath. 'It's so hard to tell. If she's bringing in her troops, she's doing what I would do: flying in low and using the wood to cover their approach. There could be a hundred faeries hiding in those trees by now, and as long as they don't trip any of the wards we'd never know it.'

'But you spotted the Blackwings earlier, right?'

'I saw two ravens,' replied Peri. 'But they arrived more than an hour apart. It could just be coincidence— Oh, hello, Rhosmari.' She swept the charts off the bed, clearing a space for Rhosmari to sit. 'What brings you here? I thought they'd be keeping you busy in the Oak.'

'Everyone's resting,' said Rhosmari, 'or trying to. But I couldn't.' Self-conscious, she sat down at the edge of the mattress – and Timothy promptly came around the other side and flopped onto his back, nearly bouncing her off again.

'Sit up, you rude thing,' said Peri, tossing a cushion at him. Timothy caught it and tucked it behind his head; Peri rolled her eyes and returned her attention to Rhosmari. 'I doubt anyone else in the Oak can sleep either,' she told her. 'But you're welcome to stay as long as you like. Once the Empress arrives, you might even be safer here.'

'No, I'll have to go back,' said Rhosmari. 'I promised Queen Valerian that I'd make a loreseed of the battle.' And then, of course, she had to explain what a loreseed was. But both of the humans were intrigued by the idea, especially Peri.

'If we'd known how to do that when Jasmine cast the Sundering,' she said, 'she'd never have been able to make us forget our past. I hope we won't need your loreseed to remind us of what really happened, but if we do, it's good to know it'll be there.'

She said *we* and *our* so readily, as though she were still one of the Oakenfolk herself. And that reminded Rhosmari of something she'd wanted to know for a long time. 'Peri,' she said, 'what made you decide to stop being a faery? I mean, I know you and Paul fell in love—' It was not easy to get through that phrase without stammering, but somehow she did it— 'but how did it all happen?'

Peri glanced over at Timothy. 'You might want to go and practise some more,' she said. 'I'm sure you're sick of hearing all this by now.'

'Actually, no,' said Timothy, crossing his legs and folding his hands comfortably over his stomach. 'Tell us a story, Aunty Peri.'

Was this how humans dealt with unbearable tension – by making jokes? Rhosmari could only marvel at their resilience. But she barely had time to finish the thought before Peri began to explain how she had hatched from a magical egg in the Oak thirty years ago, and grown up to become the fierce young hunter known as Knife.

It was a long story, and amazingly complicated. Having studied the faery records and Heather's diaries already, Rhosmari knew all about what Jasmine had done to the Oakenfolk – but Knife had been forced to discover the truth about her people's history one dangerous step at a time, with Queen Amaryllis trying to thwart her at every turn. And in the meantime Knife had met and come to know Paul quite by accident, never dreaming that their shared interest in art would lead them not only to friendship, but to an even more forbidden love.

When at last Peri finished her story, Rhosmari felt as though she were waking from a vivid and compelling dream. She gathered her thoughts with difficulty, and said, 'So Queen Amaryllis tried to make you forget Paul, and she couldn't do it?'

'No more than Jasmine could make Heather forget Philip,' said Peri.

'But how could that be? Neither you nor Heather had any magic to protect yourselves. If the same kind of spell worked to make all the other faeries forget, why wouldn't it work on you?'

'That's a good question,' Peri said. 'What do you think?'

'The power of love?' said Timothy, but he sounded sceptical. 'Sorry, I don't mean to make light of your feelings, but that sounds a little...' He made a looping motion with one finger.

Peri gave a short laugh. 'It does, doesn't it? No, that's not the answer — though it's part of the reason.' Her face sobered. 'I loved Paul, yes. But that alone wouldn't have made any difference, if I hadn't trusted him enough to give him my name. My *true* name.'

Rhosmari felt as though a heavy weight had dropped onto her chest. Her throat clenched, and little shivers ran all over her. 'You...' she whispered, forcing the words out. 'You *gave* it to him, when you were still a faery? Even knowing he could use it to control you?'

'I did,' said Peri. 'Because I wanted him to know how

much I cared for him, even though I was afraid I might never see him again. Just like Heather gave her name to Philip, when—'

Timothy sat up sharply. 'Peri – I think she's going to be sick.'

'No,' gasped Rhosmari. 'I just...give me a minute.' She breathed through her fingers until the worst of the nausea subsided, then wrapped both arms around her stomach, rocking a little. Timothy eased towards her, one hand hovering above her shoulder, but she shook her head and he backed away again.

'I'm sorry,' said Peri, looking blank. 'I had no idea.'

No, Rhosmari thought, swallowing envy like bile, *you didn't.* If either Peri or Heather had known what it was like to be controlled, they would never have dreamed of doing such a thing. Only ignorance – and infatuation – could explain their willingness to take such a terrible risk.

'Peri!' Paul's deep voice reverberated along the corridor. 'Thorn's flashing us a message.'

Peri tossed her spyglass to Timothy. 'Keep watch,' she said, and dashed out.

Timothy rolled off the bed and went to the window, brushing the curtain aside. 'I don't even know what she's looking for,' he muttered. 'It's not like the Empress's troops are going to fly over the house in formation just to let us know they're here.'

Rhosmari swallowed again, her fingers clenching and

unclenching in the bedspread. She looked about for a distraction – anything to push Peri's words from her mind – and her eyes fell to a framed picture on Timothy's nightstand. She picked it up for a closer look.

It showed a group of humans standing beneath an exotic-looking tree. A tall man leant against the trunk, his tanned face creased with maturity and gentle humour. He had one arm around the waist of a smiling woman, and his hand on the shoulder of a little girl – so these must be Timothy's parents, and his sister Lydia. And next to them stood a young woman perhaps two years older than Rhosmari, her hair a mass of glossy braids and her skin a lustrous brown even deeper than Lady Celyn's.

'Who is she?' asked Rhosmari, holding up the photograph. 'The girl?'

Timothy lowered the spyglass. 'Oh. That's Miriam. Miriam Sewanaku, our neighbour back in Uganda.'

Rhosmari looked down at the picture again. 'She's beautiful,' she said.

'Yeah,' said Timothy, turning back to the window. Then he added, very softly, 'But not as beautiful as you.'

Rhosmari's eyes widened. Had he meant her to hear those words?

'He also thinks you're intelligent and fascinating, if that helps,' said Paul as he wheeled up to the doorway. 'We're actually getting a little sick of hearing about it.' He spoke lightly, but his face was lined with tension. 'Sorry to interrupt, but we've just had news from the Oak. Another faery's gone missing.'

'Mallow, you mean?' asked Rhosmari. 'That happened just before I—' But Paul cut her off with a shake of his head.

'Not Mallow,' he said. 'Bluebell.'

'It's a good thing the Oakenfolk hadn't yet realised you weren't in the Oak, Rhosmari, or there'd have been a real panic,' said Peri, striding to meet them in the corridor. 'Losing Bluebell is bad enough, but losing you would have been catastrophic. I've told Thorn you're safe with us, but we'd better get you back there straightaway.'

'I don't get it,' Timothy said, as the three of them headed downstairs. 'Why would Bluebell disappear like that? She's never left the Oakenwyld in her life. Where would she go?'

'Thorn thinks she went after Mallow,' replied Peri. She led them down the passage to the back of the house, then across to the far corner of the sitting room, where she flipped back the carpet to reveal a brass ring set into the floor. 'Maybe to talk some sense into her, maybe to join her, no one knows. But the timing couldn't be worse. They're both likely to get caught by the Empress, if they haven't been already.' She tugged the ring and a square of the wooden flooring lifted away, shedding crumbs of foam in its wake.

'What is that?' asked Rhosmari.

'The way out,' Peri said. 'We made it for Linden when she was little, so she could visit us without having to dodge the crows. Make yourself small, crawl through this pipe, and it'll bring you to a secret corridor that runs underneath the hedge all the way to the Oak.'

Crawl through this pipe. Into a black hole little wider than a human hand, with roots and damp earth pressing down upon her. 'No, that's all right,' Rhosmari said faintly. 'I'll just Leap back—'

'You can't,' said Peri. 'After Bluebell disappeared, Queen Valerian warded the Oak so that no one could get in or out using magic. You'd have to walk across the garden, and I'm not sending you out there in plain view of the Empress and all her servants. It's too much of a risk.'

'Isn't that a bit dramatic?' said Timothy. 'We don't know if they're even there.'

'I know.' Peri's expression was grim. 'The only thing I've been looking for is a way to prove it.'

'Hunter's instincts?' Timothy asked in a dubious tone.

'Something like that. There are too many shadows in the wood. And the wind smells different. You have to know a place before you know what's normal and what isn't – and I know the Oakenwyld better than anyone. Believe me, they're out there.'

Rhosmari licked her lips and squeezed her hands together. She could not take her eyes off that missing square of floor, the round emptiness inside it. Walking into Gruffydd's Way had been difficult, but this – this was impossible.

And yet she had promised Queen Valerian that she would forecast the battle, and Campion, Linden and Wink were waiting for her to join them. And if she did not say goodbye to Garan and the others now, she might never get the chance again.

Timothy touched her shoulder. 'Are you all right? You look sort of…green.'

'I don't like small, dark places,' Rhosmari admitted with a nervous laugh. 'I just need a moment to…to prepare.'

'Would it help if I went with you?' asked Timothy, and Peri said sharply, 'Oh, no, you don't.'

But Timothy had already walked into the kitchen and taken down the electric torch. 'Why not? Hardly anybody knows that tunnel even exists, let alone that it goes all the way to the house. I'll probably be safer down there than I am here.' And with that he pulled the wooden medallion out of his pocket, and dropped it around his neck.

Nothing happened. Emotions passed like clouds over Timothy's face: puzzlement, alarm, and finally resignation. He reached to take off the medallion, but Rhosmari caught his wrist. 'Wait,' she said.

Perhaps it was the magic within her, or just her desperate need not to go into that dark hole alone. But at the moment she touched him, the medallion's power began to work – not only on Timothy, but on Rhosmari as well. The furniture around them swelled to gigantic size, and Peri loomed above them like an exasperated goddess.

'Fine,' she said. 'But Timothy – as soon as she's safely in the Oak, you turn around and come back here. Understood?'

Timothy switched on the torch and saluted Peri with it. Then he flung himself down on his belly and wriggled headfirst into the hole in the floor. 'Follow me,' he called back to Rhosmari. 'It's not that far – I can see the other end of the pipe from here. I think.'

Peri kneeled, stooping close to Rhosmari. 'It's all right to be afraid,' she said in a low voice. 'Just don't let it stop you from doing what you have to do.'

Rhosmari gave a reluctant nod. Then she got down on her hands and knees, and crawled into the tunnel after Timothy.

The pipe felt cool and smooth against her hands, its sides clammy with condensation. By the wavering beam of Timothy's torch Rhosmari could see that it was made of some greyish substance that caught the light and reflected it dimly back. But Timothy's head and shoulders were a wall of shadow, and she fought the impulse to whimper as he crawled ahead of her, moving too fast for her trembling arms and legs to keep up, leaving her behind in the growing dark—

Something snagged her skirt, wrenching her to a stop. She tried to pull free, to press onwards, but her bones were vibrating with terror, and her muscles refused to obey.

Timothy stopped. 'Rhosmari?'

'I'm caught. I can't... Something's got me. I can't move...'

'Hang on. I'm going to turn around and have a look.' A scuffling noise followed, and the light flickered wildly in all directions before coming to a halt. 'OK, maybe I can't turn around.' He paused, then said in a decisive tone, 'Right. Just stay still, try to relax, while I crawl ahead a bit. The pipe's got to connect to the hedge tunnel somewhere; maybe at the junction I'll have room to turn around.'

'Don't leave me.' Her voice was a stranger's, rasping with desperation. 'Timothy—'

'I'm going to hand you the torch, so you can see where I'm going. I'll wriggle backwards a bit, and – here, I'm shoving the torch down to you now. Can you reach it?'

Her fingers skittered across the soles of Timothy's shoes. She stretched out her arm as far as she could – and felt the torch's barrel push against her palm. 'Yes.'

'Good. Hold the light steady. I'm going to hum, so you can hear me even if I get out of sight. I'll come back as soon as I can. OK?'

Rhosmari gripped the torch with both hands, blinking her stinging eyes. She watched the muscles of Timothy's shoulders bunch and uncoil as he pulled himself down on the tunnel on his elbows, the angles of his shifting hips and knees, the black-and-white soles of his trainers... and then the shadows swallowed him up, and even the sound of his humming was drowned out by the awful silence.

'Timothy? *Timothy?*'

'What?'

Rhosmari exhaled. 'I couldn't hear you any more,' she said. 'I thought…'

'I'm almost at the end of the pipe. There's something here…' Then came a scraping sound, a creak, and a shout of *'Whoa!'* She heard a heavy thump, and then…nothing.

Terror swept over Rhosmari, and she clutched the torch so tightly her fingers throbbed. He had tumbled into a crevice, the roof of the tunnel had caved in, some lurking predator had seized him by the throat and dragged him away—

'When peace like a river…attendeth my way…when sorrows like sea billows roll…'

The song was husky and broken, but every note rang true. It was also, mercifully, getting louder. *'Whatever my lot…thou has taught me to say…it is well…it is well with my soul…'*

At last Timothy's face emerged from the darkness, dirt-smudged and blinking. 'Could you point that thing in another direction?' he asked, raising a hand against the glare of the torch. Grateful beyond words to see him again, Rhosmari tilted the beam upwards, and beneath its softened glow the two of them met face to face.

'It's really not far at all,' he told her. 'There's a door at the end of the pipe – I thought the tunnel was blocked for a minute, but when I gave it a shove, it opened up and I fell out. It's a lot wider at the other end.' He pushed himself up on his elbows and flashed her a grin. 'I don't usually sing that well, especially while lying on my stomach. I blame you.'

'Me? What do I have to do with— Oh.'

'Oh?'

'For a minute, I forgot you were a human.'

Timothy let out a whoop of laughter. 'So you do have a sense of humour, after all.'

Rhosmari hadn't meant to make a joke. She truly had forgotten that Timothy's musical talent would be enhanced by her presence. But now she realised that she had accidentally echoed the comment he had once made about forgetting she was a faery…and that *was* funny. 'I don't usually,' she said, and then more daringly, 'I blame you.'

Timothy's grin faded to seriousness, and his fingers curled around her wrists. Rhosmari's heart lurched as he leaned closer…

But he only craned his neck, trying to see past her. 'OK,' he said. 'You're stuck, right? Can you see where? Can you move at all?'

'It's my skirt,' she said. 'It's caught on something.'

'Oh, right.' He took the torch from her hands and played it down the wall. 'Looks like a join in the pipe. Try rolling over – that might pull it loose.'

Such a simple idea. She might have thought of it herself, if she hadn't been half-witted with panic. Rhosmari twisted over, then back again, and the tugging sensation vanished. 'It worked!'

'Good. Now, I'm going to back up, and you come after me. I'm right here, and I've been through this pipe all the way to the other end, and there's nothing scary about it. OK?'

He was being so patient with her – more patient than she deserved. 'I'm sorry,' she said. 'I know there's no good reason for me to feel this way, I keep trying to talk myself out of it, but—'

'Lots of people are claustrophobic,' he said. 'My mum doesn't like tight places, either. You're just lucky I didn't inherit it from her, or there'd be two of us panicking in the dark.' He turned the torch sideways between them, so it wouldn't dazzle her eyes. 'Ready? Let's go.'

Rhosmari's forearms were damp, her elbows bruised from hauling herself along. Her boots kept skidding on the pipe's slick surface – but, little by little, she advanced on Timothy as he wriggled away from her. She concentrated on his downcast eyes, the rumpled hair falling over his forehead, the soft pressure of his teeth into his lower lip as he pushed himself backwards, and gradually her fear receded. She was not trapped, not lost, not alone. She was only making her way through a tight place, with the help of a friend.

They crept along in silence, until the muscles in

Rhosmari's shoulders burned and Timothy was grimacing with the strain. Then he stopped. 'Door,' he gasped. 'Got to give it a kick.' And with a grunt and a thud, a gust of cooler air washed over them. Timothy writhed backwards out of the pipe, sliding over its edge until only his arms and his head were visible. 'Grab my hand,' he said. 'I'll pull you out.'

Rhosmari scrambled towards him and caught his fingers, then his wrists. He yanked, and she slid free, straight into his arms. He staggered back under her weight and dropped the torch; it spun crazily across the floor, flashing over the root-patterned walls and two more shut doors before rolling to a stop by their feet.

The relief of being out of the pipe was overwhelming. Rhosmari gripped Timothy's sleeves and pressed her forehead against his shoulder.

'Er...' He cleared his throat, and his voice cracked an octave as he went on, 'We should get moving. Can you walk?'

Rhosmari let go of him with an effort, then bent and picked up the torch. The hedge tunnel was even darker than the pipe, and smelled of mulch and old earth. But the walls were packed hard, and the floor looked dry. There were no cobwebs or scuttling insects, no holes that she could see. And best of all, it was high enough to stand up in.

'Yes,' she said. 'I'm all right now.'

The door at the end of the tunnel was plastered thickly with soil, and fitted so closely to the wall that if not for the brass ring that marked its handle, Rhosmari would never have known it was there. She pulled and it creaked open, revealing the East Root corridor of the Oak. 'Finally,' she murmured, and stepped forward – but Timothy caught her arm.

'I've got to get back to the house,' he said. 'You'll be all right from here?'

She switched off the torch and handed it to him. 'I know where I am now. I'll be fine.'

Timothy watched her, his face unreadable in the half-light. 'So…I guess this is goodbye.'

Rhosmari nodded.

'Yeah.' He sounded hoarse. 'OK. Well, take care.' He turned to leave.

'Timothy?' She waited until he looked back, then went on in a rush, 'I appreciate what you did for me. Very much.' And with that Rhosmari leaned forward, and brushed her lips against his cheek.

Timothy's fingers crept up to the place where she had kissed him. Then he broke into an incredulous, lopsided grin. 'Any time,' he said, and sprinted away.

Rhosmari shut the door after him, and headed for the main part of the Oak. She had just passed the empty dining hall when the air around her tingled, as though lightning had flashed by. Seconds later a pack of scullery maids fled out the kitchen door, shrieking, 'It's started! The Empress is here!'

'Don't be ridiculous,' pleaded Holly, plunging into the

corridor after them. 'It's barely even dark yet— Oh, hello, Rhosmari.' She brushed a hand across her sweat-dampened brow. 'You've heard about Bluebell, I suppose.'

'Yes, I have,' said Rhosmari. She glanced ahead to the open heart of the tree, where the kitchen workers huddled fearfully at the foot of the Spiral Stair. Beyond them, a larger crowd of faeries stood in restless ranks, all of them armed. Some carried bows carved and polished to a sheen, with quivers full of feathered shafts across their shoulders. Others wore swords and daggers of glittering steel. Weapons meant to hurt, to wound, to kill.

Rhosmari had hoped to find a way to defeat the Empress without violence, but she had failed, and there could be no stopping this battle now. The faeries of the Oak would fight to save their home, and some of them would die.

Gardener protect us, she thought. Then she began edging around the crowd, trying to find a clear path to the Spiral Stair. Thorn caught sight of her, and waved her troops back to let her pass. 'Took you long enough,' she said. 'They're waiting for you upstairs.'

Garan slipped through the ranks to join them, his cheeks flushed and his eyes fever-bright. 'The wards are holding,' he said. 'But the Empress is on the move. It is time.' He took Rhosmari by the shoulders and kissed her brow. 'Peace to you, sister.' Then he vanished back into the crowd.

'All right!' Thorn barked at her troops. 'Everyone outside and into position! Now!'

At once the faeries closed ranks and began marching off towards the exits. A tremor rocked the Oak, and Rhosmari clutched the bannister as the window-slits flashed with the dull red light of an explosion.

The battle for the Oak had begun.

seventeen

Rhosmari stood with Campion, Wink and Linden on the West Knot Branch, a rope around her waist and the loreseed clenched tightly in her hand. The moon was still inching its way up above the trees, but the stars were clearly visible, and Peri had turned the lights on at the back of the house, casting a soft illumination over the lawn. In the garden below, a host of tiny figures were moving into position; in the nearby wood, the trees were restless with birds. There was no sign of the Empress, but they all knew that somewhere in the shadows, she was there.

Rhosmari opened her fingers, balancing the loreseed on her palm. 'This is the account of the battle between the faeries of the Oak and the Empress Jasmine,' she said in a clear but quiet voice, 'as witnessed by Rhosmari daughter of Celyn of the Children of Rhys. May it stand as a testimony to future generations, that they may know what truly happened on this day.'

'Amen,' said Linden softly, as though it had been a prayer. Wink had made them all invisible to everyone else but not to each other, so Rhosmari could see that her face was strained and very pale. Stepping a few paces down the branch, which was so broad that six faeries could have walked it side by side without touching, Linden tied herself to a stout twig for support. With a last squeeze of Rhosmari's hand and a whispered, 'Gardener help you,' Wink hurried to do likewise.

Hissing and spitting sparks, a spell erupted from the enemy lines and arced high over the Oakenwyld. But instead of falling to the grass, it hovered in midair, casting a baleful light over the garden. And now the outermost wards broke, and the Empress's army rushed towards them.

'There are so *many*,' breathed Campion.

'Now!' called Thorn from below, and at once she and all the archers with her grew to human size and loosed their arrows in a long arc over the field beyond. They could hardly expect to hit anything like that, thought Rhosmari; they'd barely had time to glimpse the Empress's soldiers, let alone aim at them...

A diving hawk-faery cast a spell that rattled the branches of the Oak. Rhosmari tugged on the rope that anchored her, making sure it was secure, as the archers loosed their second volley into the air.

This time the arrows flew further, but still the Empress's army advanced, more and more shadowy figures gliding out from between the distant trees. Willowy faery women flashed in and out of visibility as they ran, while males loped along in the forms of dogs and foxes, or swooped from the treetops as birds of every size and shape. And all of them seemed heedless of their own safety, not even troubling to dodge the missiles raining down among them…

And *through* them.

'It's a glamour!' exclaimed Linden. 'Those soldiers – they're not even real!'

But the faeries of the Oak had already recognised the trick, and cast a spell of their own to undo it. Even as Linden spoke, two-thirds of the dark shapes crossing the meadow wavered and blinked out, leaving only a scattered remnant behind. One of them whirled to look behind her, feathery blonde hair gleaming – but then a haze rose up around Veronica, and she disappeared again.

The birds wheeling around the Oak had also decreased in number, and the archers were no longer wasting ammunition. A jackdaw shrieked and plummeted into the hedge, and in the distance a wounded dog-faery let out a yelp. But now the Blackwings glided in from the south-west, and though Garan and his men loosed a barrage of arrows towards them, they nimbly dodged every one. Light gathered between their outstretched wings, swelling to a blinding glare—

Another explosion shook the Oak, and green light flared around them. Rhosmari stumbled, nearly dropping the loreseed, while Campion fell off the side of the branch, her rope snapping taut. 'Campion!' cried Wink, but the Librarian panted, 'I'm fine,' and flew up to join them again.

By now most of the faeries below had grown to human size, for since the Empress's people scorned to make themselves small, it was the only way to be sure the two sides were evenly matched. It ought to have made it easier for Rhosmari to see what was going on, but there was so much mist and smoke and sparks flying about, such a confusion of fluttering wings and darting animal shapes, that she could scarcely tell allies from enemies.

'I can't see Rob,' said Linden anxiously.

'I can,' Campion replied. 'He and his troops have come around behind the Oak. They're driving the enemy back towards the wood— Oh, well done!'

But Rhosmari had no chance to find out what Rob had done well, because a small animal had just darted through a gap in the hedge – an ermine with ash-white fur, even though at this time of the year it ought to have been brown. It paused to nose at a fallen faery, who lay moaning on the grass with her wings crumpled at odd angles; then it snapped its jaws around her throat, gave her a shake and let her drop again, dead.

'Tansy,' moaned Wink. 'Oh, the poor silly fool, she should never have gone out there – she was supposed to stay in the kitchen with the others—'

The ermine paused in the middle of the lawn, coolly

surveying the chaos. Then with a shimmer it transformed into a facry, equally lean and pale, and Rhosmari's stomach turned over as she recognised Martin. He whipped around and flung a dagger straight into the crowd, sending a rebel tumbling. Then he took his bird form and darted away again.

'Coward!' Linden shouted, and for a moment Rhosmari thought she might leap off the branch and go after him. But then she put her hands over her face, and Wink hurried to comfort her.

By now the flowerbeds had been trampled into a muddy tangle, the hedges smashed in several places and one of the smaller trees splintered in two. All the work that Peri and Paul had done to make the Oakenwyld beautiful was ruined, and though Rhosmari knew it was the least of their worries, part of her ached to see it. Where were the humans, anyway? Were they biding their time for some crucial moment? Or were they already working to help the faeries of the Oak in some way that she could not see?

'Garan's surrounded,' said Campion. 'They've cut him off from the others – they're closing in—'

But at that same moment came a sound: *twang-hiss-thump*. Someone shrieked, in pain or rage. Then a hail of black stones rained down upon the garden, scattering faeries everywhere.

Peri McCormick stood on the veranda, moonlight blazing on her white hair as she tossed her crossbow aside and grabbed her rifle. With two quick shots she winged a crow and knocked a kestrel out of the air. From the window above her Timothy fired his slingshot, zinging iron pellets at the enemy, and on the opposite side of the house, Paul was doing the same.

One of the Empress's faeries who had been skulking unseen by the hedge cried out and clutched her arm, forced into visibility again. A cat yowled and collapsed into a dazed-looking faery. Three more birds tumbled from the sky – but then one of the Empress's soldiers hurled himself at Peri, dagger in hand. She dodged him easily, swung up the rifle and fired a shot past his shoulder before dropping the gun and drawing her hunting knife. He thrust, she ducked, and with two quick slashes and a kick she sent him reeling back into the crowd. Then she snatched up the gun and began reloading.

She was just about to fire again when a raven plunged down upon her, knocking the rifle from her hands. But it must have brushed one of the iron rings she wore, because as she stumbled back, the raven dropped to the ground and rose up again as Byrne Blackwing. He seized a discarded sword and swung it at her; she grabbed the poker from beneath the glass door and blocked the blow. They fought in a blur of flashing metal and rapid footwork, chasing each other around the veranda and out onto the lawn. Byrne had knocked Peri down – no, she had used his own momentum to throw him over, and she was up again—

'Thorn!' cried Wink.

'What is it?' Campion dashed over to her, almost tripping Rhosmari with the rope. 'What about her? What's happening? Where is she?'

'She fell over there—' Wink pointed blindly towards the southwest. 'Someone came up behind her and hit her on the head, and she fell down. I don't know if she's unconscious, or...'

Anxious, Rhosmari strained to see. But there was no sign of the dark-haired faery anywhere, only her troops, who had scattered in panic and were running back towards the Oak. 'Gardener have mercy,' whispered Linden, and then shrieked, 'Knife! Watch out!'

But the warning came too late. Corbin, the other Blackwing, had sneaked up behind Peri, and as she turned he thrust his dagger into her side. She crumpled to her knees, throwing up an arm to defend herself, as Corbin wrenched out the knife and stabbed it down again—

'No!' wailed Linden, seizing a twig with both hands and shaking it. 'No, no, no, not Knife, not her, oh Great Gardener, *no*—'

A *crack* split the air, and the dagger in Corbin's hand went flying. Timothy, straddling the window frame with slingshot raised, fired off another pellet that laid the raven boy flat upon the grass. Then he swung his leg back inside the house and disappeared.

A fox bolted across the garden to Peri's side, whirled

and became Rob, sword in hand. He shouted, 'Rebels! Defend us!'

Lily was the first to reach him, her glossy black hair flying. She threw up a shield around herself, Rob and the fallen Peri – but with so much iron nearby the spell was weak, and the glow of her magic flickered like a wind-blown candle. Still, it bought them a little time, and that was enough. Timothy burst out of the glass door, seized Peri beneath the arms, and dragged her back into the safety of the house.

Wink burst into sobs, her whole body shuddering as she and Linden clung to each other. 'Oh, Thorn,' she moaned. 'Oh, Knife…'

The full moon had risen above the trees now, glowing with baleful power. Something flashed out from the shadows of the wood, and Rhosmari turned just in time to see a wall of blue light sweep across the meadow, and break like a tidal wave over the Oak.

'Great Gardener!' exclaimed Campion as the spell enveloped the tree, covering it from root to high branches. 'What is *that*?'

Dizziness swept through Rhosmari as the Oak's protective wards burned away. The enormous trunk groaned and began to twist sideways, as though some invisible giant had gripped it with both hands and was ruthlessly wringing it out. The branch beneath them shuddered, and all the faeries flung their arms around the nearest twig and held on tight.

Then came a chorus of screams from inside the Oak, followed by a rumbling, splintering crash that seemed to go on and on. It sounded as though the whole inner structure of the tree was falling down. But Queen Valerian was still in there, thought Rhosmari with a stab of dread, and all the other faeries who had been helping her ward the Oak—

All at once the shaking stopped, and the tree was still. And in that moment, a voice rang out over the Oakenwyld, loud enough to bring all the fighting to a halt.

'Rebel faeries of the Oak, you cannot win this battle. Lay down your arms and surrender, or I will tear your precious tree apart.'

With an effort, Rhosmari pulled herself back up to her feet. Where was the Empress? She must be using a spell to project her voice, for she could not see her anywhere. It seemed impossible that any faery could wield such devastating power – but after what she had just experienced, there could be no doubt that Jasmine's threat was real.

Yet something seemed to be wrong with the Empress's soldiers. Some staggered about the battlefield, leaning on their weapons for support. Others stood with drooping heads and arms loose at their sides. Only a few – like Veronica and the Blackwings – remained alert, and Rhosmari caught her breath as she realised what the Empress had done.

'She's pulling magic out of her followers,' said Campion, aghast. 'Using their power to enhance her own.'

Of course. And it fit the pattern Jasmine had followed in the past, as well. When she cast the Sundering, she had used the Oakenfolk's magic to do it, and now she was drawing on her soldiers' magic in much the same way – making her strong enough to warp the Oak itself.

'But that means we can't stop her,' Linden whispered. 'Not unless we kill all of *them* first—'

'Why do you hesitate?' called the Empress, impatient now. 'Surely your choice must be obvious. Do you wish the Oak to survive, or must I break it into splinters?' And with that the trunk began to warp again, and another tremor rocked the faeries off their feet. The loreseed tumbled from Rhosmari's hand, skidding towards the edge of the branch; she flung herself flat and grabbed it just in time.

'Yet it would pain me to destroy such a magnificent Wyld,' the Empress went on, her voice all honey and butter again. 'And it is not your deaths that I desire, only your allegiance. Can we not cease this foolish quarrelling, and agree to live together in peace? I would be glad to offer you all my pardon – if you hand over to me Rhosmari daughter of Celyn as my prisoner.'

There was a terrible silence, while blood pounded through Rhosmari's ears. *This* was why Jasmine had sent her army against the Oak? Not to destroy the rebels, but to recapture her?

'If you have the power to defeat us,' Rob called out, 'then why not do it, and take Rhosmari for yourself? I think,

Empress—' his tone made a scathing mockery of the title—
'that you are weaker than you wish us to believe, both in
power and in numbers. If you destroy the Oak it will take
all your remaining strength, and leave your followers too
drained to fight. Tonight's victory may come at a terrible
cost – but it will be our victory, and not yours.'

Rhosmari's hand clenched around the loreseed. Did Rob
really mean that the way it sounded?

'Is that so?' said the Empress. 'Ah, my Robin, you think
yourself so clever, but you have always been short-sighted.
Even if you should murder every faery in my host tonight –
and I know you too well to believe that you would ever carry
out such a threat – you cannot prevent me from escaping.
And then I have only to raise another army, and come back.
It will take time, but I am willing to be patient. Especially
now that you can no longer steal away my followers...or
prevent me from stealing yours.'

The faeries of the Oak exchanged wary looks. 'What do
you mean?' Rob asked.

'Nothing but folly and empty threats.' Garan spoke up,
confident and calm. 'As long as we hold the Stone of
Naming, we can free her slaves as quickly as she can create
them.'

'The Stone?' asked Jasmine. 'You mean...this Stone?'

In a flash of light, the Empress materialised in the middle
of the lawn. Her hand was outstretched, and in it lay
a smooth white pebble.

'It's just illusion,' said Linden fervently. 'It has to be. Garan has the Stone, she's only trying to trick us into showing her where it is…'

'I know you believe you have the Stone in your keeping, Garan son of Gwylan,' the Empress continued. 'But if you look into the pouch at your belt you will find nothing but an ordinary pebble. Did you think yourself safe this afternoon, when you lay down to rest? You forgot that Bluebell had a key to every door in the Oak – and the power to beguile your mind so that you would not remember her taking the Stone from you.'

Bluebell… Rhosmari clutched the twig beside her. All along they had thought Mallow was the traitor, the one most likely to hand them all over to the Empress. Could they really have been so deceived?

'But how?' asked Wink, hushed with disbelief. 'How could Bluebell be helping the Empress? How would she even have met her? She's never been out of the Oak!'

'Yes, she has,' said Campion heavily. 'Remember those three days right after Queen Valerian was crowned, when we all thought Bluebell was hiding in her—'

But she never finished the sentence, for the Empress had lifted the Stone idly between finger and thumb, as though appraising it. 'Such a small thing,' she mused aloud. 'I wonder how easily it will crumble?' Then with sudden savagery she let it drop back into her palm, and closed her hand around it. Light flared between her fingers, and even from high up in the Oak, Rhosmari heard the terrible crack as the Stone shattered.

'No!' shouted Garan, leaping forward – but the moment his hand touched the Empress's image, white lightning exploded through him. In horror Rhosmari watched him fall backwards, mouth open in a soundless cry. Then he crumpled to the grass, and the light around him faded as the Empress brushed the gravel from her hands.

Rhosmari's legs folded beneath her. She did not even feel her knees hit the branch, or the loreseed fall from her hand. Someone caught it, and tried to help her up again, but she neither knew nor cared which of the faeries it was. Her world had narrowed to a dark tunnel, with the Empress at one end and herself at the other, and Garan lying dead between them.

Slow heat spread through her body, engulfing her like a boiling tide. Her muscles became steel, her heart a furnace. Rhosmari yanked the rope off her waist, twisted away from the hands that held her, and leaped over the edge of the branch.

Wings outspread, she dropped to a landing just outside the window of the Queen's audience chamber. Valerian sat motionless on her throne, hands braced along its carved arms. The walls of the room were cracked and the air thick with dust, but she stared straight ahead, as though gripped by some dark vision that she alone could see.

'Is it true?' she asked, as Rhosmari climbed in. 'Is he dead?'

'Yes.'

The Queen closed her eyes. 'Gardener tend you, Garan son of Gwylan,' she whispered. 'May you be planted in a place of rich soil and good water, never to be uprooted again.'

Rhosmari barely heard her. She pushed past a knot of sobbing Oakenfolk – the faeries who had stayed with the Queen to maintain the Oak's wards, but who had proved no match for Jasmine's power – and out into the passage, heading for the Spiral Stair.

Curtains draped the end of the corridor, blotting out all light from the landing beyond. Rhosmari swept them aside, took two determined steps – and reeled back, gripping the bannister as her foot skidded into empty air.

The Stair was *gone*.

'Rhosmari!' called Linden's voice behind her. 'Wait!' She plunged through the archway, and Rhosmari had to grab her arm to keep her from pitching right over into the void.

'What— *Oh*,' Linden gasped, staring down at the splintered wreckage far below. 'Oh *no*.'

'There's nothing we can do about it now,' said Rhosmari. She knew she sounded harsh, but she could not afford to let herself care. 'What do you want?'

'Rob made a bargain with the Empress,' Linden said.

'A temporary truce, for one hour. So we can look after our wounded, and decide what we're going to do.'

Only an hour. So little time – and yet it would be enough. It would have to be. 'All right,' said Rhosmari, her eyes on the shadowy hole where the Stair had once been. 'You've told me. Now you can go back to the others.'

'What are you going to do?' asked Linden.

'What I have to,' Rhosmari said, and stepped off the edge into nothingness.

eighteen

Her wings opened instinctively to slow her fall, catching the updraught and shaping it into flight. Rhosmari glided downwards, past the dangling walkways and shattered landings that were all that remained of the Stair, circling over the debris that littered the Oak's ground floor until she found a place to land.

The dust was thick enough to choke her; she coughed until her eyes watered. Then, holding her sleeve across her face, she began picking her way through the wreckage towards the East Root corridor. In one of the storerooms, perhaps, she would find what she needed; or if not, she would have to make herself invisible again and search the garden…

'Help!' cried a muffled voice. 'Someone help us!'

For a moment Rhosmari thought that the sound was coming from beneath her, and that a whole group of faeries lay trapped beneath the ruins of the Stair. But as she clambered over smashed treads and risers and ducked a fallen beam, she realised that the cries came from further ahead. She teetered her way towards them, stumbling as a panel rocked beneath her feet, and stopped at last before the kitchen door.

'The Stair's fallen down,' she called to the faeries on the other side. 'And there's too much wood here for me to move. You'll have to wait until the others can get you out.'

At first the only answers were groans. But then Holly spoke up, resolute: 'We'll be all right. Just send help as soon as you can.'

Rhosmari climbed over the last of the debris and dropped to the floor, wiping the dust from her hands. Beyond the archway the passage was clear, its root-braced ceiling and pebbled walls still intact. She conjured a glow-spell and set off towards the exit.

She had only gone a few paces before a male faery's voice, rough with exhaustion, spoke to her from the shadows. 'Rhosmari?'

'Broch,' she said blankly, as her light fell upon his face. 'How did you get here?'

'We came in through the hedge tunnel,' he said. 'Thorn showed me the way.'

'But Thorn's—' Rhosmari started to say, but then the blunt-haired faery stepped up beside him, scowling.

'I'm what?' she demanded.

Rhosmari bit her lip, willing herself strong. She could not

afford to let her composure break even for a moment, if she were to go through with her plan. 'We thought you might be dead,' she said.

'Fair enough,' said Thorn. 'I probably would have been, if this one hadn't shown up to heal me. Took a blow to the head that nearly cracked my skull.'

'*Did* crack your skull,' Broch said. He spoke with his usual dryness, but there was a wild look about his eyes, and he was gripping Thorn's shoulder as though afraid to let go.

'Yes. Well.' Thorn cleared her throat. 'Let's not get into that. So where are you off to?' She raised her brows at Rhosmari. 'I thought you were supposed to be watching the battle?'

'I—' Rhosmari began, but then a door banged open at the far end of the corridor, and a beam of torchlight sliced the darkness.

'Somebody!' Timothy's voice cracked with desperation. 'Anybody! Please!'

Broch and Thorn glanced at each other, but Rhosmari did not hesitate. She pushed past the other faeries and ran to meet him.

'Peri,' Timothy panted as she caught up to him. He was clutching his side and wheezing; he must have scrambled through the pipe and sprinted down the tunnel as fast as he could go. 'We need someone – to heal her. Right away.'

'Knife?' Thorn jogged up to them, her square face incredulous. 'What's the matter?'

'She's dying,' Timothy gasped. 'She's lost so much blood, we're afraid to move her. tried to call an ambulance but couldn't get the phone to work – mobile's no good either must be the Empress…'

Thorn whipped around and grabbed Broch by the elbow. 'We've got to get over there *now*.'

'I am not a skilled healer,' he protested, though she was already dragging him down the corridor. 'And the house is surrounded by iron—'

'Then you'll just have to keep her alive until we can get the house *un*-surrounded,' Thorn snapped back. 'Because there is no way I'm going to stand here and let Knife die.' She wrestled the bow and quiver off his shoulders, dropped her own weapons beside them, and pushed him into the secret tunnel. 'Enough jabbering! Go!'

Timothy leaned heavily against the wall. 'I've got to get back too,' he said. 'I just…have to catch my breath.' Then he slid to the floor and dropped his head between his knees.

Rhosmari looked from him to the weapons, lying forgotten in the middle of the corridor. Broch's would be too heavy, but Thorn's should do well enough. She edged towards them, keeping an eye on Timothy all the while.

'OK,' said Timothy after a moment, struggling to his feet again. 'I'm going back to the house.' He turned to her, eyes pleading. 'Come with me?'

The quiver warmed Rhosmari's shoulder, and the bow felt strong and purposeful in her hand. Even though she had made the weapons invisible, she had to resist the urge to back into the shadows, away from his searching gaze. 'I can't,' she said.

'Just for a few minutes. Please.'

Rhosmari chewed the inside of her lip. There was no way to refuse without an explanation. The only alternative was to lie – but it had been so long since she visited a theatre that she doubted she could make it convincing.

But she could stay a few steps behind Timothy as they walked through the wider part of the tunnel, and then leave the bow and quiver behind at the junction. She could visit the house for a moment or two, and then go back and get the weapons and be on her way. And Timothy would never have to know.

'All right,' she said. 'You go ahead. I'll come after you.'

Peri lay on the sofa, a blood-soaked bandage around her shoulder and another pressed tightly to her side. Her eyes were shut, her face as white as her hair; she did not even flinch as Broch's fingers touched first one wound, then the other. And all the while Paul sat with his wife's hand clasped in both his own, his eyes so haunted that Rhosmari had to look away.

'I've stopped the bleeding,' said Broch, straightening up again. He looked almost as pale as Peri now, and Thorn grabbed his arm to steady him. 'But a full healing is beyond my power. She may live a few more hours, but unless you remove the iron from the house and bring in more faeries to help heal her, she will die.'

'And how are we to do that,' demanded Thorn, 'with the Empress right on the doorstep? The minute we take that iron away she'll burn the house, or pull it down around our ears, and then we'll *all* be dead.'

'Not while the truce is on,' said Timothy. 'I can do it. I'll do it right now.' He snatched up his iron necklace and rings from the table and dashed outside, the glass door rattling in his wake.

Paul closed his eyes, pain etched deep into his face. He brought Peri's hand to his mouth and held it there a moment, then gently laid it down and backed his wheelchair away. 'I appreciate your help,' he said to Broch. 'You've done what you could. But you should get back to the Oak.'

There was a bitterness in his tone that Rhosmari knew all too well: he was close, very close, to hating all faeries just now. And how could she blame him, when he and his wife had spent years protecting and providing for the Oakenfolk, and received little but sorrow in return? If not for Peri's loyalty to her former people, she and Paul – and Timothy too – would never have been caught up in this battle.

'You can't get rid of me that easily,' Thorn told him. 'As soon as Timothy's got the house clear, I'll be back with Llinos and Rob and every other healer I can get my hands on, even if I have to drag over Queen Valerian herself. Knife is *not* going to die, you hear me?' She stomped to the hole in the floor, made herself small with a shuddering effort, and threw herself inside. Resigned, Broch followed.

'I have to go now,' said Rhosmari, still avoiding Paul's eyes. 'But the Empress won't get anywhere near this house, even once the truce is over. You and Peri and Timothy will be safe from now on. I promise.'

'Really,' said Paul. 'And how are you going to accomplish that? March out there and shoot her?'

And now she did look up, because if anyone could understand why she had to do this, he would. 'Yes,' she said, holding his accusing blue gaze as she shrank to Oakenfolk size and backed up to the mouth of the tunnel. 'That's exactly what I'm going to do.'

The bow and quiver lay where she had left them, at the junction of the pipe and the hedge tunnel. By the dim light of her glow-spell Rhosmari picked up the bow and tested its pull, examined each of the arrows to make sure they were straight and undamaged, and for the last time, reviewed her plan.

Martin had taught her that appearing vulnerable was the way to put people off their guard. And both he and the Empress knew just how vulnerable Rhosmari, a Child of Rhys who had sworn never to shed blood, could be. So when Rhosmari walked out into the open meadow and announced that she was surrendering to the Empress in order to end the battle, there would be no reason for anyone to doubt her.

Keeping her bow hovering invisibly overhead while she walked would be a challenge, since levitation was not one of Rhosmari's usual skills. But if she could learn from Martin, she could learn from the Empress, too: once she stepped out into the moonlight, even that difficult spell should become easy. Hands meekly upraised, she would walk across the field and turn herself over to the Empress's followers. She would wait until the Empress came out to meet her, and then…

There were three arrows in the quiver. But once the bow was in her hands, she would only need one shot.

And after that? asked a voice in her mind, but she pushed the thought away. Why should she care? Let Veronica and the Blackwings kill her, if they wished. By then everything that had once been Rhosmari daughter of Celyn would be dead anyway. She slung the bow over her shoulder, and prepared to Leap away.

The door of the pipe crashed open. Timothy scrambled out, the wooden medallion swinging from his neck. 'Don't,' he said. 'Don't do it, Rhosmari.'

So Paul had told him. The betrayal stung her, but she would not let anyone stop her now. 'I have to,' she replied with forced patience. 'If I don't kill the Empress, she'll go on fighting until the Oak is destroyed, and everyone is dead.

And then she'll make me her slave again, and use me to invade the Green Isles—'

Timothy set the torch down and took a step towards her. 'I know,' he said. 'Or at least…I know all those things could happen. But I also know that if you do this, it'll destroy you.'

'It doesn't matter what happens to me. Not if I can save everyone else.'

He was silent for a moment, his dark head bent. Then he said quietly, 'I'm sorry about Garan.'

He was trying to break her. Rhosmari clenched her fists, cursing herself for staying to argue with him when she should have Leaped instead. It would serve him right if she—

'I know you weren't betrothed any more,' Timothy said. 'But I think he really did love you, in the end.'

Shame welled up inside her, and the ice around her heart began to crack. 'I didn't love him,' she said, and then with sudden fierceness, 'Don't you understand, I never loved Garan and I should have, because he was good and kind, and he sacrificed everything he had to help you and Linden and the others when I was too afraid to even care. And then the Empress killed him, and I couldn't stop her—'

'Rhosmari.'

'And I *hate* her!' She was breathing fast now, almost snarling the words. 'I hate her and I want her to die!'

'I know,' said Timothy in the same soft voice. 'I do too. But what she did to Garan…*it wasn't your fault*.'

The air in Rhosmari's lungs had turned to water, filling up her chest and her eyes. 'It was,' she gasped. 'If I hadn't come here... If I hadn't... I should have...'

'Rhosmari.' Timothy reached out to her, fingers brushing her cheek. 'I've never met anyone who wanted so badly to save everyone. But you can't.' He lifted the bow off her shoulder, sliding it down her arm. 'None of us can.'

Her fingers grasped at the bow, but he had already set it aside. She clutched the strap of the quiver, twisted her body so that he could not take it away from her...and then, sickened at herself, she tore it off and flung it down. Arrows clattered across the ground as she dropped to her knees, and buried her face in her empty hands.

Timothy crouched beside her and put an arm around her shoulders. 'Good,' he said huskily. 'That's good, Rhosmari.'

'I didn't mean this to happen,' she choked out. 'Any of it. I wish I could go back and undo it all... If I'd just stayed on the Green Isles...'

'If you hadn't come, Bluebell would still have betrayed us,' said Timothy. 'And she would still have given the Empress the Stone. Garan would probably have died exactly the same way, even if you hadn't been here. But then I'd never have met you.' His voice lowered. 'And I wouldn't want that.'

She pushed herself away from him, wiping her eyes on her sleeve. 'You don't know what I'm really like,' she said thickly. 'You don't know the things I've done. I'm such a hypocrite, Timothy. All this time I've been trying to stop other people from hurting each other, and yet…'

'Hey.' His voice was gentle. 'Don't be so hard on yourself. After what the Empress did to you, I'm amazed you held out as long as you did.'

'It's not that.' She plucked at a loose thread in her skirt. 'I know how terrible it is to lose someone suddenly…and violently. That's why I can't stand the thought of fighting, because that's what it does to people. So when my mother told me that humans had killed my grandfather, I…I felt like I could never trust a human again. And yet…when my father died, eight years ago – it was my fault.'

Timothy sat back on his heels, watching her without expression. He didn't say anything, just waited for her to go on. And after a moment, Rhosmari found that she could.

'There was a cove not far from our house, back on the Green Isles. My father told me not to go there, that it wasn't safe. But he didn't tell me why, and I thought…I thought I was old enough to take care of myself. So I went anyway.'

Timothy nodded, which could have meant either that he understood, or that he would have done exactly the same thing in her place. Knowing him, it was probably both.

'The path was steep and slippery, but when I got to the bottom I found some of the most beautiful shells I'd ever seen. I was so busy hunting for them, I lost track of time. And then the tide started coming in.'

Her younger self's first instinct had been to climb up the way she had come, but the stone crumbled away under her fingers, and she'd only ended up sliding back to the bottom. She hadn't yet learned to Leap, and she didn't dare make herself small and fly away, because the wind was rising and she feared she'd be blown right out to sea. So she'd pressed herself flat against the cliffside, staring helplessly at the fast-encroaching water, until her father came looking for her.

'*Rhosmari? Are you down there?*' He'd cupped his hands to his mouth and shouted, walking along the cliff's edge. '*Don't be afraid, just...*'

And suddenly the top of the cliff crumbled away, dirt and stone pouring down like a waterfall, pummelling Rhosmari with loose pebbles and enveloping her in a smothering cloud of dust. She'd cowered behind a boulder with her hands over her head, sure that she was about to be buried alive. But the worst of it missed her, and little by little the landslide subsided. Shouts echoed from the top of the cliff as the other Children of Rhys ran to see what had happened, and cautiously Rhosmari stood up again, looking for her father.

'And there he was,' she finished. 'Lying on the rocks, with the sea washing over him. Dead.'

There was a long silence. Then Timothy said, 'I'm sorry.'

Two quiet words, that was all – and yet somehow, it was enough. Enough at least to let Rhosmari know he understood, and did not despise her.

'Timothy,' she whispered, 'I'm so scared. Scared of what

the Empress will do to me – what she'll make me do, when she captures me again.'

'She won't get the chance,' he told her, laying a hand over hers. 'Rob's only stalling for time – there's no way he's going to hand you over. We're going to keep fighting as long as we can.'

'And then Peri will die, and in the end the Empress will take me anyway.' Rhosmari rubbed her eyes. 'It's no good, Timothy. Even if I—' her voice wavered— 'killed myself, that wouldn't protect you and the others. The only way to stop the fighting, at least for a while, is to give her what she wants.'

Timothy stared at her. Then he said harshly, 'No.'

'It's the only chance we've got,' she went on, not sure if she was talking to him or to herself. 'If I give myself up to the Empress, then maybe she'll leave the Oak alone, at least for the moment. If she wants to be certain of taking over the Green Isles, she'll need all her followers behind her, so she'll take me and her army and go. And once that happens, Rob and the others will be able to go into the house and heal Peri.'

'Rhosmari—'

'And when we're away from the Oak, maybe I'll be able to think of a way to get a message to the Children of Rhys, and warn them.' She looked down at their joined hands. 'I know it isn't likely. I know I'll probably fail. But I can't stay here, and watch you all die for my sake.'

Timothy made a frustrated noise. 'And you thought Peri was crazy, giving her name to Paul,' he said. 'How is it any less crazy giving your name to someone who *wants* to enslave you?'

'I'm not giving my name to—' Rhosmari protested, and then it hit her. A strange, wild hope rose inside her breast. 'But...what if I did?'

'To the Empress? What good would that do?'

'No, not her.' She sat up, gripping his arm. 'Someone on our side, who didn't want the Empress to control me. Would she still be able to take my name, if someone else already knew it?'

'I...don't know,' said Timothy. 'I'm not even sure it would work unless you really *wanted* to give away your name, the way Peri and Heather did. But you don't. Do you?'

Rhosmari was not sure how to answer. Her stomach still churned at the thought of sharing her name with anyone. Yet now there was excitement mixed in with the dread as well.

'But what if it did work?' she asked. 'And what if we could convince the other faeries to do it, too? Could that be the key to defeating the Empress, even without the Stone?'

Timothy's face lit up as he caught her meaning. 'So maybe, even if you can't shoot the arrow that stops Jasmine, you can *be* the arrow. Not the kind that kills, but the kind that points the way.'

'Yes!' But then she remembered the enormity of the risk she would be taking, and her confidence drained away. 'Except...I don't know if I can do it.'

'Well, if it's a choice between giving your name to someone you think is trustworthy, or having it taken away by someone who definitely isn't...'

'I know.' She sighed. 'But to let anybody have that much power over you – it's huge, Timothy. It's terrifying. You have no idea what it's like.'

'To put yourself at somebody else's mercy?' said Timothy. 'You're right. I don't know. But maybe...some things are worth the risk.' And with that he crooked a finger under her chin, and brushed his lips against hers.

It was only the briefest touch, but the shock of it rippled through Rhosmari's whole body. Her breath caught, and her eyes opened wide.

'I know it's not the same thing,' Timothy said as he drew back, sounding a little gruff with embarrassment. 'I'm not arrogant enough to think that. I just wanted you to know that if anything happened to you... it would matter to me, too.'

In the dusky light of her glow-spell his face looked uncertain, and achingly young. There was no trace of the bravado with which he had faced the Elders, or the recklessness that had made him leap up the stairs to confront Martin and risk the Empress for her sake. And yet, as she gazed at Timothy, Rhosmari felt the knots of fear and mistrust that had bound her for so long loosen, and fall away.

'All right,' she said. 'I'm ready.'

'Really?' He looked surprised, but also relieved. 'Well, OK then. I'll come back to the Oak with you, and we'll find you someone—'

'No,' she told him. 'I have what I need right here.'

Then she slipped her arms around Timothy's neck and turned her face up to his, and in the breath before she kissed him, she whispered her name.

A few minutes later Rhosmari walked down the slope towards the meadow, alone and unarmed, with Timothy's parting kiss still warm on her lips. In the garden behind her, faint but clear, she could hear Rob giving out his last-minute orders. 'Llinos, you and the other Children of Rhys form a ring around the Oak. Don't let anyone through. Rebels and Oakenfolk, you're with me...'

She wished she could tell them not to worry, that there would be no more need for fighting. But if they guessed what she was doing they would try to stop her, and she and Timothy had agreed that no one must know of their plan until it had a chance to work. With a flutter of her wings and a quick prayer for courage, Rhosmari leaped to the bottom of the slope, and began hurrying through the long grass towards the enemy camp.

She had crossed the little brook that wound between the

Oak and the wood, and was almost in the shadow of the trees, when the air congealed around her, trapping her like a butterfly under glass. Helpless, she could only watch as the Empress's faeries came out of hiding to see who had dared to break the truce. At her small size they loomed over her like malevolent giants, and her stomach clenched at the gleam of their bared teeth, their hungry eyes.

'I am Rhosmari daughter of Celyn,' she told them, with all the confidence she could muster. 'And I have come to make a bargain with the Empress.'

'How brave you are,' said the Empress, spinning herself out of shadows and moonlight and walking to meet her. With a wave of one hand she dispelled the ward that held Rhosmari prisoner, and waited until she had grown to full height before continuing, 'I am glad to see that someone in the Oak has some initiative. Although it is a pity you did not come to me earlier, before so many lives were lost. How you must blame yourself now.'

Rhosmari's heart was pounding and her muscles felt like jelly, but she forced herself to look the Empress in the eye. 'You offered to pardon the rebels if they laid down their weapons and handed me over,' she said. 'They are not ready to surrender to you yet, but I am. So I am asking you to stop fighting, and withdraw – and in return, I will stay with you as long as you have need of me, and show you the way to the Green Isles.'

'Of your own free will?' asked the Empress with an arch

of her brows. 'What a generous offer. I wish I could trust you to keep your word... but I think we both know better than that.' She reached for the dagger at her belt, but Rhosmari backed away.

'Not until you promise to withdraw,' she said. 'Unless you intend to show all of your followers that you cannot be trusted to keep your word, either.'

Jasmine's lips pursed, and a cold glint came into her eye. But then she said, 'Very well. It is a bargain. Now give me your hand.'

Fear dug its claws into Rhosmari's spine. This was the moment she and Timothy had been waiting for, when their plan would be put to the test. 'Yes, Your Majesty,' she said, and turned her palm up towards the Empress.

The dagger bit into her thumb, drawing out a gleaming pearl of blood. Jasmine tipped the point of the knife delicately towards her tongue, licked it clean, swallowed...and smiled.

'What a lovely name,' she said. 'And what a shame you did not take better care of it. Now kneel and kiss my feet.'

Rhosmari had known she would have to do whatever the Empress told her, to give at least the appearance of being controlled. For that much humiliation at least, she had prepared herself. But when her body moved of its own accord, knees folding as her head lowered towards Jasmine's booted toe, nothing could shield her from the crushing weight of her own despair.

She and Timothy had staked everything on the hope that

a name given would be stronger than a name taken away. Now she knew they had been wrong, and that all the plans they had made were in vain. The Empress's power over Rhosmari was as great as it had ever been, and she would leave the Oakenwyld not merely as Jasmine's prisoner, but her helpless slave.

And now that the Stone of Naming had been destroyed, she would be trapped that way forever.

nineteen

'We had a bargain,' Bluebell insisted, as the Empress led them through the trees towards her camp. 'You promised that if I brought you the Stone of Naming, you would make me Queen of the Oak—'

'And so I shall,' said the Empress. 'In a few days' time. But first we will go to the Green Isles, and collect the rest of my army.'

Bluebell's mouth twisted into an unhappy shape, but she must have known that it was folly to argue. With a little sniff she stepped back, and nearly bumped into Rhosmari.

'Well,' she said, drawing herself up and gathering her mud-stained skirts about her. 'Look who's here. Not feeling so clever now, I suppose?'

Rhosmari ignored her, too weary and heartsick to answer. Even her hopes of getting a message to the Children of Rhys had proven fruitless, for the Empress had commanded Rhosmari to use magic only in her service. And now that she was sharing the same slow drain of energy that had weakened all the Empress's other followers, it was an effort just to keep walking, let alone talk at the same time.

'I imagine you had quite the time capturing Mallow again, after I let her out,' Bluebell went on with a little laugh. 'She was so angry! Especially after I told her that *you* were the one who made me report her to Valerian. I would never have done that on my own, you know.'

Of course not. Unlike Martin or even Rhosmari herself, Bluebell had never learned how to act a part; her rejection of Mallow's scheme to leave the Oak had been genuine, but so had her reluctance to see her former ally punished. Naturally the first thing Bluebell would have done after stealing the Stone from Garan was to set Mallow free...and if the commotion served to cover her own escape, so much the better.

'We didn't recapture her,' said Rhosmari. 'She got away.'

Bluebell's look of triumph faded. 'But if she's not in the Oak, and she's not here – then where is she?'

Rhosmari was about to reply, but the Empress gestured them to silence. A few paces ahead of them, the trees opened up into a clearing, where a host of faeries had gathered around a low-burning fire.

'We have accomplished all that we came for,' the Empress announced as she stepped in among them. 'The Stone of Naming is destroyed, and Rhosmari is once more under my control. Tomorrow we fly for the Green

Isles…but for tonight, you may go and take your rest.'

The branches above the clearing rustled, and in a rush of beating wings a hundred birds launched themselves into the sky. The remaining faeries retreated no less swiftly, until only the Empress and her lieutenants remained – including the Blackwings, Veronica, and, to Rhosmari's distaste, Martin.

'I have a special task for you,' the Empress said to him, beckoning him over. 'It will be your responsibility to see that Rhosmari never strays out of your sight. And to make that easier—' She flicked her fingers, and Rhosmari winced as a spell like an invisible hook twisted deep in her chest. Martin grimaced as though he had felt it too, but in an instant he had recovered his cool poise again.

'You think of everything, my Empress,' he said. 'Where do you want me to take her?'

'You may follow me to the village, in a little while,' she replied. 'I am pleased with you, if not with Rhosmari, and I have prepared a comfortable place for all my loyal followers to stay tonight.' She patted his face indulgently, then stepped past him to address the others.

'We must reach the Green Isles by tomorrow night,' she said. 'The Children of Rhys should not be difficult to conquer, but the success of our plan depends on stealth and speed. Once we have passed through Gruffydd's Way, it will be the task of Veronica and her soldiers to make our army invisible and soundless as we march. As soon as we reach the first household of Rhysians we will capture them, take their blood and add them to our ranks immediately; Corbin and Byrne will assist me in this. It is crucial that not a single one be allowed to escape and warn their neighbours, or communicate with their fellow Rhysians in any way.'

Under any other circumstances, Rhosmari would have found it hard to believe that such a plan could work: there were so many things that could go wrong. But in this case she feared it would be all too successful. The Children of Rhys were capable of self-defence, but they had not been trained to face an organised assault. And they would expect any threat to come from the mainland, not from their very midst.

'When we have taken over one island we will fly to the next,' Jasmine continued, 'our army growing with each conquest, until all twelve of the Green Isles are under my command. Then I will take up my throne in the Hall of Judgement, and our people will have a new homeland – a land of comfort and prosperity, from which we can never be displaced.' The firelight flickered across her face, revealing flushed cheeks and eyes aglow with anticipation. 'And to you, my lieutenants, who have chosen to serve me of your own will – you will each be rewarded with an island of your own to rule.'

'And I shall be Queen of the Oak,' breathed Bluebell, hugging her shawl about her.

Rhosmari could not bear to listen any longer. She sank down onto a fallen log, and turned her face away.

She must have drifted asleep, for when she opened her eyes again the fire had burned so low that only a few coals remained among the ashes, and the Empress was nowhere to be seen. Only Martin and Veronica stood together on the other side of the fire, conversing in low voices.

'...must value you more than I thought,' said Veronica. 'You are *very* fortunate to have found your way back into her favour, Martin.'

'But not, I take it, into yours?' He spoke casually, untroubled by her scorn. 'What must I do to persuade you of my worth, fair Veronica?'

'I know your worth already,' she said. 'Very little. You care for nothing but your own amusement; you have no interest in the Empress's ideals, or defending her empire—'

'Neither do you,' said Martin. 'We both know that the Empress is old, and growing weaker by the day; she is feeding on her followers like a leech now, desperate to achieve total control over the faeries of Britain before she dies. What is so glorious about that?' He made a contemptuous noise. 'You pretend to loathe humans as much as she does, because you hope she will make you her heir. But do you think I hadn't noticed that whenever you choose a human to prey upon, you always pick a good-looking boy, and steal his creativity with a kiss?'

'Not *always*,' Veronica retorted. 'But that is besides the point. What you should know, Martin, is that I am watching you very closely. And at the first hint of treachery…'

'Treachery!' Martin laughed. 'Why should I betray the Empress? Do you think the rebels love me any better than you do? If the Empress freed me this instant, there is only one company I would join, and it offers no threat to anyone.'

'You mean that absurd little theatre in Cardiff?' Now it was Veronica's turn to sound amused. 'How quaint. But I would not put much stock in that idea, if I were you. You may find that there is nothing worth going back to.'

'And what do you mean by that?' All humour was gone now; his words were sharp as dagger points.

'Nothing,' said Veronica, so quickly that Rhosmari could tell she had said more than she should, and was already regretting it. 'I only mean that your loyalties belong here, with your own kind. And if you ever give the rest of us reason to believe you are forgetting that, then we will make it our business to remind you.'

'Ah,' Martin said. 'Is that all. Well, you need have no fear on my account. I know my duty – and my limitations.' His footsteps crunched towards Rhosmari, and his breath stirred her hair as he leaned over. 'I know you are awake,' he murmured. 'Get up.'

Rhosmari climbed to her feet, trying to ignore the crawling sensation that came over her at the touch of his hand. 'Where are we going?' she asked, as he led her to the centre of the clearing.

'Up,' said Martin. 'What better way to travel?' And with that he transformed into his bird shape and darted away, not even pausing to see if she would follow. But he had barely reached the treetops when agony wrenched at Rhosmari's chest, as though there were a cord of nerves and flesh between them that had just reached its limit. With a gasp she transformed herself to Oakenfolk size, and flew after him.

Martin led her up above the wood and over the fields and houses beyond, circling around her in an almost teasing fashion before swooping off again into the night. It took all Rhosmari's strength to keep up with him, and by the time they reached the nearby town, her wing muscles felt as though they were on fire. They landed together on the drive of a tall brick house fronted by white pillars, and when Martin changed to human size and headed up the pathway, she did likewise.

A middle-aged woman opened the door to them, looking as weary as Rhosmari felt, and showed them upstairs to a bedroom resplendent in gold and black brocade. At that point, Rhosmari had no energy left to care whose house it was, or what the Empress had done to commandeer it. She collapsed onto the mattress, dropped her head against the pillow, and sank into exhausted sleep.

*

When Rhosmari woke again, it was morning. Her body felt rested, but her mind remained hazy, as though she were trapped in a nightmare. Even the sunlight that filtered through the blinds had a poisonous tinge to it, and the air tasted thick and cloying. And when she rolled onto her back she found a small black and white bird perched on the end of the bedpost, watching her.

She sat up, drawing her knees protectively to her chest, as Martin dropped off the end of the bed and shook himself back into faery shape. 'The Empress wants us to join her for breakfast,' he said curtly. 'Make yourself presentable.'

He was angry now, though she could not guess why. He had worked his way back into the Empress's favour, and she had promised him an island to rule. What more could he want?

Breakfast was served by the woman who had opened the door to them the night before, with the help of a bearded man who Rhosmari guessed must be her husband. The food was the finest she had seen since Waverley Hall: scrambled eggs cooked to perfect fluffiness, served with thin slices of smoked salmon and flaky rolls rich with butter. The smell of it alone was enough to make her stomach groan with hunger.

But as the humans moved about the table refilling the faeries' glasses and bringing them fresh plates for each course, the frustrated rage in the man's eyes and the terror in the woman's disturbed Rhosmari so much that she could not eat. It seemed like some twisted inversion of the hospitality Paul and Peri had shown her when she first came to the Oakenwyld, these humans' brittle silence a macabre contrast to the laughter and conversation that had so surprised her that day. And when the woman's hand trembled and a splash of orange juice fell onto the tablecloth, it was more than Rhosmari could bear. She stammered, 'Please excuse me,' and fled up the stairs to her room.

Alone, she wrapped her arms around herself, stifling a sob. She had given Timothy her name, and now she knew – if there had ever been any doubt – that she had given him her heart as well. But love had not saved her, and it would not save him either. As soon as they returned from the Green Isles, the Empress would use the Children of Rhys to force the Oak to surrender. And then she would make good on her promise to kill Timothy, and likely Paul and Peri – if she was not dead already – as well…

A hand clamped over her mouth. Out of nowhere, a harsh voice whispered, 'Don't scream. Or I'll knock you silly.'

Rhosmari's eyes darted wildly in all directions. Hardly able to breathe, let alone speak, she went stiff as coral.

'Good choice,' said her invisible captor. 'Now you listen. I'm taking you back to the Oak —' Rhosmari made a strangled protest, and she stopped. 'What do you mean, no?'

Rhosmari gulped air as the other faery released her.

'Mallow. I don't know how you got in here, or what you think you're doing—'

'Followed you from the Oakenwyld, of course,' retorted Mallow. 'And sneaked in the door with you last night. I'd have nabbed you long before this, if it weren't for that blighted Martin hanging about.' She stepped back, feet noiseless on the plush carpet. 'As for why I'm here, isn't it obvious? It's no secret I don't think much of Valerian, but at least she doesn't kill her own kind, or suck the magic out of them to make herself stronger. And I'll be hanged before I let that treacherous little snake Bluebell rule the Oak, so…' She seized Rhosmari's wrist. 'If I rescue you, that's meat for my soup, and gristle in hers.'

'You don't understand.' Rhosmari tugged vainly against the Chief Cook's hold. 'I want to come with you, but truly, I *can't*. The Empress knows my name, and she's also got me linked to Martin. The minute you try to take me out of this house, they'll both know it…and then you'll be caught as well.'

Mallow swore. 'Well, that's a fine old mess, isn't it? How am I supposed to get them to let me back in the Oak now?'

Rhosmari glanced at the closed door. Martin would be coming up the stairs any minute. 'Take this,' she said. Undoing the clasp from her hair, she pressed it into Mallow's hand. 'Give it to Timothy, with this message: tell him the Empress is going to attack the Green Isles tonight.

Tell him…that our plan didn't work, and that I'm sorry. And tell him goodbye.'

'Timothy?' Mallow's face was invisible, but Rhosmari could easily imagine the curl of her lip. 'You want me to give a message to the *human?*'

'Yes.' She spoke firmly, in the tone she reserved for her most difficult students. 'If you want Queen Valerian and the others to believe you've changed your mind, Mallow, that's one good way to prove it. Now go! Quickly!'

Mallow grumbled wordlessly…and then she was gone, with a soft inrush of air that told Rhosmari she had Leaped away. Weak with relief, Rhosmari clutched the bedpost for support.

The door opened. 'Rhosmari,' said Martin, 'it's time to go.' Then he frowned. 'What happened to your hair?'

Rhosmari straightened up and faced him, her gaze holding his until he looked away. Then she walked past him into the corridor, silent but resolute, like a martyr going to her execution.

When Martin led Rhosmari outside, the bearded man was holding the back door of his car open for the Empress, while Veronica and a nervous-looking Bluebell stood by. Jasmine acknowledged them all with a nod as she climbed into the vehicle; then the door closed, hiding her behind its tinted glass.

'Corbin and Byrne have already gone ahead to gather the

others,' said Martin as he steered Rhosmari towards the side of the house, where a row of tall cedars cast their shadow over the garden. 'We're all going to fly to Wales together – but those butterfly wings of yours are too weak for such a long journey. You'll have to ride on my back.'

'Me, ride on you? Even at my smallest size I'm bigger than—'

But before she could finish, Martin had transformed into a barn owl, stretching out both grey-white wings to show her just how large he was. Chastened, Rhosmari shrank to Oakenfolk size and climbed onto his back. As soon as she settled herself between his wings he sprang up from the ground, launching them both into the brilliant sky.

The ground spun away beneath them, houses dwindling to rooftops and lawns to mere patches of green. The sunlight dazzled Rhosmari's eyes, and the wind whipped her hair into a tangle. She clung tight to Martin, knees gripping his feathered sides and arms thrown around his neck as far as they would go.

A river threaded across the countryside, bright as molten silver. Roads sliced the land into black-edged pieces. Fields and woodland flashed past, dotted with farms and villages at first, then yielding to bigger towns and the sprawling outskirts of some great city. Could that be London already? She had lost all sense of where they were.

Then a shadow fell over her face, and when she looked up, the sky was dark with birds.

They moved together in one great flock, weirdly mismatched and just as unnaturally silent. Their wings sliced the air with deliberate strokes: crows and ravens, hawks and owls, ducks, geese and seabirds of every kind. And as Martin angled upwards to join them, Rhosmari saw that many of the others also bore a female faery on their backs.

This was the first time she had seen the Empress's whole army out in the open. Were there two hundred? Three? It was hard to be certain. But even so, it seemed that the faeries of the Oak had not been so badly outnumbered last night as they had feared. No wonder the Empress had been so willing to grant Rhosmari's request and withdraw.

After a few hours of steady flight some of the birds began to falter, and by unspoken agreement the leaders glided downwards, to settle along the bank of a slow-moving river. Martin back-winged to a landing upon the grass, and Rhosmari slid off, grateful for the chance to stretch her aching limbs.

Then the owl vanished and Martin stood beside her, small as she was. She had never seen him at Oakenfolk size before, and for a moment she could only stare. But he seized her hand and said, 'We're Leaping to Lyn and Toby's theatre. Right now.'

'To Cardiff?' They must have flown a long way, if they were close enough to the city to Leap there. 'Why?'

'Because I have to know,' said Martin. 'But enough

talking. *Go!*' And with that he vanished, and Rhosmari had to Leap with him. They slipped in and out of emptiness, appearing on the familiar back street in the heart of Cardiff.

Someone in the distance let out a shriek – they must have been spotted – but Martin ignored it. His eyes were fixed on Lyn's door, his fingers tracing the empty space where the BARDHOUSE THEATRE COMPANY sign had once hung. He swore softly and stabbed his thumb against the bell, buzzing once, twice—

The door opened. Lyn stood there with a steaming cup of coffee in hand, looking irritable. 'What do you want?' she demanded.

'Lyn,' said Martin. 'Where's the sign? What happened to the theatre?'

'Who cares?' retorted the human woman. 'If you came to audition, forget it. The company's finished.' She tried to shut the door, but Martin stepped to block it.

'You can't be serious,' he said. 'This theatre was your life. Toby's, too. Where is he?'

'Doing real work for real money, I expect,' said Lyn. 'Or at least that was the idea when he left. Listen, whoever you are—'

Rhosmari drew in her breath, a sharp intake of disbelief and pain. Beside her, Martin had gone so still that he might have been carved from ice.

'—if you want to get up on a stage somewhere and make a fool of yourself, that's your business. But it's not mine, not any more. Now get your foot out of my door before I call the police.'

Slowly, Martin stepped back. His face was ashen, and when Rhosmari touched his arm he did not even seem to feel it. He stood there like a living ghost, as Lyn slammed the door and bolted it shut.

So this was what Veronica had meant, when she told Martin there was nothing in Cardiff worth going back to. At the Empress's command, she had done to Martin's friends what she had once tried to do to Timothy – stolen away all their creative abilities until nothing was left, and left them indifferent to a passion that had once defined their whole lives. And then, in a final cruel twist, she had erased Lyn and Toby's memories of Martin as well.

'What are you going to do?' Rhosmari asked, and when he remained silent, 'Martin?'

His fingers closed on her wrist, hard enough to bruise, and the look on his face chilled her all over. 'Veronica was right,' he said. 'There's nothing for me here.'

And with that they disappeared, leaving the closed door and the vacant theatre behind them.

twenty

The beach gleamed wetly in the moonlight, and the waves
that rolled in from the open sea were frothed with silver.
One by one the Empress's army of birds straggled from the
sky and alighted on the nearby slope. No one spoke. They
were too exhausted – and too bitterly hungry.

They had flown all day and well into the night, and even
with clear skies and favourable winds, the journey had not
been easy. The last time the Blackwings had permitted the
flock to stop and rest, several fights had broken out as
the larger birds squabbled over bits of carrion too small to
satisfy anyone, while the smaller ones gulped down every
worm and insect they could find. Rhosmari, like the rest of
the females, had been forced to make do without any food
at all.

Had the Empress lost her mind, to drive them all day like
this and then expect them to fight for her as well? Rhosmari
had said as much to Martin earlier, as they watched

Veronica fire a stinging blast of magic at two hawk-faeries to keep them from tearing each other apart. But he had remained hunched in his barn owl form, the flat dish of his face inscrutable, and she wondered if he had even heard.

Now Corbin Blackwing transformed himself out of raven shape and turned to face them. His hair was dishevelled and his eyes hollow, but his voice had lost none of its harsh authority: 'The Empress awaits us. All of you, follow me.'

In the car park beside the beach sat an elegant wine-coloured sedan, the same car that the Empress had commandeered that morning. Jasmine climbed gracefully from the back seat, dismissing both car and driver with a negligent wave. She seemed not at all concerned about letting the man go, which made Rhosmari think she must have erased his memory and likely his wife's as well.

'You have made excellent time,' she said to the other faeries, as the sedan roared away and vanished down the narrow road. 'And you shall all be rewarded for it, when this night is done.' She turned to Rhosmari, eyes alight with anticipation. 'Now. Show us the entrance to Gruffydd's Way.'

It was her last chance to resist, to find the strength to deny the Empress's command. If she did not save her people, no one would. Rhosmari gathered together every shred of courage and resolve she still possessed, and willed herself not to obey.

It was no use. Her muscles flexed into motion, and though her mind shrieked and railed against her body's treachery she could not stop herself from carrying out the order. Eyes blurring, Rhosmari led Jasmine and her army across the shingle and onto the smooth, tide-washed sand.

They walked in silence, all of them back in faery shape and at full size; the only sound was the rush and sigh of the long breakers, and a distant clamour of gulls that tore at Rhosmari's heart. It was agony to be so close to the homeland she had longed for and the people she had tried so hard to protect, and know that she had only come to bring about their doom.

The familiar low cliffs approached, encrusted with lichen and tufted with grass. From here their stony slopes looked impenetrable, and yet Rhosmari knew that the entrance to Gruffydd's Way was near. If she could have dashed herself from a precipice or drowned herself in the sea rather than open that door, she would have. But she had not even the will for that.

Her feet dragged to a stop, her body turning to face the cliffside. The wave-and-circle symbol shone out to her from the rock. She raised her hand towards it…

'*Don't do it, Rhosmari.*'

She froze, fingers poised in midair. The command was quietly spoken, but impossible to ignore – and it had not come from the Empress.

'Why do you hesitate?' demanded the Empress. 'Open the door!'

Automatically Rhosmari's hand lifted for the second time. But once again the urgent whisper told her, *'Don't.'*

She heard it with her ears, not her mind. Somehow, impossible as it seemed, Timothy was here. He had raced across England and Wales to be with her, and now he was hiding somewhere among the rocks, determined to keep her from opening the secret door.

Jasmine seized Rhosmari's shoulder. 'Why do you not obey? Tell me at once!'

The words came out before she could stop them. 'Because Timothy said not to. And he knows my name, too.'

'Find him!' snapped the Empress at her followers. 'Bring him to me!'

Before she had even finished speaking, Martin changed into his bird form and flew straight up the cliffside. He loosed a spell that lit the whole slope, and all at once a scrabbling noise came from the rocks above them, flakes of shale tinkling down. She heard a small voice cry, 'Timothy!' and the answering shout, 'Don't worry about me! Go!'

And all at once there he was, pressed against the rock with his feet braced on a narrow ledge, chest heaving with panic. Trapped and helpless, in full view of the Empress and her whole army. Martin swooped towards his eyes, Timothy flung up a hand – and at the same moment his left leg trembled, spasmed and gave way.

He tumbled hard and fast down the cliffside, and landed with a thump on his back. His eyes stared wildly at the sky, mouth gaping open and closed as he fought to get his breath again. Rhosmari started towards him – but then Martin landed between them in faery form, hauled Timothy up against a nearby boulder, and laid a glittering knife against his neck. He hissed a few words in Timothy's ear, and the young man froze.

'There will be no more interference from this one,' Martin announced to the Empress. 'If he speaks again, I will kill him.'

'Well done,' she told him, and turned back to Rhosmari. 'Now open the door.'

Tears streaked her face, yet she moved without hesitation. Both Timothy and the Empress had an equal power over her, and whichever one of them spoke to her was the one she must obey. She stretched out her hand for the third time…

'*Don't*,' Timothy croaked. And with that, Martin's knife flashed across his throat. Eyes wide and staring, a line of blood vivid against his skin, he toppled behind the boulder as Martin pushed him away.

Rhosmari's heart turned inside out. The wind howled in her ears, echoing the anguish within her, and in that moment everything else – the moon and stars, the sand and waves, the Empress and all her army – ceased to exist.

'No,' she whispered. 'Timothy. *No*.'

And then the world rushed in upon her, and she realised that she had dropped to her knees and was clawing at the sand like an animal. Two faeries seized her arms and wrestled her upright; she hung limp between them, her hair a wild tangle across her face, sobbing.

'Your Majesty,' said Martin, sheathing his knife and making the Empress a little bow. 'I apologise for the interruption.'

Jasmine gave a delighted laugh. 'Martin! I have underestimated you, indeed.' Then she turned to Rhosmari and said, 'Enough folly. Show us the entrance to Gruffydd's Way.'

Even now, with her soul shattered and her mind in chaos, she had to obey. Rhosmari staggered forward, step by step, her eyes on the thin tracery of light that would open the secret door. Her fingers crept across the rock...

'Rhosmari.'

Timothy was struggling back to his feet, leaning on the boulder for support. Sand caked his hair and the scratch across his throat was still bleeding, but his eyes were clear and alive. 'I command you not to listen to the Empress, or obey her any more. From now on you must listen only to your own conscience, and do nothing but what you choose of your own free will. Forever.'

The words sang through Rhosmari's mind and loosened every muscle in her body, plunging her for an instant into a blackness cold as death and then filling her with warmth and light. She whirled away from the Empress, and flung herself into Timothy's arms.

'Kill them!' the Empress raged, and Byrne Blackwing drew his knife and started towards them – only to jerk backwards and crumple with an arrow through his shoulder.

'Do that,' said a woman's crisp voice from the rocks above them, 'and I'll kill you.'

They all looked up – and there stood Peri, with her crossbow levelled at the Empress. Her face looked strained and her hands shook a little, but the bandages were gone. 'This bolt is iron-tipped,' she said. 'And so are the arrows that Broch and Thorn are aiming at your soldiers right now. You're surrounded, Jasmine. It's over.'

'Quick!' Linden's whisper came out of nowhere, startling Rhosmari and Timothy apart. 'While she's distracted.' Sparkling heat washed over Rhosmari as the faery girl extended her own invisibility glamour to cover the two of them. 'This way – up the rocks.'

Timothy's hand closed around Rhosmari's, warm and reassuring. 'Come on. Let's get out of here.'

The three of them had picked their way up the cliffside, and were nearly to the top, when Timothy's foot slipped out from under him again. But this time Linden and Rhosmari were there to catch him and haul him up the rest of the way.

'Stupid spasms,' he said bitterly, collapsing onto the grass. 'I knew they'd be the death of me one day. It's just a good thing Martin was smart enough to step in before the Empress could kill me herself.'

'Is that what happened?' Linden exclaimed, landing beside them and making herself human size again. 'I flew as fast as I could to get help, but…for a moment I thought we'd come too late.'

'He made it pretty convincing,' said Timothy. 'At first I thought he'd really cut my throat, but the knife he used on me wasn't even sharp. I don't know why he saved my life, but he did.' He shifted closer to Rhosmari and took her hand. 'Are you all right?'

Rhosmari nodded, her heart too full to speak. Only a few minutes ago she had believed Timothy dead and all hope gone, and now here they were together, safe and free. It seemed like a dream too wonderful to be real – except for the Empress and her army still standing on the beach below.

By now there could be no doubt in anyone's mind that Peri had not been bluffing. The Empress's people were indeed surrounded, with Llinos and the other Children of Rhys in exile stationed along the promontory in front of them, while Rob and his fellow rebels blocked the lone exit from the beach behind. The Oakenfolk formed part of the larger group as well: Thorn and her archers, Queen Valerian, Campion, even Mallow – the only familiar face Rhosmari did not see among them was Wink. Without making a sound or giving the least hint of their presence, they had been closing in on the Empress and her followers – and now they had revealed themselves at last.

'You cannot escape, Jasmine,' said Queen Valerian, in a voice clear enough to carry across the beach. 'Our numbers may not be as great as yours, but our people are strong and well rested, and, unlike you, we have humans on our side. If you have any compassion for your followers, you will not ask them to fight us again.'

The Empress lifted her chin, defiant. 'I have nothing to say to a half-breed traitor.'

'Traitor to what?' demanded Peri, her crossbow still trained on the Empress. 'Every one of your followers has human blood in them somewhere, whether they want to admit it or not. It might be a few generations back, but it's still there. It's the Oakenfolk who are the purest faeries in existence, because they all hatched out of magical eggs that *you* created. And for the first sixteen years of my life, I was one of them.'

She shifted her stance on the ledge, the moonlight shining white on her hair and glittering in her black eyes in a way that made her look more fey than ever. 'I chose to become human out of love for my husband Paul, but I never forgot what it was like to be a faery.'

My husband Paul. He was missing too, Rhosmari noticed with a prick of anxiety. Had something happened to him? It didn't seem like Paul to send his newly healed wife to drive Timothy and a carful of faeries to Wales alone.

'You, on the other hand,' Peri said to the Empress, 'were born human – but you've spent nearly your whole life trying to deny it. So who's the real traitor to their race here, Jasmine of the Oak?'

A hiss went up from the Empress's followers, and some of them began edging away. But Jasmine cast them a warning look, and they all stiffened back to attention. 'Say what you will,' she said. 'And perhaps some of my more simple-minded subjects will believe it. But no one has fought harder or sacrificed more for the sake of my people – my true faery people – than I have.'

She walked towards Valerian and the rebels, her army moving in tandem with her strides. 'If at times I have seemed harsh with them, it has only been for their greater good. It is for their sake, not my own, that I am here tonight. And if I command them to fight by my side until every one of us has fallen, it is only because I believe that death would be a greater kindness than the degradation you offer—'

'The only degradation here,' said Queen Valerian, the gentleness in her tone cutting across Jasmine's rising voice, 'is the yoke of bondage you have put upon your followers, and wish to put upon us and the Children of Rhys as well. But as Rhosmari and Timothy have just proved, there is a way that all of us can escape your influence forever, a solution simpler and more powerful than any Stone. To keep you from stealing our true names and using them to control us, we have only to find one person – be it faery or human – that we trust, and give our names to them instead.'

Exclamations burst from the faeries on both sides: shocked, angry, disbelieving. Veronica looked murderous, and Bluebell nauseated. But at the back of the crowd where Byrne lay bleeding in his twin brother's arms, his fingers lifted feebly to grasp Corbin's collar, and the two of them began whispering to each other.

Jasmine's face contorted with rage. 'Kill the half-breed,' she snapped at her soldiers. 'Kill them all!'

Swords rasped from their scabbards, and arrows went on the string; birds zoomed away across the beach, darting so low and fast that nothing could stop them. Veronica drew her dagger, and Martin his knife—

'*Stop.*'

The command reverberated among the rocks and filled the air around them, ominous as thunder. Every faery froze and every head turned, as Lady Celyn stepped away from the edge of the water and strode over the sand towards them.

But Rhosmari's mother had not come alone. The other Elders flashed into visibility beside her, and then Lord Gwylan and Lady Arianllys, and in tens and twenties and finally hundreds the Children of Rhys revealed themselves, a great unbroken line of them stretching from one side of the beach to the other, outnumbering both armies twice over.

The Children of Rhys had come to join the war.

*

'No,' breathed Rhosmari. Before Linden or Timothy could stop her, she shrank to Oakenfolk size and leaped over the edge of the low cliffs, spreading her wings to break her fall. She landed on the shingle, caught her balance, and changed back to her usual size again, running across the sand towards her mother.

'Empress!' called out Lady Celyn. 'As you can see, you and your followers are outnumbered. I offer you one last chance to surrender.'

Jasmine stood still as the Lady Elder approached, the sea wind lifting her blonde curls and making her look like a tragic heroine in some ancient tale. Then she spat, coldly and accurately, into the sand at Celyn's feet.

'Stay back,' warned Rob, stepping to block Rhosmari as she pushed her way to the front of the rebel lines. 'You will not help your people by exposing yourself to danger.'

'But that's my mother,' she said. 'I have to talk to her. I have to explain—'

'Seems to me she's got a pretty good grasp of the situation already,' said Thorn. 'If I were you, I'd leave her to it.'

'You will not fight,' the Empress was saying contemptuously to Lady Celyn. 'You cannot touch me or my followers without breaking your most sacred oath. Do you think that by merely standing here, you can frighten me into submission? You may talk of last chances and peace treaties until the end of time, but I will *never* submit.'

341

'You underestimate us,' said Lady Celyn. 'Yes, we have sworn not to shed blood. But that does not make us weak.' And with that she nodded at her fellow Elders, and they all raised their hands.

Magic blazed from their palms and arced towards the Empress. But before the light could touch her, Jasmine leaped back and flung up a magical shield to protect herself. The Elders' power rippled over and around her, but it could not penetrate that barrier – and as the struggle intensified, the Empress's army began to stagger.

Intent on their spell-casting, the Elders did not notice. All the other faeries on the beach seemed equally unaware, or perhaps did not realise the seriousness of the threat. But Rhosmari remembered how she had felt when the Empress was drawing on her power, and she sensed that what was happening right now was much, much worse. Jasmine had said that she would rather see her people die than let them be ruled by anyone else – and obviously, she had meant it.

Rhosmari glanced around, panic rising. What could she do? Martin had just sunk to his knees, and even Veronica was swaying now. Soon all their strength would be gone, and their hearts would stop beating.

And yet…would that be such a bad thing? Martin might have saved Timothy's life, but Rhosmari could never forget how he had betrayed her. And she already knew how cruel Veronica could be. Knowing the Empress was evil, they had still chosen to side with her – and now it seemed only just that they should pay the price.

But if she let Martin and Veronica die, then at least two hundred other faeries, many of whom had not wanted to serve the Empress any more than Rhosmari did, would die with them...

'Stop!' she shouted at the Elders. 'She's killing them! Stop your spell!'

But they could not hear her. The light from their hands blazed white-hot now, pouring over Jasmine's shield in a sizzling rush, and all the other faeries were staring at the spectacle as though mesmerised. At the edge of the beach, the last of the Empress's soldiers toppled, and lay still. If Rhosmari did not act now, it would be too late – but she could think of only one way to stop Jasmine, and it would cost her dearly.

Helpless rage filled her, the same hatred that had burned in her after Garan's death. This was all the Empress's fault. She was the deceiver, the enslaver, the murderer. She was the one who deserved to be cut off from her people – why should Rhosmari have to pay the price? Blinking back angry tears, she grabbed the bow out of Thorn's hands, nocked the iron-tipped arrow to the string, and sighted along it. Then, with a shuddering breath, she let it fly.

She was shooting into the wind, on a beach at night, with a bow she had not even tested. If her aim had wandered even a hand's breadth, no one could have blamed her for the outcome. But the arrow struck true, piercing through the Empress's magical defences and burying itself deep in her right shoulder.

Jasmine screamed as the protective spell around her shattered. She collapsed to the sand – and the Elders' spell engulfed her in a dazzling wave of power.

'For centuries you have stolen power from others to feed your own ambitions,' Lady Celyn said in a ringing voice. 'Now your own power will be taken away.'

Light exploded across the beach, and Rhosmari and the other faeries covered their eyes. When at last their dazzled vision cleared, the Empress was staggering across the sand towards them, the arrow still jutting from her shoulder. Her youthful glamour had vanished, her grey-streaked hair hung in tangles, and the sagging skin around her mouth and eyes made her look as old as Sarah.

'You think you have beaten me,' she rasped. 'You know nothing of what I can do.'

The other faeries recoiled, but Rob sheathed his sword and walked to meet the Empress. 'It's over,' he said quietly, catching her as she stumbled. 'Come, and I will heal you.'

Until that moment, Corbin Blackwing had been scarcely noticeable at the back of the Empress's army, as he kneeled upon the sand with his injured brother cradled in his arms. But it must have dawned on him that Jasmine's defeat would be his own as well, for now he lowered Byrne to the sand, rose – and changed into his raven form. Before anyone could stop him, he had taken flight.

Black against the darkness, he made an almost impossible target. But as Corbin flapped past her, Peri swung up her crossbow, and her shot clipped the raven's outstretched wing. Forced out of bird shape by the touch of iron, the Blackwing tumbled through the air and fell heavily onto the shale.

But even without magic Corbin's faery strength was formidable, and in an instant he was up and running again. Spells and arrows hurtled after him as the rebels gave chase, but he dodged them easily. He leaped onto the ramp that led away from the beach, sprinting for the car park and the open road beyond—

Then with three powerful thrusts of his hands Paul McCormick came wheeling down the ramp and threw his arms around Corbin's waist in a flying tackle. They hit the shingle in a flurry of limbs and a wild spinning of wheels, and as Paul drove his fist into Corbin's jaw, the male faery went limp.

'That's for stabbing my wife,' Paul said coldly, pushing himself up on his hands as Wink ran down the ramp after him and turned the wheelchair upright. He had barely hauled himself back into the chair again when Peri came running across the sand, leaped onto his lap, and kissed him so hard they nearly tipped over. They were still embracing when Broch and Llinos dragged Corbin to his feet and took him away.

Rhosmari did not wait to see what happened next. Her gaze on the Children of Rhys still gathered by the edge of the water, she handed the bow back to Thorn, and walked across the beach to meet her mother.

'But has the Empress not been punished already?' Arianllys was asking, as Rhosmari came up to them. 'Her power is gone, and she will not live long in any case. To leave her as she is now will surely be justice enough.'

'If any of us has the right to decide her fate, you do,' replied Lady Celyn. 'But for the sake of—' She stopped as Arianllys touched her arm. Then slowly she turned, and her eyes met Rhosmari's.

'Mother,' said Rhosmari, going down on one knee and bowing her head. 'I have disobeyed you, and I have put our people in great danger, and I have shed blood. I know I am not worthy to return to the Green Isles. But—'

She never got the chance to finish the sentence. Heedless of her fine robes and the other Elders watching, Lady Celyn dropped to the sand and pulled Rhosmari into a tight embrace.

'My daughter,' she whispered. 'Oh, my daughter, you have suffered so much, and all because of my pride. Forgive me, as I have already forgiven you.'

Dazed, Rhosmari allowed her mother to lift her back to her feet. Then Lord Gwylan came forward, and gripped her hand warmly.

'If not for you, Rhosmari, we would never have been prepared for the Empress's coming,' said Garan's father. 'Mallow gave your message to Timothy, and Timothy told the Oakenfolk, and all your human and faery friends journeyed here together so that Queen Valerian could bring the news to us in time.'

Valerian. Of course. Of all the faeries, she was the one to whom the Elders of the Children of Rhys would be most likely to listen; she had committed no violence and betrayed no one's trust, and her selfless commitment to her people could not be denied. They had rejected Timothy and Linden's pleas for help and abandoned Garan and his followers to exile, but not even the strictest laws of the Green Isles could keep them from answering Queen Valerian's call.

'I'm so sorry about Garan,' said Rhosmari, swallowing past the lump in her throat. She understood now what her mother had meant, when she said that Lady Arianllys had the most right to decide the Empress's fate.

'We will miss him very much,' Arianllys replied. 'But I foresaw that he would die, and that the Stone of Naming would be destroyed, on the day he left the Green Isles. Still, I could not help praying that the vision had been false, and that you might find a way to prevent it...but now I know that it could not have happened any other way.' She touched Rhosmari's cheek. 'I only wish my son had lived to see his dream of freeing all the Empress's slaves fulfilled.'

Behind them, the Empress's army sat exhausted on the sand, too weak to fight even if they had wished to. The faeries of the Oak had tossed their weapons into a pile upon the rocks, and were watching them closely. Peri stood tall and straight with her crossbow slung across her back and an arm around each of Linden and Timothy's shoulders, talking to Queen Valerian.

And a little distance away stood what remained of the Children of Rhys in exile, Broch and Llinos and some thirty other young males, carrying themselves with brittle dignity as they faced the families they had left behind and the Elders who had declared them traitors to their own people. But Garan, with his sea-green eyes and ready smile, was not among them, and never would be again.

'So do I,' said Rhosmari quietly.

'This war is ended,' said Lady Celyn, her gaze sweeping over the faeries gathered upon the beach. Next to her, Jasmine stood between two of the Council Guard in smouldering, impotent silence. 'The Empress's power is broken. She will be punished as her crimes deserve, and so will those who willingly aided her in her schemes.'

'Punished?' said Martin, his eyes narrowing as he turned a pebble over between his fingers. 'Do you mean... executed?'

Of course, thought Rhosmari. He had good reason to be afraid of what would happen to him – especially now that he knew that the stern-faced Elder before him was Rhosmari's mother. A flicker of sympathy went through her, and she was about to reassure him when Lady Celyn spoke:

'We do not deal in death, even in the name of justice. Nor will we torture, cripple or starve those we keep prisoner. But prisoners they will be, in cells warded and bound with iron, in a place set far apart from all human or faery habitation. And from this there will be no escape.'

Martin nodded slowly. 'I see,' he said, and squared his shoulders, as though preparing himself for his fate. He walked over to stand beside the Empress, tossing the stone in his hand – then with a twist of his fingers he transformed the pebble to a silver dagger, and stabbed it into Jasmine's heart.

The murder was so unexpected, so brutally decisive, that for a moment the faeries around him were too shocked to move. Before anyone could lay hands on him, Martin whirled and brought the knife down a second time. Then he flashed into his bird form, too swift and tiny for anyone to catch, and darted away. By the time Veronica toppled to the sand with Martin's blade hilt-deep in her throat, he had vanished into the night.

twenty-one

An hour later the beach was quiet and clean as though the conflict had never taken place. The bodies of Jasmine and Veronica had been removed, and what remained of the Empress's army rounded up by Rob and the rebels under his command. It would take some time to determine which faeries had followed Jasmine by choice, and which had only been slaves – but judging by the general lack of mourning for the Empress, there were far more of the latter than the former.

Rhosmari stood with her mother upon the promontory, gazing out at the ocean waves and the distant, shadowy shapes of the Green Isles. Small lights winked along their shores and flickered among the woods and slopes, as the Children of Rhys returned to their homesteads to reclaim what little remained of the night.

'I saw Fioled, when the others were leaving,' she said. 'I tried to talk to her. But she wouldn't even look at me.'

Lady Celyn was silent.

'I can't ever go back to the Green Isles.' Rhosmari searched her mother's face, but without any real hope. 'Can I.'

Celyn sighed. 'I would that it were otherwise,' she said. 'You shot to wound, not to kill, and you did so in a noble cause. But you did shed blood, and in the eyes of many of our people, that makes you no longer a Child of Rhys.'

'But not in yours?'

She cupped Rhosmari's face in one hand, thumb gently stroking along her cheek. 'You are my daughter,' she said, 'and I would sooner disown myself. When I found you in Gruffydd's Way, and you accused me of being just like the Empress...'

Shame coursed through Rhosmari. 'I should never have said that. I was wrong.'

'You were more right than you knew,' replied her mother. 'If your words had not pierced my heart and forced me to examine myself, I could have become just like her. For I was born human, Rhosmari, and your grandfather, who died trying to make peace between two humans who were quarrelling, was human as well. And in my desire to protect you from prejudice and violence, I denied you that part of your heritage.'

Rhosmari stared at her mother, too astonished to speak. It seemed an almost inconceivable irony that for weeks she had struggled with mistrust and prejudice against humans, never knowing that she was part human herself…

'But your grandfather was a noble and compassionate man,' Lady Celyn told her. 'Just as your father was. And I believe that both of them would be proud of you.' She kissed Rhosmari's brow. 'As am I.'

'Will I ever see you again?' Rhosmari asked, blinking away tears as her mother stepped back. 'Or is this goodbye?'

'Our people are not quick to change their ways,' Celyn said. 'Yet change is coming, whether we wish it or not. Now that the Stone of Naming has been destroyed, we must decide how best to protect ourselves without it: whether to keep ourselves aloof and our true names secret, or to follow the path of trust that you and Timothy have shown us. And the faeries of the mainland will have to make that same decision as well.'

She drew a deep breath and continued, 'I cannot be certain of the outcome before I have consulted with the other Elders, but Gwylan and Ariannllys and myself at least are united in believing that you would make a fine ambassador for our people, to keep us informed of what is happening in the outside world. And perhaps, in your own way, to bring to our fellow faeries a little of the peace of Rhys.'

'You mean,' said Rhosmari slowly, 'I can still visit the Green Isles? Even if I can no longer live there?'

'Perhaps. As I said, I can promise nothing as yet. But…' She touched Rhosmari's face again. 'Even if you cannot cross over to me, you can always call, and I will come to you.'

Rhosmari put her hand over her mother's. 'I'd like that,' she said.

'What I still don't understand,' said Wink as the faeries of the Oak watched the the Council Guard leading the shackled Blackwings, Bluebell, and other supporters of the Empress away, 'is why Martin did it. I mean, none of us liked the Empress, and I can't even say I'm sorry that she's dead. But her power was gone already, so why kill her?'

Because of Lyn and Toby, thought Rhosmari, but she did not say it. It would be hard to make anyone else understand how much that little theatre and its human owners had meant to Martin, or how cruelly that venture – and that friendship – had ended.

'I can think of one reason,' said Timothy. 'If I could command Rhosmari even though I don't have any magic, then the Empress could still use her followers' true names to command them even once her own magic was gone. Martin must have guessed that Jasmine was planning to bide her time until the Children of Rhys thought she was helpless, and then use that advantage to escape.'

'Yes, but what about Veronica?' asked Campion. 'Why would he turn on her?'

'She was the Empress's heir,' Rhosmari said. 'Martin told me once that he believed that the Empress had already taught Veronica the spell she used to bind her followers, and maybe some of their true names, as well. So if she ever escaped, she could have become just as dangerous as Jasmine.'

'I suppose. But it was still murder, the way he just...' Wink shuddered at the memory. 'And then he flew off like he didn't even care. Doesn't it seem wrong to you, that anyone could do so many terrible things, and still get away free?'

Rhosmari's gaze turned to the horizon, where the stars were beginning to fade. 'Free?' she repeated softly, as Timothy put his arm around her shoulders and drew her against him. 'No, I don't really think he is.'

'Regarding the power of true names,' said Queen Valerian, 'Lady Arianllys spoke with Campion a little while ago on this matter, and told her something that I think you all should hear. Campion?'

The Oak's Librarian coloured as all the faeries turned to look at her, but she cleared her throat and spoke up. 'Yes. It seems that in the most ancient lore of the Children of Rhys, written in the old faery language from which all our true names are taken, there is a passage which tells how thousands of years ago the faeries used to give their names willingly to their rulers as part of their oaths of service.'

'There is no surprise in that,' said Broch, ignoring Thorn's elbow in his side. 'That was why the Children of Rhys needed the Stone of Naming in the first place, so they could free themselves from that bondage.'

'But it was never meant to be bondage,' Campion replied. 'That's the surprising part. Originally, the faeries surrendered their names to their rulers – but only so the rulers could then turn around and set them free. Just like Timothy did with Rhosmari tonight. It was never supposed to be about controlling people, or forcing them to do things they didn't want to. It was meant to be a gesture of trust.'

All the faeries were quiet, considering her words. At last Queen Valerian said, 'If we want to be certain that no one like Jasmine can ever rise among us again, we may do well to renew that old tradition. But I will not ask my subjects to do anything that I am not willing to do myself. So I ask you all to be my witnesses as I call forward the two I have chosen to hear my name: Wink – and Perianth.'

Peri, who was still sitting on Paul's lap, got up abruptly. 'Your Majesty?' she said.

'I can think of no one I would rather trust with my name than you,' replied Valerian. 'And no one whom I am more certain will never abuse it. You have sacrificed your freedom for ours long enough. Now it is time for you, too, to be free.' She stretched out her hands, drawing Peri and the misty-eyed Wink to her side; then she cupped a hand to each of their ears in turn, and whispered a few words too softly for anyone else to hear.

'Oh,' Wink burst out, gulping with emotion. 'That's the most *beautiful* name.'

Peri, however, had more presence of mind. She faced the

355

Queen and said in her brisk, measured voice, 'Your Majesty, I accept the gift of your true name. And with that name I set you free.' Then she bent to one knee on the sand and said, 'My name is Perianth.'

It was a ceremonial gesture, nothing more; they all knew her true name already, since now that she was human it carried no special power. But now that Peri had set the example, the faeries in the crowd began stepping tentatively forward to do likewise. Thorn came first, followed by Linden and Campion; and then, with a visible effort of courage, Rob. One by one they whispered their names in Queen Valerian's ear, bowed before her, and waited while she spoke the words that would release them; and once the other faeries saw that the Queen was setting them free without hesitation, they quickly joined the queue to do likewise. In the end only Mallow hung back, looking very red in the face, and Rhosmari wondered what would happen if she refused. But Queen Valerian only gave her a slight, compassionate smile, and began to turn away.

'No,' said Mallow hoarsely. 'Wait...Your Majesty.'

As the Chief Cook made her way through the crowd and kneeled before her Queen, Timothy sidled up to Rhosmari and took her hand. 'I noticed you didn't give your name to Valerian, either. Does that mean I'm your ruler?'

She flicked his palm lightly with her fingers. 'No, you tyrant, it does not. It means that if I'm going to be the ambassador to the mainland from the Green Isles, I should probably be giving my allegiance to the Elders instead. If they'll let me.'

'What an interesting idea,' said Timothy. 'Do you know, when I met Linden, she'd just been appointed as the Oakenfolk's ambassador to the faeries beyond the Oak. But who's the ambassador to the faeries from the human world? Do you think there's an opening for the post?'

Rhosmari smiled and leaned her head against his shoulder. 'If there is,' she said, 'I think you're qualified.'

acknowledgements

I am grateful to my lovely and insightful editor, Sarah Lilly, and all the enthusiastic staff at Orchard Books UK; and to my agents, Josh and Tracey Adams (in the US) and Caroline Walsh (in the UK).

My deepest thankfulness and appreciation also go to my brother Pete Anderson and my fellow author Deva Fagan, who faithfully read each chapter of this book as it was written, shared their thoughts on how it was progressing, and gave me the courage to believe that it might actually be a good story; as well as to my second-round critics Saundra Mitchell, Kerrie Mills, Brittany Harrison, Liz Barr, Erin Fitzgerald, and James Bow, who helped me figure out where Rhosmari's story wasn't quite right and how to make it better.

As always, there are a million little details of research and inspiration that go into making up a book. Liz de Jager was kind enough to share with me her holiday photos from Wales. Emily advised me on the finer points of Welsh nomenclature, as did Helen Hall and the other helpful members of dysgu_cymraeg on LiveJournal. Claire Margerison helped me find a new name for my fictional pug, and Claudia Gray inspired me to put pugs in my books in the first place. Many kind members of the little_details community counselled me on matters of archery, along with honeysucklebowyer, Markus77 and CraigMBeckett from the Primitive Bows forum on PaleoPlanet. But these are only a few of many who helped me along the way, and I am grateful to you all.

Finally, I want to thank the fans who wrote to express their enthusiasm for the previous two faery books and ask if there would be another one – hearing from my readers is always a pleasure, and I'm honoured that you take the time not only to read my books but to let me know how you feel about them. This story is for you, too.

R.J. Anderson, 2011

About the Author

Rebecca Anderson was born in Uganda, raised in Ontario, went to school in New Jersey, and has spent much of her life dreaming of other worlds entirely.

As a child she immersed herself in fairy tales, mythology, and the works of C.S. Lewis, J.R.R. Tolkien and E. Nesbit; later she discovered more contemporary authors like Ursula LeGuin, Patricia A. McKillip and Robin McKinley, and learned to take as much pleasure from their language as the stories they told.

Now married and the mother of three young sons, Rebecca reads to her children the classic works of fantasy and science fiction that enlivened her own childhood, and tries to bring a similar sense of humour, adventure, and timeless wonder to the novels she writes for children.

www.rj-anderson.com
www.orchardbooks.co.uk

From the bestselling author of *Knife, Rebel* and *Arrow* comes
an extraordinary book for older readers

978 1 408 31275 9 £6.99 PB June 2011
978 1 408 31371 8 eBook June 2011

ONCE UPON A TIME THERE WAS
A GIRL WHO WAS SPECIAL.

THIS IS NOT HER STORY.

UNLESS YOU COUNT THE PART WHERE
I KILLED HER.

www.discoverthetruth.co.uk
www.orchardbooks.co.uk
ORCHARD BOOKS

Read on for an exclusive extract of ULTRAVIOLET...

zero (is translucent)

Once upon a time there was a girl who was special. Her hair gleamed like liquid honey and her eyes were blue as music. She grew up bright and beautiful, with clever hands and a confidence that impressed everyone she met. Her parents adored her, her teachers praised her, and her schoolmates envied her many talents. Even the oddly shaped birthmark on her upper arm seemed like a sign of some great destiny.

This is not her story.

Unless you count the part where I killed her.

one (is red)

When I woke up this morning, I felt like myself again. The fluorescent lights didn't freeze my skin. People had voices, instead of barks and roars. I washed my face, and brushed the tangles out of my hair. I felt good for a whole ten minutes, and then I remembered.

Dear God, what have I done?

My first glimpse of Pine Hills came through a lattice of evergreen boughs and the orange haze of migraine. The van bumped along the forest road, loose stones popping beneath its tires, while I pressed the side of my face against the window and breathed shallowly. Then something pale flashed at the corner of my vision, and I struggled upright for a better look.

The whiteness turned out to be a sign, with embossed letters that shifted into rainbow hues as I squinted at them: PINE HILLS PSYCHIATRIC TREATMENT CENTRE. A line of complacently looped script beneath read *Bringing Hope to Youth in Crisis.*

Beyond the sign, a cluster of institutional buildings sidled into view. At first they looked separate, a peak-roofed longhouse surrounded by cabins; but as we drove closer I saw that they were all connected, like a hydra in the process of budding. In front of the hospital the trees surrendered to grass and asphalt, and behind it the forest recoiled from a clearing enclosed by chain-link fence. As the van edged past I saw a girl pacing around the courtyard, all skinny limbs and hair like a splatter of ink, talking and gesturing wildly with her cigarette.

There was no one with her.

I put a hand to my forehead, flinching as my handcuffs clinked and starbursts filled my vision. This was not happening to me. I didn't belong here. I wanted to hurl myself at the driver, rattle the bars between us and cry, *There's been a mistake, you don't understand, take me home.*

But that would only make me look every bit as crazy as everyone thought I was. So I squeezed the panic down inside me, forced the lid back on and snapped it tight.

Calm, Alison. Whatever happens from now on, you have to stay calm.

The van slowed to a stop, and the side door rumbled open. Humid, pine-flavoured air washed over me, to the tune of droning cicadas and the liquid burble of a chickadee. I stepped out into the grip of my police escort, who marched me across the asphalt to a door at the side of the building. It growled open at our approach, and closed behind us with a steely click.

As the officer took out his key and fumbled with the cuffs on my wrists I looked around, shivering a little in the air-conditioned chill. At first glance the room looked like a dentist's office, with plaque-coloured walls and wintergreen furniture. But the sofa bled stuffing from a gash in its side, while the chairs and table looked as though they'd been flung across the room at least once before anyone thought to bolt them to the floor. The wall beside the reception desk had a dent in it the shape of a size twelve running shoe. I hoped I wasn't about to meet that shoe's owner.

My handcuffs snapped open. The constable pocketed them, signed a clipboard handed to him by one of the nurses, then shouldered back out the door. I was left alone with the two women behind the desk, who sized me up as though I were a time bomb. At last the smaller one said, in a cheerful voice soured by insincerity, 'Alison Jeffries, right?'

I nodded gingerly. The scintillating patterns behind my eyes were shifting from peach to tangerine, and my head felt as though it had been clamped in a vice.

'OK. I've got some forms here we'll need to fill out...'

Over the next few minutes they took from me my name, my history, and everything I owned except, unfortunately, my headache. I was searched with clinical thoroughness, and my clothing and shoes locked away. Even the scent of the world outside vanished from my skin as I showered and changed into the shapeless pyjamas they'd given me.

Feeling like a damp scarecrow, I shuffled out to be met by the taller nurse, who escorted me down the hallway to an examination room. There a lanky physician looked me over from crown to soles and several humiliating places in between. He took my blood pressure, and looked grave when I told him I had a migraine. He gave me two blue pills and a seat in a darkened corner, and I was still sitting there when the door opened and another white-coat came in. I looked up, into the muddy hazel eyes of the nicest man I would ever learn to hate.

'Hello, Alison,' he said. 'I'm Dr Minta.'